THE AIR AROUND THEM CRACKLED
WITH ELECTRICITY

The men who had gathered around as the two Masters of Sinanju squared off felt the hair at the back of their necks rise from the palpable energy.

Neither of them had yet struck a blow. To the spectators, the younger Master of Sinanju seemed strong and agile, but the old Master exuded a sense of quiet confidence and grace.

Chiun had yet to attack. One thing was certain, though—Remo would be damned if he'd be the one to strike the first blow. If Chiun was so sure of his allegiance to Man Hyung Sun, he would have to be the first to lash out.

Only then would Remo defend himself.

Other titles in this series:

Created by
WARREN MURPHY
and RICHARD SAPIR

THE

Destroyer™

MISFORTUNE TELLER

A GOLD EAGLE BOOK FROM
WORLDWIDE®

TORONTO • NEW YORK • LONDON
AMSTERDAM • PARIS • SYDNEY • HAMBURG
STOCKHOLM • ATHENS • TOKYO • MILAN
MADRID • WARSAW • BUDAPEST • AUCKLAND

First edition May 1999

ISBN 0-373-63230-4

Special thanks and acknowledgment to
James Mullaney for his contribution to this work.

MISFORTUNE TELLER

For Sharon Fowler, who might not know how much her years of support and encouragement have meant, but should.

For Jack Fowler, who got the ball rolling.

And for the Glorious House of Sinanju.
E-mail address: housinan@aol.com

1

When a political insider told Michael Princippi that after losing the 1988 presidential race he had as much chance as Mickey Mouse of getting himself renominated to the same lofty post, he sneered condescendingly and boasted a superior knowledge of politics.

When a newspaper columnist pointed out to Michael Princippi that after finally being passed over as a "never-ran" in both 1992 and 1996 he had about as much of a chance of staging a comeback in the year 2000 as Halley's Comet, silent movies and the dodo, he told the man to eat his political dust.

And when, on the day that would begin the strongest push for unification of North and South Korea since 1946 and would also spark a near meltdown between the U.S. and both Korean governments, someone told him that he would soon achieve a power he could never understand and release a force so deadly that it could quite literally mean the destruction of civilization, he would have said that it was about damned time. But what he truly needed to get the ball rolling was for someone to sign his nomination papers.

"It's a bit premature, wouldn't you say, Governor?" his lawyer asked him guardedly on that fateful afternoon.

"What are you talking about?" Princippi demanded. He was a slight man who stood five foot two in his stocking feet and had the personality of a clogged shower drain.

"Well, people still remember you," the lawyer said, uncomfortable with having to broach the subject. "Maybe we should wait a few more decades. I hear they're doing some amazing things with cryonics these days," he suggested amiably.

Princippi's fish-belly face soured. "Where did you go to law school?" he asked.

The lawyer stiffened. "Is that really relevant?" he asked. It was a sensitive subject. The attorney knew that Princippi had at one time had access to the best legal minds in Massachusetts. The former governor had found his current attorney in a booth at the local Sears.

Princippi shook his head. "Look, my mind is made up. The stage is set for the comeback of the century. Of the *next* century," he added.

"Maybe," the lawyer said. He did not sound convinced.

As he appraised the attorney, Princippi's eyes suddenly narrowed. The lawyer was sitting on a wobbly old chair in the ex-governor's Brookline, Massachusetts, kitchen.

"Is it raining out?" asked the man once known as "the Prince" by his constituents.

Princippi had just noticed that the lawyer's cheaply tailored, off-the-rack suit appeared to be soaked right through. A few roundish patches glistened under the dirty white sunlight that poured through the filthy kitchen window. The attorney shifted. His shoes squished.

"Not really," he hedged. He carried his arms away from his sides, deliberately keeping his hands away from the slick-appearing wetness of his suit.

"Why are you soaking wet? Jesus, you're getting water all over my floor!"

The lawyer sighed. "It's saliva, sir," he said. In deference to his client, he lifted his shoes so that only the tips touched the ancient, cracked linoleum.

Princippi's bushy black eyebrows bullied their way up onto his forehead. "What?" he asked.

The lawyer decided not to sugarcoat his reply. "Those nomination papers you gave me for people to sign? I told pedestrians they were for you, just as you instructed." He paused, suddenly unsure whether or not he should go on.

"And?" Princippi stressed.

"They spit on me," the lawyer blurted out. "A lot. I think some people circled the block just to take a second run." He glanced down at his oozing wet suit.

Princippi shook his head firmly. "No, no, no," he insisted, his eyes beginning to glaze over. "No. That simply cannot be true. Did you tell them that the papers were for their Prince?"

"I did everything you told me."

"You did something wrong." Princippi appeared to have dropped into a daydream. He stared blankly into space as his attorney spoke.

"Yes," the lawyer sniffed tartly. "I allowed you to draw me away from my practice. My booth at Sears wasn't much, but at least I didn't have people hocking loogies on me all day. This is revolting." He picked up his faux-leather plastic briefcase from the Formica tabletop and tipped it to one side. Viscous liquid slopped out of a hole in one corner, puddling into the musty, dirt-encrusted linoleum cracks in the floor. "These people hate you," the lawyer added. With a loud slap, he dropped the briefcase back to the table's surface.

Princippi did not appear to notice his lawyer's outburst. He was lost in thought.

In times of intense personal strife, he had a habit of winking out of reality for long moments. He considered it to be a psychological defense mechanism. It shielded him from the vicissitudes of a painful world. A psychiatrist might have better described it as a grand delusion.

He was having "the Dream."

Princippi was in the Oval Office. Standing at the window in silhouette. JFK, circa 1961 and 1962—

Bay of Pigs, Cuban Missile Crisis. Very statesmanlike.

The brightness of the sun streaming through the window exploded around his image, enveloping it, obliterating it. Nothing remained. Just a sheet of blinding whiteness.

All gone. Snatched away in a heartbeat. He had nearly had it all. Now he had nothing. Just a crumbling house and a two-bit mall lawyer.

The trance was broken. Michael Principi was back in his grimy kitchen. He was staring at the filthy floor. His eyes were focused on a pair of soaking-wet shoes.

Principi did not even raise his head as he spoke.

"You are discharged from my service," he informed the lawyer, his face a somber mask. "Please type up a letter of resignation."

The lawyer snorted derisively. "Yeah, I'll get right on it," he mocked. "First, there's the matter of my fee."

"Yes, yes, yes," Principi said, waving his hand dismissively. "Take it up with Doris."

"Doris quit last week. You hadn't paid her in three months."

"My wife, then."

"She's still in rehab, Governor. Remember the paint incident?"

Principi looked up. His eyes betrayed his concern that the latest episode involving his substance-abusing wife might become public. "Get it out of the slush fund," he said.

"The slush fund melted," the lawyer said. "And before you take the Doris route with me, I'm sure the *Boston Messenger* would be interested in some of the dirt I've seen around here. Especially concerning your lovely wife."

"Y-you're a lawyer," Principi stammered. "You can't betray a confidence like that."

"You hired me as a campaign staffer after you hired me as a lawyer," the attorney pointed out. "Campaign staffers aren't bound by confidentiality."

"I'll sue."

"Great. Who's going to represent you?" The lawyer crossed his arms across his wet chest and waited smugly.

Principi sat gasping for a few long moments, lost for an appropriate response.

Finally, he simply got up. He left the aluminum folding lawn chair with the clumps of frayed nylon that hung from beneath in cobweblike clumps and walked silently up to his bedroom. His feet were lead.

He found a few hundred dollars in an old envelope stashed between his ratty mattress and creaking box spring. He was downstairs with the cash a few moments later.

"Viper," the ex-governor spit morosely as he turned over the wad of crumpled bills.

"Pleasure doing business with you," the lawyer said. He stuffed the money in his soggy pocket. Quickly, he gathered up his briefcase and left.

After he was gone, Princippi sunk to his cheap aluminum kitchen chair. He stared dejectedly at the floor, images of abject poverty battling the Dream for control of his thoughts. Poverty won out.

As he sat in gloomy depression, a few nylon straps snapped beneath his bottom. He barely noticed.

TWO HOURS LATER, Michael Princippi was tinkering under the hood of his rusting 1968 Volkswagen Beetle. He had no idea what was wrong with the car, but there was no way he was going to take it to a mechanic. After his stint as governor, working types seemed to hate him more than most. Besides, it was cheaper this way. And Princippi was nothing if not cheap. At least when it came to his own finances.

Former governor Princippi was not mechanically inclined. Nonetheless, he was in the process of tugging furiously with a pair of pliers at some filthy black thing with other longer things sticking out of it when he became aware of someone standing near him. He glanced up suddenly, banging his head on the underside of the hood. Sheets of rust dropped into the sunlight like startled bats.

"Who the hell are you?" Princippi demanded

of the man standing in his driveway. He blinked rust from his eyes.

"Hi!" said the earnest, chirpy young man. "Would you like to change your life for the better?"

Princippi sized up the intruder.

Early twenties. Pale. A little above average height and weight. Bizarre clothing.

The kid wore a flowing white gown with an open pink robe draped over it. A long braided ponytail stuck like a handle from the back of his otherwise bald head.

The governor tipped his head. "Are you a registered voter?" he asked.

"No, sir," replied the young man.

"Then get lost," Princippi suggested. He went back to work beneath the hood.

Maybe the thing he had been working on didn't actually have anything to do with the way the car ran. He yanked at it again, more furiously this time. One of the strange twisty things on one side snapped in half.

"Damn," Princippi complained.

"Everyone wants to know how to change his life for the better." The voice was closer now and more insistent. Near his ear.

Princippi continued working. "My life *is* going to change," he grunted. "And when it does, the Secret Service won't let nut-jobs like you within a country mile of me."

He yanked harder at the little metal thing hanging off of the larger thing. It snapped off. As it did so, there was a rumble of an engine.

For an instant, Michael Principi thought he had fixed his car. He realized momentarily, however, that the sound was coming from farther down his driveway.

The ponytail kid was standing next to Principi. He was looking around the hood. "Ah, our ride," he enthused.

Principi glanced around the other side of the hood. A dark blue, windowless van was backing up the driveway. One rear door was open. Principi could see a pale forearm holding the door ajar.

This was ridiculous. The Brookline in which Michael Principi had lived when he was governor had not allowed this kind of riffraff to drive around willy-nilly. Sure, on his watch other nearby towns might have had more nightly gunplay than a spaghetti Western, and convicted murderers had been given the keys to their own cells, but, dammit, Brookline had always been safe.

Principi ducked back beneath his hood. "Look, I am in the middle of planning my triumphant return to politics, so if you don't intend to vote for me, get out of here before I call the cops."

The young man didn't leave. Instead, he said something strangely enigmatic.

"I'm sorry, Governor, but I'm about to change your life. Whether you want me to or not."

Princippi was almost going to lift his head from the grimy engine to ask what the kid was talking about when he noticed something odd. Through a gap beneath the engine, he suddenly saw a pair of sandals as the white robe rose a few inches around the man's ankles. The kid was standing on his toes for some reason.

All at once, Princippi heard a familiar creaking sound. It spurred him to action.

He tried hastily to climb up from the engine well. Too late. The back of his head slammed solidly against his rapidly closing hood.

Princippi saw stars. He saw bright light. As he lay, stunned, on the driveway, he saw figures in pink-and-white robes swoop from the rear of the van and gather him.

Then he blacked out.

IT SEEMED LIKE only a moment later when he came to.

He was lying on his back in the rear of the blue van. The vehicle was bouncing along a street somewhere. There were no windows.

Blandly smiling faces sat on benches on either side of him. They stared down at the former governor.

He took a good, long look at the shaved heads,

the flowing robes, the dim expressions. The tambourines.

Tambourines?

"Oh, my God," Michael Princippi wheezed. The air spun crazily around him. "I've been kidnapped by Loonies."

And as the world swirled a midnight dance of fear, darkness took hold of him once more.

2

His name was Remo and he was leaving Germany for what he hoped would be the last time in a long, long time.

Remo sat behind the weirdly angled steering wheel of a rented truck. He fidgeted as he drove.

From all outward appearances, Remo was an ordinary man. Lean and dark haired, Remo looked somewhere in his early thirties. Deep-set dark eyes lurked in a skull-like face that many had said was cruel, but nothing greatly beyond the norm. The only things visibly different about him were his freakishly thick wrists. These shifted now as he twisted in the uncomfortable truck seat.

The seat seemed to have been designed specifically to make one's lower back ache.

Remo was a Master of Sinanju. A man trained to the very height of physical and mental perfection. Most times, such a thing as an uncomfortable truck seat would not even remotely begin to bother him. But although Remo's perfectly attuned body did not experience the pains of ordinary men, he had ridden in this bouncing German truck so long that he was beginning to get a growing sense of prickling discomfort in his lumbar region.

This was the last truck in a seemingly endless convoy he had single-handedly driven from Bonn to Berlin. He could not remember how many times he had traveled the six-hundred-mile round trip in the past few weeks. This last journey was made to seem all the longer by the passenger who had insisted on chaperoning him.

"Cannot this carriage go faster?" the squeaky voice in the seat beside him demanded.

"I'm going as fast as the speed limit," Remo said with a sigh.

"The signs are configured in kilometers. You are used to miles. Perhaps you are improperly converting the speed in your mind."

"I'm going the speed limit, Chiun," Remo insisted.

"Humph."

The sound of displeasure emanated from the inscrutable face of the Master of Sinanju, Remo's passenger and teacher.

He was a delicate bird of a man. One hundred years old if he was a day, but possessed of piercing hazel eyes much younger than his wizened shell. Vaporous cotton-candy hair clung to a spot above each ear. His otherwise bald skull was enshrouded in an almost translucent film of walnut-hued paper flesh. A wisp of beard bobbed at his pointed chin.

The old Korean clasped his bony wrists with the opposing hands and stared glumly out the window. He remained silent for approximately ten seconds.

"Are we there yet?" Chiun asked.

"No!" Remo snapped. "Dammit, Chiun, why didn't you just wait for me in Berlin?"

"I did not trust you," Chiun said simply.

"You trusted me with the first gazillion dollars worth of booty," Remo replied.

"It is not that I thought you would steal any of my treasure," Chiun told him. "You are disgustingly honest and ill concerned with money. I find both character traits more than a little appalling, by the way," he added.

"Compliment taken," Remo said.

Chiun continued, "I did not trust that you would be thorough in your final search. I wanted to be certain that you did not carelessly leave behind a stack of gold bars or a crate of diamond tiaras when we at last shake the dust of this benighted land from our sandals."

"I'm not a six-year-old, for crying out loud," Remo complained. "Why do you think God gave me these?" As he drove he pointed at his eyes.

Chiun shrugged. "I am not privy to the thoughts of deities. A joke, perhaps?" he suggested.

"Har-de-har-har," Remo griped. "Make fun of the round eyes. I notice you weren't yucking it up when I was moving all your damned gold for you."

"That was business," Chiun said. "This is pleasure."

Smiling, he settled back into his seat.

Remo was grateful for the silence. He had been stuck in Germany with the Master of Sinanju for far too long. They were getting on one another's nerves more and more lately. His drawn-out trips to a desolate storage facility in Bonn had been his only breaks from the aged Korean. And they weren't much for breaks.

In Bonn, Remo had spent his time loading literally tons of gold and priceless jewels into his rented truck. He had to work at night to avoid prying eyes. Every once in a while, the owner of the facility would wander over and Remo would steer the man politely away. The steering had gotten less and less polite as time wore on.

Driving, Remo thought of the storage facility's owner. He was a greasy little German with a Kaiser Wilhelm mustache and a pastry-fed backside. Surprisingly, Remo hadn't seen him before leaving on this last trip. It was surprising because the man usually made himself known.

Thunder thudded somewhere in the distance. A snaking stream of lightning cut through the cheerless gray sky.

Dreary fat raindrops splattered loudly against the windshield. The wipers were attached at the top of the frame—unlike those in America. They squeaked angrily and doggedly across the sheet of bowed glass.

Remo had always thought that the British Isles were famous for their lousy weather. But he was willing to wager Germany could give England a real run for its money. He could not remember one decent day since they had arrived in Germany.

The dismal cast of the sky translated to Remo's attitude. He wanted nothing more than to get the last of the thousand-year-old junk in the back of the truck moved off German soil.

The treasure Remo was transporting across Germany was part of the legendary Nibelungen Hoard. A few weeks earlier, he and the Master of Sinanju had been involved in a race with a secret neo-Nazi organization to retrieve the incredibly valuable fortune. The neo-Nazi organization—called IV—had wanted the money to further its nefarious schemes. Chiun had simply wanted the money. In the end, Chiun had won out.

An eleventh-hour deal made with an interested and greedy third party had reduced Chiun's treasure to half the actual Hoard. However, even after halving the loot, there was a tremendous amount left over.

When he learned that their portion of the Hoard was in a storage facility in Bonn, Remo's employer had insisted that it be moved immediately.

"It's too risky, Remo," Harold W. Smith of the supersecret American agency CURE had said.

"Risk shmisk," Remo had said dismissively. "It's sitting in a half-dozen sheds collecting dust. No one's going near it."

"What if someone gets curious? What if they investigate to see what is in the storage facility? Good Lord, what if someone has already done so?"

"Smitty, don't burst a blood vessel," Remo said. "Chiun and I will deal with it first chance we get."

"Do it now."

"Isn't there anything else more pressing?" Remo begged.

"No," Smith insisted.

In their encounter with the neo-Nazi organization, Smith had been attacked and injured. At the moment he was hospitalized after undergoing emergency surgery to remove fluid from around his brain. With nothing urgent on the table for his two field agents to handle, the recuperating Smith had given Remo and Chiun time to move the Hoard from Germany to Chiun's ancestral village of Sinanju in North Korea. Smith, however, did not offer to help in any way. He did not want to create an international incident that could in any way be traced back to the United States. CURE's participation in the smuggling operation was to be strictly hands-off.

Remo had no idea how much their share of the Hoard came to. Millions, certainly. Billions, probably. That much raw wealth in the wrong hands could spell disaster if dumped into a single nation's economy. An economic domino effect could even go on to topple the world economy. This was Smith's real concern, Remo knew.

Fortunately, both Smith and Remo knew that Chiun had as much of a chance of spending the vast stores of Nibelungen wealth as he had of parting with the rest of his ancestors' five thousand years' worth of accumulated spoils that were even now languishing in the Master of Sinanju's Korean home. That was to say, there was no chance whatsoever.

Chiun's personal riches did not dissuade him from studying every nook and cranny in the storage sheds to make certain not a single ingot of the Hoard had been left. Since they had climbed into the truck cab, Chiun had been eager to return the last meager portion of gold to his tiny village.

Driving without a break for several hours now, they had just come upon a dreary, sprawling industrial city.

"Is this Berlin?" Chiun asked, perking up.

"You know it isn't," Remo said tiredly.

"All Hun cities look alike to me," Chiun replied.

"It's Magdeburg," Remo told him. "We've got another eighty miles to go."

Chiun's face pinched in displeasure as he stared

across the visible portions of the gloomy German city.

The Gothic spires of the Cathedral of Saints Maurice and Catherine rose high above the other flat roofs. Industrial grit and grime seemed to be attracted to the steeples as if they were magnetized.

"I see they allowed that monstrosity to be completed," he commented with displeasure. He nodded to the cathedral.

"Gothic architecture doesn't do much for me," Remo admitted, glancing up at the steeples. "Still, you've got to admit it's pretty impressive."

Chiun turned to him, hazel eyes flat. "Do I," he said. His voice was devoid of energy.

Remo shrugged. "Sure," he said. "It's like the pyramids. I don't know how they managed to do anything so huge back then. I mean, we consider ourselves lucky when we get the government to deliver the mail on time."

Chiun extended a bony finger to the steeple. It was still far in the distance. They were not even going to drive within miles of the massive cathedral.

"That eyesore is representative of everything that went wrong with Europe in the last millennium," he said. "It is the direct product of the vile pretender Carolus the Dreadful. And you would defend such a thing?"

"Hey, I only said it was impressive," Remo said.

"It is ugly," Chiun insisted.

"Whatever." Remo shrugged.

They drove on in silence. The cathedral receded behind them along with the city of Magdeburg. They had just crossed the Elbe River and were proceeding along to Berlin when Chiun spoke once more.

"Do you not wish to know who Carolus the Dreadful was?" the Master of Sinanju asked.

"Not particularly."

"You in the West know him as Carolus Magnus—Charles the Great. He was not great, however," Chiun added quickly. "He was quite awful."

Remo scrunched up his face. "Charles the Great," he said. "Wasn't that Charlemagne?"

"See how easily the vile name spills off your white tongue," Chiun accused.

"I thought Charlemagne was a great ruler," Remo said.

"White lies. Perpetuated by whites." Chiun pitched his voice low, as if imparting some heinous secret. "The truth is, Carolus was in league with the Church of Rome."

"That's no secret, Chiun," Remo said. "Everybody knows that. Didn't he even get crowned emperor by the pope, or something?"

"Another reason to dislike him," Chiun sniffed.

"Which, the pope part or the emperor part?"

"Take your pick," Chiun said with a shrug.

"Any individual with vile papist inclinations cannot help but be socially maladjusted. Look at you, for instance. The carpenter's sect had you for but a few years early in your life and you still cannot slough off your peculiar notions of right and wrong. Honesty. Pah!"

"Thou shalt not steal, Little Father," Remo reminded him. "That's what Sister Mary Margaret taught me."

"A nun," Chiun scoffed. "If she was so smart, why could she not land a man?"

"They have to take a vow of celibacy, Chiun," Remo said, knowing full well that the old Korean was already aware of this. "And don't dump on Sister Margaret. She practically raised me."

Chiun harrumphed again. "At least her vow prevented her from breeding more squalling papists."

"What about the emperor part?" Remo said, steering Chiun away from Sister Mary Margaret.

The Master of Sinanju glanced over at Remo. "You know at one time Sinanju had much work from Rome."

Remo nodded. The House of Sinanju had been home to the greatest assassins the world had ever known for more than five millennia. Remo and Chiun were the latest in a long line of Sinanju Masters that dated back to prehistory.

"When Charlemagne had himself crowned emperor, it was thought that he would give rise to an empire as great as that of ancient Rome," Chiun said. "This in spite of his dubious flirtation with Catholicism."

"Didn't he?"

"Certainly not. The fool set up educational systems in monasteries and encouraged literacy among his advisers. He aided the Roman church in winding its wretched tentacles throughout his vast conquered territories. His lunacy led to what is called the Carolingian Renaissance."

"I take it from your tone there wasn't much work for the House back then," Remo said.

"Work?" Chiun balked. "The fool created a civilization. Assassins cannot function where men are civilized. Even when he embarked on his idiotic crusades, he conscripted local help. The House never got a single day's work from the impostor Carolus."

Chiun was silently thoughtful for a pregnant moment. "Well, perhaps one," he admitted.

Remo tore his eyes away from the gray roadway. "Are you telling me we bumped off Charlemagne?"

Chiun turned a level eye on Remo. "The man believed in education and religion. His interference in history led directly to the Christian West, the Magna Carta and—worst of all—American democracy. You tell me."

Remo looked back to the road. "We did in Charlemagne," he said, shrugging to himself.

"A blot on the European continent that has

never been erased. He gave an insufferable air of smugness to you whites that lives to this day.''

"Listen, can we get through this last trip without the race-baiting?" Remo begged.

"You brought it up," Chiun challenged.

"All I said was I thought that cathedral was impressive," Remo said.

"It is ugly," Chiun stated firmly.

"Yes, that's right." Remo exhaled, surrendering at last. "Of course. I don't know why I didn't see it before. It's ugly. Ugly, ugly, ugly. It is the ugliest thing I've ever seen, and Charlemagne deserved to have his head lopped off for doing whatever it is he did that caused it to eventually get built. There, happy?" Remo demanded. He gripped the steering wheel in frustration.

Chiun tipped his head thoughtfully to one side. "It was not *that* ugly," he said lightly.

The scream that threatened to explode from Remo's throat was drowned out by the sound of a high-pitched siren directly behind them. When he looked into the big side-view mirror, Remo saw the small shape of a German police car trailing the rented truck.

"What the hell's wrong now?" he asked aloud.

"Do not stop," Chiun commanded. "It could be a bandit in disguise who has learned of the Hoard and wishes to claim it as his own."

"It's a cop, Little Father," Remo said, frowning. "We've probably got a taillight out or something." He pulled the big truck over to the side of the road.

Remo climbed down to the wet pavement, grateful to get out from behind the wheel if only for a moment. He heard Chiun's door close, as well. They met up at the closed rear of the truck.

The markings on the door of the police car identified it as belonging to the small town of Burg, which was roughly halfway between Magdeburg and Brandenburg. The policeman himself was dressed in a dark blue uniform with gold piping. As he stepped out of his own vehicle, the officer pulled an odd-shaped blue cap onto his graying hair. It reminded Remo of a French Foreign Legion hat.

"You vill open the rear of the truck, *bitte,*" the German police officer announced as he stepped up to Remo and Chiun.

Remo raised an eyebrow. "Is there something wrong, Officer?" he asked.

Standing behind him, Chiun tugged at the back of Remo's black T-shirt. "I told you not to stop," he hissed.

Remo shrugged Chiun's hand away.

"Open it," the officer said, nodding to the door. His hand was resting on his gun holster. Remo noted that the silver snap had been popped before the cop had even gotten from the car. He had been expecting trouble from the start.

"I'm sorry—" Remo began.

He didn't have a chance to finish. The gun was quickly and expertly drawn from the holster. The policeman leveled it at Remo's chest. "I vill not ask again."

"Why do they all sound like Major Hochstetter the minute they get a gun in their hands?" Remo mumbled to Chiun.

"Do not let him see the Hoard, Remo," Chiun insisted.

There had been cars zipping past the busy roadway the entire time they had been stopped. Remo noted the speeding vehicles with tight concern. "I don't have a choice," he said to the Master of Sinanju. He lifted an eyebrow as he looked at Chiun. Reluctantly, Chiun nodded.

"Das is correct," the cop said firmly.

As Chiun stepped back, Remo turned away from the police officer. He found the key to the rear door in his pocket and unlocked the padlock. Turning the latch, he lifted the rolling door several feet from the rear platform.

"Inside," the cop insisted. "Bose of you."

Remo and Chiun glanced at one another. They climbed up from the wet roadway and into the damp, murky interior of the truck. The police officer came in behind them, gun still aimed at the two men. The muted Doppler sound of cars racing by hummed through the shadowy metal walls of the truck. Water splashed from the highway onto the sides of the road.

When the officer caught sight of the open crates of gold and gems packed inside the cold truck, his mouth dropped open. Even though it was only a fraction of the larger amount of the Nibelungen Hoard, it was still a huge amount of treasure. He stared, shocked, at the stacks of ancient wealth.

"I am confiscating all of dis," he announced, voice numb. He had to concentrate to keep the gun aimed at his two prisoners. He wanted more than anything to ram his black-gloved hands into the nearest crate of gold coins.

"Of course you are," Remo said indifferently. "What I'd like to know is where did you hear about this?"

"Hmm?" the cop asked, glancing up. "Oh. My brusser."

Remo looked at the man's chest. "What the hell are you talking about?" he asked.

"My brusser told me," the cop repeated. He had turned away from Remo once more and was staring, awestruck, at the glittering gold.

Remo was dumbfounded. "You wear ladies' underwear, and it talks to you?" he asked, incredulous.

"Not *brassiere,* imbecile," Chiun interjected, in a hissing whisper. The Master of Sinanju turned to the policeman. "Can I assume that your brother is the owner of the storehouse where my treasure was secreted?"

"*Ja,*" the cop said. "He vas upset dat you put

your own locks on the place. I helped him to set up a surveillance system outside the sheds you had rented. In dis vay ve vere able to see vat you had stored there vile it vas being loaded onto the truck. However, it did not look like so much." He shook his head in awe.

"Where is your brother now?" Remo asked.

"Vaiting for us," the cop said. "Somevere safe."

"Does anyone else know about this?" Remo asked.

The cop looked up, abruptly annoyed. "Dat is irrelevant. Ve vill go now," he said.

The Master of Sinanju was growing impatient. "Dispatch this one, Remo," he said.

"We've got to find out if anyone else knows," Remo insisted.

"No one knows but this imbecile Hun and his untrustworthy sibling. Make haste."

"You. Qviet," the officer said to Chiun. He pointed his gun at the Master of Sinanju.

"Buddy, wait—" Remo began. Too late.

The gun had been the last straw. In the instant the barrel had been aimed at his frail chest, Chiun's fingers flew from the confines of his kimono sleeves. Fingernails like deadly talons and as sharp and strong as titanium knife blades swept around to the officer's neck. The first rush of nails took out half the man's throat. Blood erupted in a gushing font onto the nearest crate of gold.

As he felt the shock of raking pain in his neck, the officer tried to shoot. Only then did he realize that his gun was no longer there. Nor, it seemed, was the hand that held it.

Chiun's other hand had dropped down onto the man's wrist, severing the policeman's fist just below the cuff of his blue uniform. The impulse to squeeze the gun that was no longer there caused spurts of blood to pump from the raw wrist stump. In another moment, the officer joined his hand and gun on the floor of the truck, a tiny bubble of crimson at the center of his forehead indicating where Chiun's final blow had been struck.

The Master of Sinanju stepped away from the body as it fell to the damp floor.

"Couldn't you have waited another second?" Remo griped. "We don't know how many more like him are out there."

"They are irrelevant. My gold is all that matters." He turned to go. "See to it that that thing does not bleed on my treasure," Chiun added. Kimono skirts billowed as he hopped down from the truck.

Muttering, Remo rolled the body away from the crates.

Moments later, with the truck's rear door sealed once more, Remo joined Chiun in the cab.

"What did you do with the brigand's vehicle?" the Master of Sinanju asked.

"What did you expect me to do, eat it?" Remo asked. "I shut off the lights and locked it up."

"It will be noticed," Chiun said, concerned.

"Well, duh," Remo said.

Chiun rapped his knuckles urgently on the dashboard. "Hurry, Remo!" he insisted. "Make haste to Berlin lest some other highwayman attempts to take that which is rightfully mine!"

"Sure. Lock the barn door after the horse is at the glue factory," Remo grumbled.

Leaving the persistent light mist to accumulate on the parked police car, Remo pulled the truck back into traffic.

Berlin was still some sixty miles away.

He had awakened more than two hours before.

The shock of his being kidnapped by Loonies had worn off the second time around, so when Mike Princippi opened his eye only to see a fat pale toe peeking from the end of a cheap sandal two inches from his face, he had merely blinked at the digit. The toe wiggled back.

Princippi pushed his cheek from the floor of the van. The imprint of a metal truck seam lined his grayish skin.

Kneeling, the former governor eyed his captors.

They looked back at him with benign—almost deranged—smiles. The men were jostled on their plain seats as the van continued to speed down the unseen road to a destination known only to the Loonies.

Princippi cleared his throat. "What—?" The words caught for a moment. He coughed again, trying to work up his courage. "What do you want from me?" he asked.

One of the men smiled. Princippi recognized

him as the man who had spoken to him in his driveway, though with the matching clothes, haircuts and insipid smiles it was hard to tell for sure.

"Want?" the young man asked. "We want nothing of you, friend Michael. What we want is to give you something."

Princippi licked his lips. "Can't you give it to me here?" he asked. He eyed the closed van door. "Stop the car and we'll have a little presentation ceremony right now."

"The gift we give you cannot be given by us," the man said. "I am Roseflower, by the way. If by knowing my name you will become more at ease."

"Roseflower, huh?" Princippi scoffed. "Is that the name your parents gave you or is it your Loonie name?"

The former governor seemed to have found the one thing that erased the smiles from the faces of the men around him. As one, the mindless grins receded into pale faces, replaced by expressions of pinched disapproval.

"That is not an acceptable term," Roseflower said.

"What isn't?" Princippi asked. He racked his brain, trying to remember what he had just said. The gathered men did not seem to want to help him in any way. All at once, the light dawned. "Loonie!" he announced.

The expressions grew more dour. Seeing this, Princippi frowned, as well.

"We do not appreciate that appellation," Roseflower said stiffly.

"I thought that's what you were," Princippi said, his voice betraying uncertainty.

"The proper name is Sunnie," Roseflower insisted. "That other is a derisive designation created by the enemies of our leader."

"Okay, so you're Sunnies," Princippi conceded with a shrug of his slight shoulders. "Can I see a little more of the name reflected in your dispositions?"

The rest seemed to follow Roseflower's lead. His smile returned, thinner now than before. Bland grins appeared on the faces of the others.

"Are we friends again?" Princippi asked hopefully.

"Of course," Roseflower said. His idiotic smile widened. The others followed suit.

"Friends would do anything for one another, wouldn't they?" Princippi asked hopefully.

"I'm not going to let you go, Michael."

Dejected, Princippi's shoulders sunk even farther into his slight frame.

"Some friend *you* turned out to be," he grumbled.

He spent the rest of the long trip in gloomy depression.

THE VAN DID NOT STOP for several more hours. When it finally did, Princippi hoped it was at a gas station. The minute he heard the words "Fill it up," he planned to scream for all he was worth.

Hope gave way to despair when the rear doors of the van were at last pulled open.

Cool air and bland artificial light poured into the fetid interior. Princippi noted that the air smelled vaguely of gasoline and car exhaust.

His legs ached from alternately kneeling and sitting on the hard floor of the van. Helpful hands brought him to his feet and guided him down onto a cold, flat concrete floor.

It was a parking garage. Underground by the looks of it. Black oil stains filled the spaces between angled parallel white lines. A large red number 2 was painted on the wall near a set of closed elevator doors, and 2nd Basement Level was stenciled in cheery green letters beneath it.

His Loonie escort guided Princippi to the elevator. The doors opened as if by magic. He was whisked upward.

The elevator carried them from the subbasement parking garage up to the seventh floor. When the doors opened once more, they revealed a sterile corridor of eggshell white. Princippi was trundled out onto a rugged blue wall-to-wall carpet.

As he was hustled along the hallway, the former governor noted several large signs spaced along the walls that read Editorials, Features, Advertising and the like. Arrows below the names indicated the direction in which one might find each department.

He began to get a sinking feeling in the pit of his stomach far deeper than the one he had felt all day. If this was what he thought...

Doors parted at the end of the corridor, and he was escorted into what was obviously the city room of a large newspaper. Unlike most papers this size, however, there was not a hint of staff on duty.

A row of huge sheets of opaque glass lined the entire far wall of the large room. The pink-robed men led him past rows of vacant desks with their attendant idle computer terminals to the single door that nestled amid the glass.

The name on the door gave Michael Princippi a chill: Man Hyung Sun, Publisher.

He barely had time to read the words before the door was opened for him. He was quickly ushered inside amid his phalanx of robed Loonies.

Princippi recognized Sun right away. The infamous millionaire rose from behind a huge gleaming desk, his face beaming.

The man was notorious. A cult leader from the 1970s who was thought to have been discredited, Sun had made a quiet, determined comeback in the past two decades, acquiring even more wealth and followers than he had controlled in the supposed heyday of his notorious cult. One of the baubles the Korean had purchased for his amusement was the foundering newspaper, the *Washington Guardian*. Princippi assumed that this was where he now was.

"Governor, I trust you are well?" Sun said as he stepped out from behind his desk. Unlike his followers, Sun wore a well-tailored conservative business suit. His face was bright and guileless. The cult leader was approaching eighty but looked a good fifteen years younger.

"Not really," Princippi said. "What do you want from me?" Though it disturbed him to do so, he took Sun's offered hand. The grip was firm.

"Right to the point," Sun said, pleased. "I like that. They called you a technocrat during the presidential race. As if it is an offense to be punctilious."

The man's cheery attitude was infectious. Princippi was beginning to forget he had been knocked unconscious and dragged unwillingly through five states by the cult leader's mindless followers.

"Yes," the former governor agreed, casting a glance at the line of men behind them. Bare arms crossed over pink-and-white-robed chests. They seemed quite harmless now. Princippi nodded amiably. "I agree. It's too bad there aren't more Chinese in America. You people understand precision." He smiled cheerily.

"I *beg* your pardon," Sun said, hooded eyes abruptly dead.

Princippi got the sudden sense that he had said something desperately wrong. He bit his cheek. "Aren't you Chinese?" he asked weakly.

As had happened with his followers in the van,

Man Hyung Sun's smile evaporated. "Korean," he said flatly.

Princippi hunched further in on himself. He glanced at the Loonies behind him. They were no longer smiling, either. Pink had started to appear quite menacing once more.

The ex-governor resisted the urge to say "What's the difference?" Instead, he mumbled an embarrassed apology. This seemed to mollify Sun. The smile returned, cracking the wide moon face of the cult leader.

"We should not squabble," Sun said. "For this is a great moment. A truly momentous meeting. There has been a turning point in the great cosmic cycle." He closed his eyes. A change appeared to come over the Korean. The smile in his fat face grew wider and settled into lines of great contentment. "Do you not sense it?" Sun asked.

Princippi glanced over his shoulder at the line of Loonies. "Um, yeah," Princippi agreed uncertainly.

"I am glad," Sun replied. "For it has spoken to me, as well. It told me to seek you out." He inhaled deeply and exhaled loudly. "Your mere presence stirs it to greater life within me. My mind and heart thrill in you."

Princippi started to get an even worse feeling than any of the ones he had experienced so far today.

Being bashed on the head by his own Volkswagen hood was okay. Kidnapping? Not a problem. Getting hauled in before a notorious cult leader? Piece of cake. There were far worse things that could happen to a would-be presidential candidate. He hoped one was not about to.

Mike Princippi cleared his throat. He glanced at the line of smiling men behind him. *Men* being the operative word there. There was not a single female face beneath a shining chrome dome.

"Er, is this some sort of gay thing?" Princippi asked nervously. He quickly held up his hands. "Which is perfectly all right if it is, don't get me wrong. Some of my best friends...you know? It's just that it's not my cup of herbal tea." He chuckled weakly.

Again, Sun's smile faded. This time, however, it was not a look of disapproval but one of mild confusion.

"You have felt it, have you not?" the cult leader asked.

"Only when I go to the bathroom," Princippi said. "And never around other guys." He shrugged to the Loonies. "Sorry," he added to the silent line of men.

"The presence," Sun guided. "In your mind?"

Princippi turned away from Roseflower and his friends. Something had begun to tingle in the back of his mind. Something dreadfully familiar. Something that he always tried to ignore.

"What are you talking about?" he said, trying to appear innocent. Inwardly he was alarmed.

"Do not lie to me," Sun said. "It is there now. I can feel it, as well."

Principi tried to suppress the weird sensation in his brain. It was a gentle, persistent stinging. As if rogue synapses had begun to spark and fire like faulty wiring in a set of tangled Christmas-tree lights.

"This is getting a little too weird for me," Principi said. "May I go now?" He smiled weakly.

Sun shook his head. "You have fought it for too long," he said. "It was wrong of you to do so. It has kept us apart. And without you, I cannot be whole."

The Korean stepped up to Principi. The ex-governor, though not a tall man himself, was almost as tall as the cult leader.

Principi realized that the strange stimulation in his brain grew stronger the closer he came to Sun. He tried to quell the fire, but knew from experience that it would not do much good. Not when it was this strong.

Sun raised his hands to the sides of Principi's head. When the former governor balked, he felt strong arms grab him from behind. The Loonies had clamped hold of him.

The sparking in his brain exploded in a crescendo. It was like the dying moments of a fireworks display played out behind Michael Princippi's eyes. But the crescendo did not end. As Sun rubbed at the ex-governor's face, the pops of brilliant light continued to ignite steadily. For some reason, they were all lit in flaring shades of yellow.

"What is this supposed to be? Some kind of mind meld?" Princippi asked. He tried to make it sound like a joke, but the truth was he was deathly afraid. Sweat beaded on his pasty forehead, dripping in rivulets down his face and around Sun's pressing hands.

"He told you to come to me. To seek me out. Why did you not?" Sun asked. His eyes were closed.

Through the haze of yellow that danced across his retinas, Princippi looked over at Sun. The Korean seemed almost to be in a trance. "This is crazy," he said.

A hand withdrew from his face, only to return sharply. Mike Princippi felt the stinging force of the slap against one gray cheek. The yellow clouds of fire burned more brightly, reveling in the pain inflicted.

"Tell us!" Sun demanded. When he opened his eyes to peer accusingly at Princippi, the former governor recoiled.

Something had happened. It must have been a strange optical illusion. The result of the bursts of light before his own field of vision. That was the only logical explanation.

The Korean's irises appeared to have taken on

a bright yellow hue. They were like twin beacons of glowing yellow fire, boring through to his very soul. And the words spilled out before Princippi even knew he was speaking them.

"I thought you'd think I was insane," he blurted, not knowing on what level he had even thought this. He only knew that somewhere in the darkest depths of his repressed mind, it was true.

"And so you kept me from him? *Him* from me?"

"I didn't *know*," Princippi begged. "I thought it was like a Son of Sam thing. You know, the dog telling me to go out and kill, or some crackpot junk like that. It all sounded too nuts."

"In spite of what you have already been through?" Sun demanded.

"*Especially* after that," Princippi said, knowing exactly what it was Sun was referring to.

All at once, Sun pulled his hands away from Princippi's head. The flashes of fire burst one last time and then collapsed inwardly, into a pit of great darkness. For the first time in a long time, the schizophrenic sensation of someone else sharing his mind was no longer with Michael Princippi. It gave him a feeling of great relief. And, oddly, an equal mixture of intense loneliness.

The demonic yellow glow in the eyes of Sun grew weak, as well. It died momentarily, like twin vanishing embers in a spectral fire.

Sun looked away from Princippi, across one of

the governor's weak shoulders. "The Boston Museum of Rare Arts," he said sharply. "Greek room. Not on display. It is in a rear chamber with other artifacts. Go."

Roseflower and two of the other men left wordlessly. The rest stayed.

The former governor and presidential candidate knew precisely what it was Sun had sent the men to retrieve. He had donated it to the museum himself. Somehow, Sun had gleaned this from his own thoughts.

"Now we wait," Sun said. He walked back around his desk, settling into his chair.

Principi spoke freely now, without reservation. "You know the people who were involved with this before are either dead or aren't talking. No one wants to be linked to the Truth Church or the crazies who ran it. It's over." He said this last bit as a warning.

"That is where you are wrong, Governor," Man Hyung Sun announced with certainty. He folded his hands with calm precision on the surface of his gleaming mahogany desk. "It has only just begun."

Sun gave him a smile so disconcerting it made Principi want to dash for the nearest urinal.

4

The truck careered wildly down Kantstrasse. The Theater des Westens soared past on the left as Remo floored the big vehicle. He aimed for the Kaiser Wilhelm Memorial Church.

"Hold on!" he yelled.

Without shifting gears, he whipped around the sharp corner and out across Kurfurstendamm. Cars driving in both directions slammed on brakes or swerved from the path of the seemingly out-of-control truck.

From around the facade of the huge church, dozens of tiny police cars soared. Bumping into one another, grinding paint on paint, they bunched up again. Like a swarm of angry wasps, they roared in the direction of the runaway truck, lights and sirens flashing and wailing.

Remo had taken the curve too sharply. The right wheels of the truck bounced once against the curb and began rising slowly into the air. The world took on a weird angled look as the vehicle began to tilt onto Remo's side.

"Lean over!" Remo commanded. Still holding the wheel, he flung himself toward the Master of Sinanju.

"Do not get too familiar," Chiun complained as the back of Remo's head popped into his field of vision. He tipped his own head to see around it.

"Dammit, Chiun, *lean!*" Remo commanded. Still on two wheels, they had managed to cross over to Tauenzienstrasse.

"You told me to hold on," Chiun pointed out. Though they had been outrunning the police for more than ten minutes, he was still as calm as a crystal pool.

"It was a figure of speech!" Remo yelled. *"Lean!"* He felt the van moving farther over. Another few seconds and they would be flat on one side and skidding at a hundred miles per hour.

Chiun sighed. "Very well." He tilted toward his door.

The Master of Sinanju's ninety-pound frame seemed to do the trick. With his weight added to Remo's, the truck collapsed back onto all four wheels, settling in an angry bounce of tires and grinding shocks.

Something broke free from beneath the truck. In the side-view mirror, it seemed to skip back into their wake and beneath the tires of one of the leading police cars.

As it bounced over the long strip of twisted metal, rubber erupted in hot bursts from both sides of the police cruiser. The car did a perfect 180-degree turn into the nose of another oncoming cruiser.

The crash was spectacular. A dozen police cars slammed into one another, buckling and crumpling like paper cups. The rest skipped around the huge crash site, driving even more determinedly after Remo.

"I hope they've got air bags," Remo commented as the horrid scene faded to a rapid speck behind them.

"They eat a diet of pastry and pork," Chiun explained indifferently. "Germans are their own air bags."

"You realize if they catch us they're going to find him in the back," Remo said. He jerked his head over his shoulder to indicate where various body parts of the dead Burg police officer were even now bouncing around amid the remnants of the Nibelungen Hoard.

"They had better not catch us," Chiun warned.

"I'm doing my best," Remo said, irritated.

He swerved in and out of traffic as he drove wildly down the wide street. Cars seemed to move almost instinctively out of his way. Those that did not were batted by the fenders of the truck. The metal was already a crumpled mess.

"That cop's brother must have ratted us out," Remo said, narrowly avoiding a collision with a van that was pulling out of a side street. The other vehicle slammed on its brakes. "Either that or somebody saw us at the cop car."

"I was nowhere near the constable's vehicle," Chiun pointed out. "I am innocent in that matter."

"Yeah, you only killed him," Remo snapped sourly.

"Oh, of course," Chiun sniffed. "Blame me for the dead highwayman. How like you, Remo."

"You killed him!" Remo snapped.

"A technicality," Chiun said dismissively. "Do not assault my delicate ears with trivialities."

"I've got another triviality for you," Remo said. "Your buddies aren't going to be too happy to see us show up with all of this going on around us."

"Do not concern yourself with them," Chiun said with certainty. "They will do as they are told."

"You hope," Remo said.

He cut around another sharp corner, more slowly this time. The truck's tires remained firmly on the street; however, the pursuing police cars seemed to leap dramatically ahead. They buzzed around the corner and into Remo's wake.

"This road appears closed," Chiun mentioned.

Remo had gotten the same impression. There was no vehicular traffic on the long thoroughfare. It hadn't been this way during any of his other trips. Far up ahead, Remo thought he saw why.

"Is that what I think it is?" he said anxiously.

"Where?" Chiun asked, peering through the

windshield like a Gypsy looking into the heart of a crystal ball. "Before the line of parked police vehicles or after it?"

"That's what I thought," Remo groaned.

He could see them clearly now. There were two rows of them. One lined up before the other. They stretched from one side of the street to the other, effectively blocking the avenue to through traffic.

Berlin police officers were standing with rifles before the cars, faces taut. Hazy rain dribbled across the stabs of flashing blue light issuing from the roofs of the dozens of parked cruisers.

"We could bail out here," Remo suggested rapidly. "They'd never catch us."

"And abandon my treasure to these sticky-fingered Huns?" Chiun asked, incredulous. "Never!"

"That's what I thought you'd say," Remo sighed. He hunched down behind the steering wheel. "Brace for impact."

When it became obvious that the truck was not going to slow down, the order to fire was given by the commanding officer on the scene. The gunfire started before they even slammed into the first line of cars. Rifle fire crackled through the damp evening air.

Quarter-size pockmarks erupted across the nose of the rushing truck. The windshield spiderwebbed then shattered in a spray of thick greenish chunks.

Remo and Chiun had ducked behind the dashboard. Glass exploded across their backs as they tore into the defensive police line.

Berlin police scattered out of the path of the truck like timid matadors from a crazed bull. The vehicle lurched as it slammed the first row of cars. Bullets riddled the doors and side panels as the large truck roared past.

Fortunately for Remo, the police cars were of the small European style. They were flung from the crumpling nose of the truck as it plowed forward into the second line. It pushed these aside, as well. More slowly now, it continued onward, bullets and shouts following it.

When he got back up, Remo saw the pursuing police cars winding their way through the twisted wreckage. Wind whipped around his stern face through the open front of the truck. He turned from the side-view mirror.

"This is getting worse and worse," Remo commented. "They'd just better not lock the gates before we can get there," he warned.

Chiun shook his head firmly. "They will not lock the gates," he insisted. "For they would not dare."

"ARE THE GATES SECURE?" Ambassador Pak Sok asked nervously. He was a squat man with a face as flat as a frying pan bottom. He wiped at his sweaty forehead with his handkerchief.

"Quite secure," replied the ambassador's assistant, who was also an officer of the Public Security Ministry.

Sok did not seem convinced.

It was not that he thought his aide was lying. Although he did not trust his assistant in most matters, Sok knew that he would not lie about something as trivial as a locked gate. He simply was not convinced that a locked gate would make any difference. In fact, it might only make things worse.

As ambassador for Choson Minchu-chui Inmin Konghwa-guk, otherwise known as the Democratic People's Republic of Korea, Sok was his country's highest-ranking diplomat in Germany. He enjoyed all the perks of his posting, including access to Germany's uncensored television broadcasts. It was on the TV that he had seen an image that made his heart sink.

The television was on now, sound down. In the large living room of the North Korean embassy, Sok turned away from the tall multipaned window, looking back at the screen.

A white truck continued to race desperately down Germany's streets, relentlessly pursued by an ever growing convoy of police vehicles. A news helicopter had been following the action from the sky for the past twenty minutes.

To Sok it looked almost like the internationally famous chase that had taken place in America a few years back. But this time the truck was driving at breakneck speed, not at a snail's pace. And there was not an ex-football player cowering in the vehicle. Sok would have *preferred* that it be an American celebrity unknown to him. Unfortunately, he knew all too well who was in that truck.

"He cannot hope to come here," Ambassador Sok's aide said, watching the screen intently. The truck was racing down familiar streets. It was only a few blocks from the embassy.

"I would hope not," Sok agreed, his voice betraying his jangled nerves. He turned from the television back to the window. His fingers gripped tightly at the thick silk fabric of the red floor-length curtains. Vines crept artfully away from the walls and across strategic portions of windowpane. "You are *certain* the gates are locked?" the ambassador asked.

"Yes, yes." The aide nodded. He bit a thumbnail as he stared at the TV screen. Eyes growing wide, he suddenly grabbed for the remote control.

Sok heard the gunshots beneath the serious German voice of the reporter. He wheeled around in time to see the truck barrel into a line of parked police cruisers. Cars flew in every direction as the truck pummeled its way through to the other side. It skidded sideways momentarily and then righted itself, racing away from the smashed cars.

"Where is that?" Sok asked.

"About two—"

"Wait," the ambassador demanded, raising a quieting hand. "Turn that down," he ordered.

The aide did as he was told. When the sound had been muted once more, they continued to hear the muffled gunshots. A moment later, Sok's heart sunk as he heard the frantic squeal of tires. Turning back to the TV, he saw the truck finishing up a crazed turn around a very familiar corner.

"They are here," the ambassador said, his voice dead.

"THE GATES ARE CLOSED!" Remo yelled as the truck screamed up to the North Korean embassy.

"They do not leave them open on a normal day," the Master of Sinanju pointed out. Gusts of air from the open windshield whipped fiercely at the gossamer tufts of hair above each ear.

"The guards have guns!" Remo shouted.

"Do they not always?"

"Not pointed at us!" Remo replied.

At least ten embassy guards were standing in the long driveway just inside the closed gate. Kalashnikov rifles jutted through the spaces in the tall wrought-iron fence, aimed directly at the nose of the approaching truck.

Remo's mirror had been picked off by a Berlin police officer. A big enough slab of glass remained that he was able to see the cruisers closing in behind.

"There's not enough time to stop," Remo warned Chiun.

"Do as you must," the Master of Sinanju conceded. ''Just do not lose any of my precious treasure.''

''That's the least of my worries right now,'' Remo said.

Turning the wheel sharply to the right, Remo jumped the truck onto the curb at an angle. The big vehicle tipped slightly to one side. Rapidly, he cut the wheel to the left. The vehicle leveled off as it raced across the sidewalk.

Beyond the gates, the eyes of the Korean embassy guards grew wide as the truck barreled remorselessly toward them. As one, the guards opened fire.

They did not have much time to shoot.

The truck crashed the gates a second later, scooping up four guards and flinging them roughly aside. The others scattered like flung jacks into the bushes as the truck flew crazily up the drive.

The brakes were hit the instant the truck struck the gates. Tires screamed in protest as the vehicle screeched toward the ambassador's residence. Black streaks of smoking rubber spread in crazy zigzags as the truck tried frantically to both stop and remain upright while doing so.

In the end, it could not do both.

Halfway up the driveway the big truck toppled over onto its passenger's side. Sparks popped and paint ripped away as the vehicle slid toward the ivy-covered brick walls of the Korean embassy.

Inside the vehicle, Remo and Chiun kept their

bodies loose. The moment the truck hit the driveway, they met the impact with an equal repulsive force. They immediately joined with it. The two Masters of Sinanju floated as safely as babies in a pool of amniotic fluid as the truck skidded to a slow, determined stop.

A slight impact at the last moment indicated that the truck had tapped against the wall of the embassy building. Sideways now, Remo could see oddly vertical bricks piled up through the smashed windshield.

The sudden intense silence was filled almost instantly by the sounds of car after car squealing to a stop back beyond the blown-open gates of the embassy. Shouts in both German and Korean filled the air.

Sitting sideways on the upended truck seat, Remo Williams listened to the yelling voices outside. He had one hand braced against the roof of the truck. "We're not out of the woods yet," he commented. He glanced over to the Master of Sinanju—more a glance down than sideways now.

Beyond Chiun's broken window was driveway. The old Korean had braced one bony hand similarly against the roof.

"You did that on purpose," Chiun accused.

"Did what?" Remo asked, his brow creasing.

"You deliberately tipped this vehicle over onto its side." He looked at the pavement, which was framed in his window like some strange modern painting rendered in asphalt.

"Geez, Chiun, we've got more important stuff to worry about right now," Remo complained.

Scuffling footsteps sounded immediately outside the truck. For a moment, Remo thought that the Berlin police had dared to venture onto embassy grounds. But all at once, a familiar red face appeared in the remnants of the front windshield. Remo recognized Ambassador Sok.

"Sorry. We thought this was the McDonald's drive thru," Remo said with an apologetic shrug.

The Korean diplomat was very undiplomatic in his expression. Clearly, he would have found this whole incident more pleasing if Remo and Chiun had perished in the crash.

His face pinched disapprovingly as he rose wordlessly from his bent posture. Almost as soon as he was gone, he began shouting down to the gathered police. He spoke in English, the accepted international language.

"Diplomatic immunity! Diplomatic immunity! These are Korean diplomats and this is sovereign North Korean soil! Please to stay beyond fence!"

Sok's voice grew more faint as he hustled down the drive to the twisted remnants of the embassy gates. He was greeted with shouts and jeers from the Berlin police.

Somewhere far above, Remo heard a helicopter rattling loudly.

"Let's take stock, shall we?" Remo suggested heartily. "So far we've pissed off the Germans, the Koreans and—when Smith finds out about this—America, as well. All that for a few scraps of yellow metal. Whaddaya think?" he asked with growing sarcasm. "Was it all worth it, Chiun?"

On the seat below him, the elderly Korean turned a baleful eye up to his pupil.

"Yes," droned the Master of Sinanju simply, adding, "and I am not talking to you."

5

"No way," Dr. Wendell, the surgeon who had performed the emergency procedure, had insisted. "I will not be a party to it. If you leave, it is with my strongest reservations."

"Listen to reason," suggested Dr. Styles, the general practitioner who had diagnosed the edema. But though he used his most rational tone, his words fell on deaf ears.

"Folcroft Sanitarium is more than suited to handle these cases," the doctors' patient had declared.

The doctors pushed hard for an extended stay—unusual in the modern era of "everything as outpatient" medicine. But this was an extreme case; the patient was at the sensitive time of life when the seriousness of something such as excess fluid on the brain could not be overstated.

Already, while in the care of New York's Columbus-Jesuit Hospital, he had fallen once on the way to the bathroom. Of course, it had been the night after the operation and he should not have been out of bed in the first place, but their patient was determined.

"Determined to kill himself," Dr. Wendell muttered to Dr. Styles in the hallway prior to their last attempt to keep their patient in the hospital one more day.

He was running a big risk leaving, but their patient had made up his mind. Apparently, that was that.

Of course, he could suffer more dizzy spells that might cause him to fall down a flight of stairs. The fluid could build up once more. Most insidious of all, years down the road he might even develop a tumor at the site. Who knew? In such cases, it was always best to play it safe.

"This is craziness," Dr. Styles said. "You've only been here two days."

"Where are my trousers?" Harold W. Smith asked in reply.

Smith was an absolutely terrible patient. Full of intelligent questions and eager to get everything over with as quickly as possible. Even brain surgery.

The old axiom was true. Doctors did make the worst patients. The fact that the gaunt old man was listed as "Smith, Dr. Harold W." on all of his hospital forms went a long way toward explaining his attitude. But though Smith held the title of doctor, no one—not even his personal physician—seemed to know what he was a doctor of.

He was director of Folcroft Sanitarium in Rye, New York. That much was clear. For it was into the care of this respected but terribly exclusive and secretive care facility that Harold Smith was given over.

Smith accepted the mandatory wheelchair ride out of the hospital without complaint. A parsimonious man, he reasoned that the orderly assigned to escort him from Columbus-Jesuit would be paid whether he wheeled Smith to a waiting car or not. Better that the boy did his job as he rightly should rather than use for idle purposes the ten minutes it took to bring Smith downstairs. And—though Smith hated to admit it—the Folcroft administrator was not sure if he could have walked down on his own.

Dr. Lance Drew was waiting for him downstairs.

Dr. Drew was the chief physician at Folcroft, answerable directly to Smith. He instantly took over from the orderly, aiding his frail-looking employer into his car. It was a forty-five minute drive from the city to Rye.

When the familiar high wall of Folcroft appeared beside the road, the sight seemed to hearten Smith.

He was not an emotional man by any stretch of the imagination. Few physical objects held much meaning to the taciturn Harold Smith. But Folcroft was different. It had—in a large way—been his home for more than three decades. Rarely did a day go by without Smith's passing between the somber granite lions set above the gates of the venerable old institution.

In a sense, this was a homecoming. Although he had never entered the grounds in quite this way before, he felt more energized than he had in a long time. Even when he was feeling perfectly well.

Taking the car past the small guard shack, Dr. Drew drove rapidly up the great gravel driveway to the main building. He parked at the front steps, hurrying around to the passenger's-side door.

At first, Smith was determined to negotiate the stairs on his own. He found, however, that he was having trouble simply getting out of the car.

"Please take my arm," Smith asked eventually. His reserved tone belied his embarrassment.

Dr. Drew did as he was instructed. When he reached a helpful hand for Smith's battered leather briefcase—the only luggage the Folcroft director had brought with him to the hospital—Smith pulled it away. His strength in this seemed quite surprising.

"I will carry it," he insisted.

Drew only shrugged. He held firmly on to Smith's biceps as Smith clasped the doctor's forearm for support.

"Careful, careful," Dr. Drew instructed soothingly when they were at the stairs. "Take them slowly. We have all day."

Smith found Drew's tone patronizing in the extreme. He would have liked to have said something, but all of his energies were being devoted to negotiating the staircase. It had never seemed so high before.

Once inside, Smith settled into a room in the special Folcroft wing. Virtually deserted now, it only held patients on an infrequent basis.

There Smith worked, not only on his recovery, but on the small laptop computer that he kept stored in his precious leather briefcase.

Like the physicians at Columbus-Jesuit, Dr. Drew discouraged Smith from working. There was nothing, he said, that would not keep until the Folcroft administrator had made a complete recovery.

"Hydrocephaly is no small matter, Dr. Smith," Dr. Drew said.

"I am aware of that," Smith replied as he typed away at his keyboard. He was careful to keep the text on the small bar screen turned away from the Folcroft doctor.

"It is an accumulation of cerebrospinal fluid inside the skull. Your skull. Where your brain is?"

"I do not appreciate sarcasm," Smith replied crisply, eyes leveled on his computer.

Dr. Drew merely threw up his hands and left.

Of course, Smith knew how serious his medical condition had been. It was the result of an obstruction caused by a severe blow to the head. The unrelieved pressure had caused Smith much discomfort for many days, including vision problems, nausea, vomiting and a relentless, pounding head-ache. The headache had been the thing that finally propelled him to the doctor and ultimately to surgery.

But the bandages were gone now, the small incision scar was a puffy memory of the operation and the patch of gray-white hair that had been shaved from his pate was on its stubbly way to filling back in. It was three weeks after the operation now, and Smith was firmly on the road to complete recovery.

Besides, he had work to do.

Not Folcroft business. If it became necessary, his secretary was well trained by her employer to handle long absences. The work that occupied all of Smith's time as he sat alone in the virtually abandoned wing of the big old institution had nothing to do with the grounds or building in which he had toiled tirelessly for thirty-plus years. Truth be told, every last brick of Folcroft could have toppled over into the cold black waters of Long Island Sound and the lifework of Harold W. Smith would still go on.

Unbeknownst to all who worked there save Smith himself, Folcroft was merely a cover. A public face for a most private enterprise.

It would have shocked the staff to learn that the place to which they reported to work every day was in reality the greatest and most damning secret in the two-and-a-quarter-century history of the United States Constitution.

Folcroft was the home of CURE, a supersecret agency of the U.S. government.

In the dusty basement of Folcroft, a hidden bank of four mainframe computers augmented with optical WORM-drive servers toiled endlessly and anonymously. Locating, collecting, collating information from the World Wide Web. The Folcroft Four, as Smith had dubbed the computers in a rare display of creativity, stretched their fiber-optic tendrils literally around the world. The data gathered was brought back electronically to Smith for his perusal.

Ordinarily, Smith would have accessed the information from a hidden terminal in his office desk. But Harold Smith was nothing if not adaptable. Circumstances had forced him for the time being to utilize the small laptop setup that he ordinarily used when away from Folcroft.

As director of CURE, Smith was charged with safeguarding the nation against threats both internal and external. In the most dire circumstances, he was allowed to employ the most powerful force in the U.S. arsenal. But at the moment, there were no dire issues facing either CURE or America. It was for this reason that Smith had allowed the agency's two secret weapons time to retrieve some personal property from Germany.

The Nibelungen Hoard. Smith still did not quite

believe that Remo and Chiun had found the Hoard. If the legends were true, it was a dangerous amount of wealth for anyone to have.

The same madman whose attack had caused the fluid buildup on Smith's brain could have used the gold to destroy the economy of Germany. Adolf Kluge was dead now, but that would not prevent another from taking up his banner of destruction. This was the reason Smith had insisted Remo and Chiun transport the Hoard to Chiun's native village of Sinanju as quickly as possible. It would be safe there, languishing amid the other treasure for millennia to come.

The past few months had been very trying. For all of them. But it seemed as if a turning point had at last been reached. And if not that, at least it was a lull. There had been so few of them in the past thirty years that Smith had decided to enjoy this one.

As he typed at his laptop, the CURE director sighed contentedly.

Seconds later, a nurse raced into the room dragging an emergency crash cart behind her.

"Oh," she said, wheeling the cart to a sudden, skidding stop. A look of intense concern crossed her face. "Are you all right, Dr. Smith?"

"What?" Smith asked, looking up from his computer. "Yes," he said, confused. "Yes, I am fine."

"I thought I heard you gasping for air," she

said, her tone apologetic. "It sounded like an asthmatic attack. Or worse."

Smith's gray face puckered in slight perplexity. "I made no such sound," he said.

Dr. Drew raced into the room a moment later. He skidded to a stop next to the nurse. When he saw Smith sitting up calmly in bed, he turned, panting, to the middle-aged woman.

"Did you call a Code Blue?" he demanded.

"I'm sorry, Doctor," she apologized. "I thought he was going into respiratory failure."

"I do not know what it is you heard, Nurse," Smith said. "But I assure you I feel fine."

Turning away from the doctor and nurse, Smith resumed typing. As his fingers tapped swiftly away at the keyboard, he thought again how calm the world scene was at the moment. As he did so, another pleased sigh escaped his gray lips. It sounded like a dying moose attempting to yodel up a rusted radiator pipe.

Dr. Drew and the nurse glanced at one another in immediate understanding. Without another word, the nurse rolled the crash cart back out into the hallway, leaving Dr. Drew alone with Smith.

"How are you feeling today, Dr. Smith?" Drew asked. He was forced to compete with Smith's clattering keyboard for attention. He tried not to show his irritation.

"As I said, Doctor, I am fine," Smith said. His

eyes did not lift from the text on his computer screen.

To Dr. Lance Drew, it was like battling a television for a teenager's attention.

Drew made a soft humming noise. "While I'm here…" he said more to himself than to Smith.

The doctor went over and collected a blood-pressure cuff from a netted holder in the wall. Smith stopped typing long enough with one hand to allow Dr. Drew to slip the cuff up onto his left biceps.

"It would help if you didn't type," Dr. Drew complained as he adjusted his stethoscope under the inflatable bag.

It was as if Smith didn't hear him. The constant clattering noise and the slight arm motion would make it difficult. Frowning, Drew watched the indicator needle as much as listened to the uneven heartbeat of his employer.

Typing furiously at his laptop, Smith had been careful enough to inch the computer to one side in order to keep his work away from Drew's prying eyes. For a moment, the endless staccato drumming of his arthritic fingers against the keyboard paused as he read an AP report the CURE system had flagged.

There had been a break-in the previous night at the Boston Museum of Rare Arts. Three guards were dead, but no valuable artifacts had been taken.

The strangeness of the report was what brought it to the attention of the CURE mainframes. As best as could be determined by a curator, the Greek exhibit of the classical art collection was all that had interested the burglars. And even with the kind of focus the robbers had apparently had, they had ignored the most valuable Greek pottery and Roman glass on display, choosing instead to steal what was being described by the museum as a "common stone artifact."

It was not a job for CURE. Smith was certainly not going to recall Remo and Chiun from Europe to go looking for a useless museum piece.

Smith was about to leave the article when his computer suddenly did so for him. The AP story winked out, replaced by another story, this one attributed to Reuters.

He read the straightforward lines of text quickly, wondering what it was his computers had found so intriguing. It did not take long for him to realize why the Folcroft Four had pulled the story from the Web.

"What's wrong?" a concerned voice beside Smith asked.

Smith's eyes shot up from his computer, shocked. Dr. Drew was standing there. Stethoscope earpieces hung down from either side of his head.

"What?" Smith croaked.

"Your blood pressure," Drew explained. "Your heart rate just shot through the roof."

"No," Smith said, swallowing. "No, I am fine." The words were hollow.

Smith was trying desperately to think. Already his head had begun to ache, bringing back too recent memories of his painful ordeal.

"Is there something I can do?" Dr. Drew offered helpfully. Detaching his stethoscope, he leaned to one side, trying to get a peek at Smith's computer.

Smith instantly slapped the thin folding screen down over the keyboard and hard drive, obscuring the text.

"I'm fine!" Smith snapped. "That will be all."

Dr. Drew stiffened. For a man used to respect, Smith's rudeness at times was intolerable. With only a cursory nod to his patient and employer, he left the hospital room.

As soon as the Folcroft doctor had exited the room, Harold Smith shut down his remote computer. He had wasted far too much time in bed. It was time to get to his office.

Dropping his bare feet to the floor, Smith stepped uncertainly over to the closet in search of his suit.

6

Fifteen minutes later, Harold Smith was out of his pajamas, dressed in his familiar gray three-piece suit with attendant Dartmouth tie, and sitting in the more comfortable environs of his Spartan Folcroft administrator's office.

The headache he was experiencing was not as it had been. The pain now was like the ghostly afterimage of the dangerous bout of hydrocephaly. Still, it was enough to remind him of all he had been through.

Smith held firmly to the edge of his desk with one bony hand while with the other he clamped his blue desk phone to one ear. He waited only a few moments for the scrambled satellite call to be picked up by the North Korean embassy in Berlin.

"Apprentice Reigning Master of Sinanju, please," he said to the Korean voice that answered. There was no need for secrecy. A sophisticated program ensured that the call could not be traced back to Folcroft.

It was the word *Sinanju* that did it. Although the

man who answered apparently spoke no English, he dropped the phone the minute it was spoken.

Moments later, Remo's familiar voice came on the line.

"What kept you?" he said by way of introduction.

"Have you lost your mind?" Smith demanded.

"Cripes, what's the matter, Smitty? Someone squirt an extra quart of alum in your enema this morning?"

"Remo, this is serious," Smith insisted. "I have the news on in my office right now." He glanced at the old battered black-and-white TV set. "They are playing videotape of what can only be you and the Master of Sinanju in a high-speed chase with Berlin police."

"Edited or unedited?"

"What?" Smith asked sourly. "Edited, it appears," he said, glancing at the screen. "Why?"

"'Cause over here we're getting the full treatment. They've rebroadcast the whole chase virtually in its entirety a bunch of times since last night."

"Remo, you almost sound proud," Smith said, shocked. "You must know that this is outra—" He froze in midword. "My God," he gasped.

"The gate crash, right?" Remo guessed. "Beautiful piece of driving if I do say so myself."

On the screen of Smith's portable TV, Remo's rental truck had just burst through the twin gates of the Korean embassy. Guards were flung to either side as the truck flipped over, skidding in a spectacular slide up to the front wall of the brick building. Every inch of the incredible crash had been recorded by a German news helicopter.

"This is beyond belief," the CURE director announced. His stomach ached. If his head reeled any more, it would tangle in the phone cord. At this moment, strangulation would be a blessed relief.

"I thought so, too," Remo said proudly. "It was touch and go for a little while there, but we came out of it okay. Except Chiun is a little ticked at me. But he'll get over it."

"No, I will not!" the squeaky voice of the Master of Sinanju yelled from the background.

"Remo," Smith said, trying to infuse his voice with a reasonable tone. It was not easy. "I do not know what to say. You have recklessly and deliberately compromised yourself. According to what I have read, this footage is playing the world over. The German authorities are screaming for your heads."

"Can't do it," Remo said. "Extraterritoriality. As official representatives of the North Korean government we are exempt from the laws of our host nation. That would be Germany. Legally, they can't touch us."

"You are not Korean diplomats," Smith explained slowly.

"I am Korean," Chiun called. "And am quite diplomatic."

"Tell Master Chiun that—semantics notwithstanding—he is absolutely, unequivocally not a representative of the North Korean government," Smith deadpanned.

"You're not a diplomat, Little Father," Remo called.

"Do not 'Little Father' me, flipper of trucks," Chiun snapped back.

"He says he's not talking to me," Remo explained to Smith. "Of course, as usual, that only lasts until he can come up with the next insult."

"Nitwit," Chiun called.

"See?" Remo said.

"This is insane," Smith said, aghast at Remo's flippant attitude. "How can you not realize the seriousness of this situation? My God, Remo, they *filmed* you."

"Videotaped, actually," Remo said. "And while we're at it—no, they didn't."

"I can see you!" Smith snapped. The image of the battered truck was replaced by a vapid news anchor.

"You see a truck, Smitty," Remo explained patiently. "You didn't see either of our faces. You know how Chiun and I can avoid being shot by cameras."

"That is irrelevant," Smith said. "You are found out. According to reports, the Berlin police have the embassy surrounded. The German government has gotten involved in the situation. North Korea is stonewalling for now, but that will not last. The two of you are sitting in the middle of a growing storm of international scrutiny."

"Not for long," Remo said confidently. "We're getting out tonight."

"How?" Smith asked, instantly wary.

"Don't you worry your pretty little head," Remo said soothingly. "Just rest assured that those police barricades won't stop us. We should be fine on this end as long as we don't get turned in first."

"Is there a danger of that?"

"Unlikely. The ambassador is scared to death of us. He knows all about Sinanju, so he doesn't want to cross us. The guy who worries me is his aide. I think he's with the secret police or something."

Smith closed his eyes as he considered the predicament. "I told you I was not comfortable with your going to the North Korean government for help," he said.

"You're the one who told us we were on our own."

"And I stand by that. CURE's facilities are not at your disposal when you wish to smuggle the Nibelungen Hoard out of Germany," Smith said, restating his earlier position.

"Which is why Chiun turned to North Korea," Remo said. "It's easier this way, Smitty. That dipshit Kim Jong Il pees his pants whenever he hears

Chiun's name. He couldn't wait to loan us his personal jet. Diplomatic pouch. No searches. Zip, bang, boom into Pyongyang Airport. Every trip has been flawless. We were home free until today.''

Eyes still closed, Smith pinched the bridge of his nose. "How much treasure is left?" he asked wearily.

"Not much," Remo said. "Luckily, we were on our last run. A couple of boxes. Maybe twenty, twenty-five in all. About as big as orange crates."

"You can get them out undetected?"

"Bet on it," Remo said.

"I would prefer not to," Smith said dryly. He exhaled a loud, painful puff of stale air. "Do what you have to as quickly as you possibly can. I want you both off of German soil and back here at the absolute earliest. Is that clear?"

"Not a problem," Remo said amiably. "Consider us already gone. By the way, you don't sound too chipper. How are you feeling, Smitty?"

Smith did not even bother to reply. With an exhausted stretch of his tired arm, he dropped the blue receiver back into the old-fashioned cradle.

7

Whenever Dan Bergdorf slept, he had nightmares.

The dream pattern was always the same. He was in the middle of some grand disaster movie from the 1970s. Not the actual film itself, but the *making* of the film. Dan would be on a plane with Burt Lancaster, directing an epic crash. Cameras would roll, Dan would call "Action" and all at once the dummy bomb from props would somehow wind up being real. The explosion would rip through the fuselage, and the plane would make a screaming beeline for the ground thirty thousand feet below. Unlike in the movies, all aboard perished.

Sometimes he was putting out skyscraper fires with Steve McQueen. Other times he was crawling through greasy passageways of a capsized luxury liner with Gene Hackman. Always, the phony disaster would wind up being all too real. At the terrifying moment his dream alter ego perished in whatever the latest calamity might be, Dan would scream himself awake.

Sweating, panting, disoriented, Dan would realize as he came back to his senses that it had all been a bad dream.

And as the horror of reality sank in, he would realize that his sleeping nightmares were nowhere near as bad as his waking one.

Unlike in his dreams, Dan did not work in motion pictures. He was an executive producer of special projects for a small television station in Passaic, New Jersey.

WAST-TV Channel 8 had tried to make a name for itself in the syndication market a few years before. Right out of the box, they had a major hit that the station's top brass was certain would propel them into the vanguard of television's burgeoning new frontier.

New York radio shock jock Harold Stein had branched out into low-budget TV. The marriage between the raunchy radio-show host and Channel 8 seemed to be one made in heaven. Or perhaps somewhere farther south. In any event, *The Harold Stein Show* was a syndicated sensation. In some markets, it even beat out the tired *Saturday Night Live* in the ratings.

As executive producer for the *Stein* show, Dan and Channel 8 had ridden the crest of a wave that would surely take them all on to bigger and better things.

Or so they thought.

After only two seasons working on the hour-long show, Stein called it quits, citing his intense displeasure with the cheapness of the program as his primary reason. Channel 8's stock and reputation instantly took a nosedive.

After a few years of desperate scrambling—in a twist right out of Charles Dickens—the failing station was bought up by a mysterious benefactor. An immediate infusion of cash from this unknown source instantly brought Channel 8 back into the black. Prospects brightened. Some new staff were even hired. For the first time since the Stein debacle, Dan Bergdorf had allowed himself to get his hopes up. That lasted until the day he was brought into the general manager's office to meet the new owner.

All hope for a future in legitimate television and films vanished the moment he learned who his new employer was.

Dan instantly recognized Man Hyung Sun. It was the night of that very first meeting that the dreams had started.

His nightmares had only gotten worse over the years. By the time Sun showed himself as the owner of Channel 8, it was already too late for Dan. He was branded a Loonie by every station in the country.

The flurry of résumés he sent out was ignored. Phone calls to supposed friends who had made it in the industry were not returned. Dan became an outcast. With no other prospects in life, he was forced to remain at Channel 8.

At WAST, Dan was put in charge of special projects. That was the Channel 8 term for infomercials.

These program-length commercials usually involved cellulite cream, "magic" abdominal exercises or real-estate scams. Apparently, the glut already on the market was not enough to prevent Channel 8 from making a tidy little profit on these syndicated half-hour ads. It seemed that people could not get enough of them.

Dan, of course, was not one of those people.

"What kind of asshole is up at 3:00 a.m. watching 'Professor Brilliant's Amazing Patented Exfoliation Sensation'?" he demanded of his secretary one day after seeing the New York ratings for the infomercial.

"Have you seen it?" she asked. "It's pretty funny."

"I don't have to watch it, honey," Dan deadpanned. "I was there when they shot that disaster. First, it ain't that funny. Plus, Professor Brilliant's wig looks like a dead poodle. Plus, the sets are cheesier than a Wisconsin dairy farm. Plus, get me a cup of coffee now or you're fired."

His attitude at work was at least that bad every day since the Loonie takeover. Worse on days after one of his celebrity-filled disaster nightmares.

On the day he met with former governor and presidential candidate Mike Principi, Dan Bergdorf was still recovering from the night he had spent stumbling through earthquake-ravaged Los Angeles with Charlton Heston and Ava Gardner.

"Governor Princippi," Dan said, trying to force images of tumbledown buildings and devastated streets from his mind. "It's a genuine pleasure to meet you."

After the men shook hands, Dan took a seat on his office couch, indicating that Princippi should sit in a comfortable overstuffed chair.

"I must say, I'm a bit surprised to see you here," Dan admitted. He pitched his voice low. "We don't generally get people of your caliber at Channel 8." His voice dropped even lower, as if imparting a shameful secret. He was. "I voted for you, by the way," Dan added.

Clearly, the ex-presidential candidate was not interested in discussing his disastrous campaign. "Do you know what this is about?" Princippi asked officiously.

Dan clapped his hands on his knees. He shrugged. "To tell you the truth, I'm in the dark. Something about cutting an infotainment spot, I imagine. What did you have in mind?"

"It isn't my idea," Princippi stated firmly.

Dan raised his hands. "No explanations necessary. I'm just a producer here. Probably something your people cooked up, right? Well, I can guarantee you a spot classier than those Ross Perot cheese-ball segments. Laying the groundwork for 2000, eh? I tell you, I'll vote for you again."

"It is nonpolitical," Princippi interrupted. He was beginning to fidget in his chair.

Dan seemed disappointed. "Really?" he asked.

"It's more along the lines of—" Princippi cut himself off. His pasty face had flushed red. "They really didn't tell you anything?"

Dan shook his head. "General manager told me I was meeting with you, that's all. Top guy himself wanted me to. I guess ole king Loonie has seen some of my work. Probably 'Thirty Days to Thinner Thighs.' That gets a lot of airplay in Washington. He's still near Washington, right?"

Princippi glanced at the closed door. "Actually…" he began uncomfortably.

TEN MINUTES LATER, Dan found himself pacing back and forth on one of the Channel 8 stages, trying to force images of a sweating, screaming George Kennedy from his mind.

The Loonies had descended.

Men in pink saris draped over flowing white robes stood crammed like vapid, gaily colored sardines all around the perimeter of the small stage. The focus of their attention was the lone man standing in the wings, waiting to go on.

Man Hyung Sun. The leader of the Sunnie cult himself was waiting patiently for a cue from the stage manager.

It had been bad for Dan Bergdorf before, but never this bad. Sun might have owned Channel 8 but he had only visited the station once seven years ago. Since the Korean cultist was not involved in the day-to-day operations of the station, Dan could pretend that he was working for someone else.

The station manager.

The program director.

Anyone but Sun.

"Look at them," Dan mumbled as he glanced at the sea of blank, beaming Sunnie faces. "They're frigging drones."

On the set, Mike Princippi was pretending to be involved in a high-level meeting of political strategists. Reading from cue cards, he and the three other men were wondering how they could possibly hope to outthink their crafty opponent.

To the right of the action, the stage manager dropped a hand rapidly, pointing a finger at Sun. The cult leader took his cue without missing a beat. He strode magnificently into the shot, much to the feigned amazement of the men already being videotaped.

"Oh, hello," Mike Princippi said. "Aren't you Reverend Man Hyung Sun?"

Offstage, Dan groaned quietly.

The set was beyond obscenely cheap. Ratty, space-filling nylon drapes hung in sheets across the gaps in the artificial wall backdrops. The color of everything was washed-out green and drab blue. The furniture was strictly cable access. No question about it.

This was going to be the blackest smear on Dan's résumé to date. He'd never recover from this one. With a sinking feeling in his stomach, he watched for the cult leader's reply along with the anxious, awestruck Sunnies.

"I am he," Sun intoned to the overly eager men. "I am the future. I am your future. I know your destiny." Sun turned dramatically to the camera. He pointed directly at the lens. "And yours."

Hold…and…

"Cut!" the director shouted.

The gathered Loonies immediately burst into wildly enthusiastic applause.

Sun took the ovation as his due. He did not even look at his followers as he stepped back, allowing the stage hands space to do their jobs.

On the set next to Sun, Mike Principi looked as if someone had just told him his wife had been picked up again for drinking liquid ant repellent in the ladies' room of the local Stop 'n' Shop.

Stage hands swept in to set up for the next scene. And beyond the row of furiously clapping Loonies, Dan Bergdorf was in a pathetic, mute fog.

Dan was picturing himself in a field with Michael Caine. Both he and the actor were being descended on by a swarm of South American killer bees. With each slap of applause from the Sunnies, Dan literally felt another single bee sting.

Sting after sting after sting.

Until his pathetic career in television at last fell over and died.

8

Rim Kun Soe was displeased.

He had been posted to Berlin to assist Ambassador Sok after an embarrassing incident involving a representative of North Korea's Culture and Art Ministry.

More than a month before, the Culture and Art Ministry agent had been implicated in a scandal involving smuggling, accepting bribes, abetting an enemy of North Korea and a host of other infractions. More grave than any of his crimes against the Democratic People's Republic was his crime against the Master of Sinanju. Keijo Suk—the Culture and Art Ministry representative to Germany—had sneaked into the Master's home while he was abroad and had stolen an ancient artifact. For his theft, Suk had paid in blood.

The upshot of the whole sordid affair was a shake-up at the Berlin mission. Many of the older staff were recalled to North Korea. Anyone who was a friend or even an innocent associate of Suk was sent back home only to learn that he or she had been dismissed from the foreign service.

One of the few people to stay after the debacle was over was Ambassador Pak Sok. This did not mean that Sok was above suspicion, by any means. Rim Kun Soe had been specifically assigned by the Public Security Minister's office to keep an eye on the Ambassador. After all, Keijo Suk's indiscretion had taken place on Pak Sok's watch. It was possible that the ambassador had been compromised, as well.

Rim Kun Soe had not been settled into his quarters at the Berlin mission for more than three days when evidence of the betrayal of Ambassador Sok became apparent.

There was a knock on the door. Impossible, given the fences and guards around the embassy building.

Soe had answered the door only to find an ancient Korean standing on the broad steps. He was in the company of a much younger man who was obviously not Korean.

"I would speak with the ambassador," the old one had intoned.

"Who are you, ancient one?" Soe had demanded. "How do you come to stand here without alerting our guards?"

"Guards see only what guards see," the old man had said by way of explanation.

"Yeah. And mares eat oats and does eat oats,"

the young one had said, peeved. "Can we get this over with?"

American. Obviously. Soe had instantly screamed for the guards. That had been a mistake.

Three armed men arrived. Stunned to see the pair who had somehow penetrated their security, they had instantly raised their weapons. That, too, was a mistake.

The old one stood placidly, eyes resting flatly on Soe's increasingly shocked face, while the young one turned to the North Korean soldiers.

Soe never even saw the hands move. All he managed to glimpse were the obvious aftereffects of the young man's flashing hands.

Six small somethings banged against the door that Soe held open. He found out later that they were kneecaps.

The three men fell to the ground, mouths open in shock.

Guns hopped from hands as if charged with electricity. The young one steepled the rifles together above a nearby rosebush before turning back to the screaming soldiers.

Toe kicks to foreheads finished the trio. Afterward, the young American took the bodies and leaned them against one another much as he had done with the rifles. They formed a macabre tripod on the opposite side of the steps from their weapons.

The soldiers had not fired a single shot.

Soe puffed out his chest, pulling his eyes away from the carnage. "I will die, as well, before I betray Korea," he announced courageously.

"Don't tempt me," the American said, grabbing Soe by the face and pushing him back inside the embassy.

Inside the mission, Ambassador Sok was called. Rim Kun Soe accused him of giving aid to the enemy.

Sok denied the charge.

Only after an emergency call to Pyongyang placed by the old intruder himself was it determined that this was none other than the Master of Sinanju in their midst.

On the telephone, Kim Jong Il, Supreme Leader of the DPRK and secretary-general of the Korean Workers' Party, had himself insisted that the embassy and its staff be put at the disposal of the great Sinanju Master. In an ironic quirk of fate, Soe— who had been placed in Berlin because of the criminal actions of another—was put in charge of a smuggling scheme far greater than the one that had gotten him posted to Germany in the first place.

It was the aide to the ambassador who had made arrangements for each shipment of Chiun's gold to be slipped in secret aboard Kim Jong Il's private jet.

There was too much treasure to be sent at one time. The plane never would have gotten off the ground if they had attempted to send the Nibelungen Hoard to North Korea all at once. As it was, the two dozen flights had probably been overloaded. Luck had been with them so far.

At the far end, Soe learned from friends in the security ministry that a caretaker for the Master of Sinanju met every shipment. Soldiers were conscripted into service to haul the treasure back to Sinanju. It was an incredible waste of men and resources, all for one small man who somehow had all of the North Korean government wrapped around his bony fingers.

Rim Kun Soe greatly resented the Master of Sinanju. The old one represented greed more typical of the decadent West than of Soe's beloved Korea. He also had an infuriating habit of casting aspersions on Soe's native city of Pyongyang. These generally involved members of his immediate family.

Soe would have delighted in killing the old one.

And, as bad as the Master of Sinanju was, his pupil was even worse. An American of polluted lineage, he was surly, smart-mouthed and easily annoyed.

Soe had been looking forward to the day when this dubious enterprise was at last over. That was supposed to have been today. Now that was in doubt.

Standing in the basement of the Berlin embassy, the ambassador's aide made certain the crates had been secured as per the instructions of the Master of Sinanju's protégé.

The wooden lids were nailed tightly shut. There were no holes through which a single coin or gem could drop.

Soe hefted the nearest crate.

Heavy. It would take two men at a time to bring them out to the wall of the embassy.

He dropped it back to the floor, feeling the heaviness in his straining arm muscles.

"You and you," he said, tapping the chests of the nearest pair of waiting soldiers. "This one." He pointed to the crate he had just lifted.

Dutifully, the men lifted the heavy chest.

"Do not make a sound," he instructed.

They nodded their understanding. The Berlin police still had the embassy surrounded. Soe did not wish them to be alerted to the activity on the far side of the thick embassy walls.

The two soldiers carted the wooden crate across the floor and up the granite-slab stairs to the rear garden.

"You next," Soe said, pointing to the next pair of guards. There was only one more set after them. "Go in staggered rounds. Do not try to carry them out all at once."

As the next soldiers lifted the second chest and headed for the door, Soe left the basement.

He found the Master of Sinanju sitting on the floor of the embassy library.

"I have done as you instructed," Soe said.

"Your men did not help themselves to my treasure?" Chiun asked. His cobwebbed eyes were closed in meditation.

"I watched them myself," Soe insisted. "They did not steal from you. Nor would they, after what you did to their compatriots."

A faint nod. "Fear breeds honesty," Chiun admitted.

On his way to the library, Soe had not seen the Master's pupil. Although the two of them appeared to bicker constantly, they were rarely far apart.

"Where is your American lackey, O Master?" Soe asked.

Chiun opened his eyes. There was bright fire in their hazel depths. "Watch your tongue, Pyongyanger," the old Korean warned. There was a chilly edge in his voice that seemed to actually lower the room temperature.

"I have heard you call him worse," Soe pointed out.

"I may call him what I wish. You may not."

"My apologies, Master of Sinanju," Soe said, bowing.

Chiun's steely gaze bore through to Soe's soul for a few long seconds. At last he drew his thin papery lids across the frightful orbs. "My son is securing us transportation," the elderly Korean said.

"Forgive me, O great Master," Soe said. "But

there are many police officers outside. This embassy is at the center of a scrutiny far greater than that of the Vatican mission in Panama several years ago. Even General Noriega surrendered eventually. How do you hope to get out alive?"

"Know you this, son of a Pyongyang whore. The Master of Sinanju and his heir are not pineapple-faced despots cowering behind the skirts of the Church of Rome. We will leave when I have deemed we should leave. Until then, be certain that your men take not an ounce of gold, lest your neck suffer the consequences of their actions."

The security ministry agent frowned at the peaceful form of the ancient Korean. How easy it would be to put a bullet in his frail old skull. As easy as it would be rewarding.

In the end, he followed his orders. Rim Kun Soe left the old one to his meditation, wondering as he bowed from the library how the young one could possibly hope to get that much gold out of the North Korean embassy unnoticed.

REMO HAD NO IDEA how they were going to get all that gold out of the North Korean embassy unnoticed.

Under cover of darkness, he scaled the wall at the rear of the embassy, hopping down to the pavement between a couple of milling Berlin police officers. The uniformed men did not even notice him.

Merging with the shadows, he slipped through a

line of parked cars, turning backward as he reached the police cordon. Flapping his arms, he was finally noticed by a young police officer who assumed he had slid between the security barricades. As he had expected, Remo was escorted out into the milling crowd of curious onlookers.

Outside looking in now, Remo stood with his hands on his hips wondering how the hell he was going to haul the remainder of Chiun's booty out of the embassy without alerting every cop in Berlin.

There were twenty-six crates in all. Each one as heavy as lead. Remo frowned as he scanned the area.

The crowds were thinner now than they had been. That was a blessing. Although people had been interested the night of the chase and crash, they weren't curious enough to endure the cold on the second full evening.

Unfortunately, the Berlin police had not followed suit. Their interest was as high as it had been the day before. Maybe higher. There was a huge number of police officers milling about outside the ivy-covered walls.

As he looked at all the crisp dark uniforms huddled together outside the high wall, Remo wondered if crime had suddenly been eradicated around the rest of the city. That was the only thing that should have allowed so many men to spend so much time here.

He realized that an end to criminal activity in Berlin wasn't very bloody likely. At least not if the Germany he had seen over the past few weeks was any indication. The only way to end crime would have been to throw a net over the whole damned country.

The day's endless drizzling rain had turned into spits of fat gray snowflakes. As they came in contact with the wet ground, they melted across the saturated pavement.

Already there were indications that the snow would accumulate to slush before the night was through. Remo didn't intend to be around to see it.

It would be easy enough to go out and rent another truck. But then what would he do with it? Drive it through the police lines and right up to the twisted and propped-up embassy gates?

There were about a billion cameras outside the gates at the moment with one cop for every camera. He wouldn't get anywhere near the front of the mission with another rental.

Truck, truck, truck, he thought. As he looked around, he rotated his freakishly thick wrists absently.

There were those tiny European police cars that would be laughed off the road back in America. A larger paddy wagon was parked for some reason away from the nearest cluster of cruisers. Probably preparing for a riot if one broke out. In Germany that was always a wise precaution.

A thought occurred to Remo.

It was a long shot, but it was the only chance they'd have short of sitting out the whole diplomatic fiasco.

Remo slipped back through the police lines, moving stealthily to the rear wall. He kept to the shadows once more, remaining just beyond the periphery of police eyes.

He scaled the wall rapidly, slipping back inside the embassy grounds near the spot where he had instructed Rim Kun Soe to leave the treasure crates.

They were stacked together on the wet lawn in neat piles. Thirteen piles of two each.

A line of huge fir trees grew at the interior of the high wall. Remo grabbed a stack of cases in each hand and slid over to the wall.

Dumping the crates four high into one arm, he used his free hand to scale the wall. He set the cases upon the wall, returning for the next four.

Once all of the crates were lined up amid the jutting branches of the fir tree, Remo dropped back to the sidewalk outside. He went back through the police lines, this time avoiding the police entirely. He found the paddy wagon parked where he'd left it.

The door was unlocked. Remo was ready to hotwire the truck—one of the few mechanical skills he had ever bothered to develop—but was surprised to find the keys dangling in the ignition. He also found a police officer's cap sitting on the passenger's seat.

Pulling the cap down over his eyes, Remo started the truck. Since he was not near the main gates, no one seemed to notice as he backed over to the rear wall.

At the wall, Remo let the engine idle as he sneaked back out of the cab. The rear of the truck was directly beneath the line of crates. Remo could see the lighter wood jutting from the shadows of the big trees.

Without hesitation, he scampered back up the wall.

He had opened the rear doors of the paddy wagon already. Atop the wall, he grabbed one crate at a time and flung it down into the open interior of the truck.

They should have made a racket when they landed, but Remo somehow managed to skim the huge boxes into the back of the police vehicle as easily as if he were skipping flat stones on the surface of a still lake. In less than a minute, he had loaded up all twenty-six.

He got back to the ground, closed the rear of the paddy wagon and was just putting one foot back inside the cab when his luck finally ran out.

"Entschuldigen Sie?"

Remo was greatly tempted to just ignore the voice and get in the truck. He decided against it. No one—not Smith, not the Koreans, not Remo himself for that matter——wanted a repeat of the previous day's performance. Instead he turned, smiling amiably.

"Hi," Remo said to the lone policeman standing in the shadows behind him. "Lotta weather we've been having lately, wouldn't you say?"

The young man was far away from the rest of the cops that were assembled near the main gate. His face clouded when he heard the American voice coming from Remo's mouth.

The cop couldn't have been much out of his teens. His wide baby face was filled with uncertainty, even as he reached for his side arm. "You will stay still, *bitte*," he ordered, voice quavering.

"Sorry," Remo said, shrugging apologetically. "*Nein* can do. I've got places to go, heirlooms to smuggle."

The young officer had made the tragic mistake of stepping close to Remo as he issued his last order. He had not even unholstered his weapon before Remo shot forward.

Faster than normal human eyes could comprehend, Remo had slapped the gun back into the police officer's holster. Spinning the man in place, he grabbed a cluster of nerves at the base of his neck.

The cop's eyes grew wide in shock. Almost as quickly, his lids grew heavy. He sank gently to the sidewalk. Remo propped the sleeping officer up against the wall.

Hurrying forward to the truck cab, he got

quickly inside. No one stopped him as he drove out through a weak point in the police lines. Remo was on the street with the embassy behind him in a matter of moments.

"And they make fun of the Maginot Line," he said.

Tossing off his policeman's cap, he steered the truck up a shadowy side street.

IN THE EMBASSY, the Master of Sinanju heard the car horn beep two times fast, three times slow.

It was about time. The stooges of Pyongyang were beginning to get on his nerves.

Rising like a puff of steam from the library carpet, he hurried outside.

FOUR MINUTES LATER, Chiun slipped in beside Remo in the dark cab of the parked paddy wagon.

"Took you long enough," Remo complained, pulling away from the curb.

"The police are more agitated than they had been," Chiun said aridly. "It seems some lout knocked unconscious one of their fellows without having sense enough to hide the body."

"Don't carp," Remo advised. "Because of me, your gold is safe."

"Only when it is in Sinanju will it be safe. Until that time, make haste."

"Fine," Remo said. "Just try not to kill any cops on the way to the airport."

"I make no promises," Chiun sniffed.

"Jesus, Mary and Joseph," Remo sighed.

"And do not invoke the gods of Charlemagne," Chiun warned. "It is unseemly not only in the eyes of my ancestors, but in those of the greater deities."

Remo thought of a few things he would have liked to invoke. Instead, he held his tongue.

He drove slowly, and the taillights of the Berlin police paddy wagon turned back out on the main drag. The truck quickly disappeared in traffic, heading off in the direction of Tegel Airport.

9

The unmarked private elevator whisked Michael Princippi up through the glass-enclosed atrium of Man Hyung Sun's exclusive Fifth Avenue apartment building.

Through smoky one-way glass, Princippi could see placid fountains gurgling soothing, colored water far below.

The centerpiece of the lobby area was a huge marble fountain that shot water four stories into the air. Princippi was above the apex of the spurting water by five stories and was moving swiftly toward the penthouse.

He hung away from the glass wall, huddling into himself near the closed elevator doors. Princippi never thought he could feel more miserable than he had back when he lost the 1988 presidential race. He was wrong.

The Loonie infomercial had hit the airwaves the previous day. Tongues were already wagging about his participation in the program-length commercial.

"The buying of American politics," FOX's Brit Hume had dubbed it. He had done a five-minute cable hit piece on the former governor that re-opened all the old wounds of his failed campaign. The reporter had stopped just short of bringing up Mrs. Princippi's substance-abuse problem.

As far as his wife was concerned, it was a good thing she was already hospitalized when the news struck. She had been discovered that morning in a maintenance closet at the Betty Ford Clinic mixing a cocktail of Clorox and Pine Sol.

"If it wasn't over before, it is now," Princippi announced glumly. As if in response, the elevator doors slid efficiently open.

Sighing, Princippi stepped out into the hallway.

The hall was more a foyer. It stabbed off to the right, where the servants' elevator was located, and went equally far on the left, where it stopped at a fire door. Directly across from the elevator was a closed oak door. And standing directly in front of the door was the Loonie, Roseflower.

It was amazing how much bigger and more menacing he looked since the abduction. It was the soothing pink robes that had fooled him. Draping, they hid a lot.

The kid obviously worked out constantly. Crossed over his barrel chest, his huge bare forearms were like pale tree trunks. They could easily have lifted Mike Princippi into the air and snapped him like a twig.

"Good morning, Michael," Roseflower said.

The idiotic smirk again. For some reason, the smile was more disconcerting than if the Loonie had scowled at him.

"Hello," Princippi said, trying to smile, as well. As was usually the case, his smile lacked sincerity or warmth.

Roseflower didn't seem to mind.

"Reverend Sun is expecting you. Have a wonderful day."

The Loonie bodyguard stepped aside, allowing Princippi to enter the penthouse apartment.

Michael Princippi couldn't wait to close the door between him and the perennially perky lapdog.

"Come in," Sun's voice called from deep within the apartment before the door had even shut.

The cult leader's city residence was tastefully and expensively furnished. A broad curving staircase of highly polished wood led to an upstairs balcony lined on one side by a delicately carved balustrade.

Sun's voice had come from this direction. Princippi climbed the stairs, noting as he went the original works of art that were tastefully displayed along the wall.

Upstairs, the smell told him which way to go.

It was a sickly stench. Rotten eggs left too long in a garbage disposal. Sulfur.

Princippi had read before that particular odors were known to trigger specific memories, emotions of a time long ago. He had not really believed it until that moment. He now knew that it was abundantly true.

They were not so much memories that came to him now as he followed that sick sulfur stench to the far end of the hallway. It was more a feeling. Stirring awake after a long slumber. The emotion he felt was fear.

Princippi found Sun in a small room off of the cultist's opulent bedroom.

The room was only tiny in comparison to the rest of the apartment. Actually, it looked as if it was supposed to be a good-size closet. But the clothes were all gone. A few wooden hangers hung on empty racks.

Sun was in the middle of the room. The Korean sat on a plain three-legged stool.

The room was fetid. A greasy yellow smoke clung visibly to the foul air. It was not like smoke produced by burning. It was more a Hollywood interpretation of what smoke should be. A sort of dry-ice fog.

The stench was like a solid mass that Princippi had to push from his path as he stepped inside the room.

"Close the door," Sun ordered. His voice was muffled.

Reluctantly, Princippi did as he was instructed.

Sun's head had been invisible beneath a thick bathroom towel until now. Sitting on his low stool, he was bent forward, the towel draping across something at his feet. He was like a man fighting cold symptoms. Three humidifiers hummed incessantly around him.

Once the door was closed, Sun came up from beneath the towel. He was breathing deeply at the air of the room—a hiker catching his breath atop a mountain.

"What news have you for me?" Sun asked, draping his towel across the mysterious object at his feet.

"I, um, just talked to Bergdorf at Channel 8. The, uh, Sun Source infomercial has been distributed around the country as per your instructions."

Princippi was finding it difficult to speak. Sun's eyes held the same weird yellow glow they had taken on back at the *Washington Guardian* offices. It looked as if someone had screwed two yellow Christmas bulbs into his eye sockets.

"What of the switchboards? Do the people of this land seek out my oracular wisdom?" The yellow eyes flashed hypnotically.

"Switchboards?" Princippi gulped. "Um, yeah. Yeah, they're doing okay. I guess. You know, there are business people more suited to this. These psychic hotlines are a big deal. I'm sure you could lure someone away from Kim Smiley or the Amazing Mystico. Maybe even some of Dionne Warwick's old people might want to jump from that sunken ship."

"We have chosen you," Sun announced.

Man Hyung Sun had recently taken to speaking in the royal *we*. Michael Princippi was one of the few people who understood why.

"Okay, fine," Princippi said, forcing affability. "But could we maybe tone down my public participation a little? The press is having a field day with this. It's really going to put a hitch in my plans for the presidency."

"We have judged it should be so," Sun said, ending the argument. He pulled the towel off the hidden object on the floor, draping the rank fabric around his neck.

Princippi recognized the stone urn instantly. He hadn't seen it in almost a year. Chiseled Greek characters ran up the sides, worn with age. A thick yellow film rose from the heavy urn, inspired by the closeness of the humidifiers.

The former governor gulped nervously as he looked at the ancient piece of carved rock. Inside was a clumpy yellow crystalline substance. It sparkled in the wan room light. The color of the wet sand matched the fierce brightness in the cult leader's eyes.

"What of Boston?" Sun asked suddenly.

Princippi had to tear his eyes from the urn. "Huh?"

"Boston," Sun repeated. "Has the Sun Source program run there?"

"Uh, yeah," Princippi said, swallowing. His

heart was pounding. "Just like you said. We bought more time there than anywhere else. A couple of stations are carrying it, morning and late night." Fear, coupled with the swirling sulfur smoke, was making him dizzy. He needed to go to the bathroom again. The ex-governor wished Sun would hurry up and cover the urn with his smelly towel.

"That is where we shall find them," Sun said in satisfaction. "And we shall finally have our revenge."

The smoke grew stronger. Squinting in displeasure, Princippi flapped one hand in front of his face as he covered his mouth and nose with the other. "Find who?" he asked.

But Sun did not answer. He had pulled the towel back over his head, draping the far end over the ancient urn. The cult leader breathed deeply at the sickly fumes.

10

The cab from Boston's Logan International Airport dropped Remo and Chiun off on the sidewalk in front of their Quincy, Massachusetts, condominium.

They had taken the North Korean jet from Germany to England, switching to a commercial flight at London's Heathrow Airport. The private Korean jet flew east into the sunrise while Remo's 747 headed in the opposite direction across the Atlantic. They landed a little after 3:30 a.m.

It was the dead of night by the time they climbed the stairs to their home.

"You hungry?" Remo asked once they were inside.

"Rice," was all Chiun said in response. He left Remo to make their meal while he went off to the living room.

As Remo was rummaging through the kitchen cupboards in search of a pot, he heard the familiar blare of the TV coming from the other room. Fifteen minutes later, Remo set a bowl of steaming rice and a pair of chopsticks at the feet of the Master of Sinanju. He joined his teacher cross-legged on the floor before the big set.

"What are we watching?" Remo asked. Unlike Chiun, he used his fingers to eat his rice.

"Drivel," Chiun replied. He hauled a thick clump of rice to his papery lips.

"I guess TV hasn't changed much since we left," Remo observed.

On the television, a pudgy man who was—physical evidence to the contrary—trying to pass himself off as an exercise expert, screamed at an enthusiastic audience about something called the Butt Blaster. Said Butt Blaster was apparently the cure-all to flabby derrieres around the nation. By investing only two minutes a day, the pudgy man promised that those who used his product would have bottoms as tight as a snare drum. He had models behind him to prove his case. They looked as if they exercised for breakfast, fasted for lunch and starved themselves while exercising for supper.

"How many of those things do you think broke during taping?" Remo asked, nodding to the strange exercise contraptions on the screen.

"How long is this program?" Chiun asked.

"Infomercials usually run half an hour," Remo said.

"One hundred and sixty-three," Chiun announced firmly. "See?" He aimed a long ivory fingernail at the action on the television. "The metal on that one gives even as the fat announcer blabbers on."

Remo instantly saw what he was pointing at. A stress fracture had appeared on one of the workout devices. Theirs were the only sets of eyes on the planet that would have seen the tiny crack. Long before it broke entirely, the scene changed. The actor sweating in the background of the shot suddenly had a brand-new Butt Blaster. It wasn't even the same color as the original.

"A great value at only $29.99!" screamed the raspy-voiced pitchman. "Plus $59.99 postage and handling," he said, suddenly speaking so low and quickly that the words were virtually indecipherable. His blond ponytail bobbed excitedly as he browbeat the studio and home audiences into purchasing his product.

"You want to know something, Chiun?" Remo said. "In spite of stuff like this, I'm glad we're home."

Remo meant it. They had spent a great deal of time traveling in the past few months. From Europe to South America to Asia and back to Europe. It had been a grueling, frenetic cycle. He wanted nothing more than to sit back and relax for a couple of weeks.

Chiun did not respond to Remo's comment. The half-hour-long exercise advertisement had come to an end. The Channel 8 Productions logo was followed by a burp of dead air before the too loud intro music of yet another infomercial began.

By this point, both their bowls were empty. Remo got to his feet, collecting their dirty dinner dishes. He was straightening up and turning to go when a familiar voice caught his attention.

"...what we can do," said the insipid voice on the TV.

"It would help if we could somehow know the future," came the reply.

"Keep dreaming," said the dull voice.

Bowls in hand, Remo turned back to the screen.

The face was as he remembered it. Dull, gray. Giant black bushy eyebrows, more appropriate to a Muppet than to a politician, hung over beady, porcine eyes.

Remo scrunched up his face. "Isn't that Mike Princippi?" he asked uncertainly.

"Hush," Chiun instructed.

"I've always had trouble with the future," the TV Mike Princippi was saying.

"Knowing the future would not only help in politics, but in all walks of life," his television companion opined.

"No way," Remo said, sinking back to the floor. A light had begun to dawn. "This can't be what I think it is."

"The future is hard to predict," Princippi said. He was obviously reading from cue cards. "If I knew how, I'd be President right now." Even though he laughed along with the other men on the set, his eyes were sick.

"Dammit, I was right!" Remo enthused. "It's a psychic-hotline infomercial. I'll be goddamned if Mike 'the Prince' Princippi isn't on TV hawking some crackpot fortune-teller's 900 number." He positively bubbled with excitement.

Chiun turned a baleful eye on him. "Do I take it you do not approve?"

"Are you kidding?" Remo said. "This is great. I love when politicians have to sink even lower than politics. It's almost impossible to do."

"Why is it you believe he has sunk at all?" Chiun asked.

"Look at him!" Remo said happily. He flung out a hand at the TV. "The guy is on a psychic infomercial squirming like fish on a line. He looks about as happy to be there as the guy who beat him looked in the presidential debates four years later."

Chiun looked back at the screen. "Perhaps," he admitted. "It is also possible that he is ill."

"Of course he is," Remo said. "I'd be sick, too, if I had to endorse that check." His broad smile stretched so far across his face it threatened to spill beyond both ears.

"Why are you so gleeful?" Chiun asked suspiciously. "It is not like you."

"You don't get it. This is the American dream, Little Father," Remo explained. "We live to see our politicians fail. Especially a smug little creep like Princippi. It's the grease that oils the gears of this great democracy.''

Chiun shook his head. ''This nation is unfathomable,'' he said. He turned his attention back to the television.

On the screen, Mike Princippi was saying, ''I wish we could outthink my opponent.''

There was a sudden flurry of movement from the right side of the screen. All at once, a new figure strode onto the set. He was short and wore an expensive business suit on his pudgy frame.

As he noted the nationality of the latest player to join the others, Chiun's interest was immediately piqued.

''Chiun, isn't that—?'' Remo began, suddenly worried.

''Silence!'' Chiun commanded.

Princippi was in the middle of saying, ''Oh, hello. Aren't you Reverend Man Hyung Sun?''

''I am he,'' Sun intoned seriously.

''This is worse than I thought,'' Remo muttered. The glee he had felt before had begun to dissipate the moment the cult leader made his appearance.

''...future. I am your future. I know your destiny.'' Sun pointed out at the television audience. ''And yours.''

The image quickly cut from the studio-produced scene to an outdoor segment. Pink-robed Sunnies interviewed men and women on the street about the amazing prognosticating abilities of the Reverend Man Hyung Sun.

Everyone was thrilled with the information the seer's hotline helpers had given them. Throughout the anything but spontaneous interviews, a 900 number flashed at the bottom of the screen. It was accompanied by the phrase "Your personal psychic is standing by."

The videotaped outdoor segment lasted for only a few minutes. When it was done, Man Hyung Sun reappeared. He and Mike Princippi were sitting together in a faux living-room environment. It held many of the same furnishings as the faux conference room in the lead segment.

"Holy flying crap," Remo murmured.

"Must you continue babbling?" Chiun complained, peeved.

"Chiun, don't you get it? It was bad enough when it was just Princippi up there. Now he's having a powwow with the head of the freaking Loonie cult. Before it was a joke. Now it's just plain embarrassing."

"Perhaps the Greekling is wiser than you," Chiun pointed out. "If Sun is indeed a seer, he could have prescience to alter events yet to be."

"Sun is a con man," Remo said, rolling his eyes.

"You do not know that."

"I know enough, Little Father. That guy shanghais kids into his dippy cult. He had the mindless drips banging away on tambourines in airports all over the place back in the '70s and '80s, remember? He was also found guilty of tax evasion, I think. He's an A-number-one asshole-creep-con-man-millionaire-rat-bastard. With a capital *B*."

"He is Korean," Chiun said somberly.

Remo frowned. "So what?"

"He would not shanghai anyone. *Shanghai* is named for the vile Chinese practice of putting men aboard ships against their will."

"Okay, so what do Koreans call it?"

"Unexpected oceangoing journeys filled with wonder and delight."

"Fine," Remo said. He pointed to Sun on the television. "That's what he does with mush-brained teenagers."

Princippi was in the middle of asking Sun about his qualifications as a clairvoyant.

"I have been aligned with cosmic forces for as long as I can remember," Sun said. His English was better than that of most Americans. "Through heightened perceptions impossible for mortals to understand, I have seen these forces recently arrange themselves in such a way as to foretell a great end. And a new beginning. For those viewing this program, know you this—the Omega Time has come."

"What the hell is he going on about?" Remo asked.

"Silence!" Chiun commanded. His voice was sharp.

"I am the Sun Source," Sun proclaimed. He looked out at the camera as he spoke.

In their living room, both Remo and Chiun were surprised by his words. They glanced at one another. Chiun's face was severe, Remo's puzzled.

When they looked back at the TV, Sun was finishing his spiel. "The *pyon ha-da* is upon us. Birth of death, death of birth. Call now. Operators are standing by."

The pink-robed Loonies reappeared. The same videotaped man-on-the-street segment as before began playing. Chiun did not watch it this time. Gathering up the remote control, he clicked off the television. He was deep in thought.

"I can't believe it," Remo said, shaking his head. "Mike Princippi. How the almost mighty have fallen. You think Smitty knows about this?"

Chiun looked over at Remo, annoyance creasing his wizened features. "Do you not know what this means?" he asked impatiently.

Remo was surprised by the harshness of his tone.

"Um, no matter how bad you've got it, there's always someone worse off than you?" Remo suggested.

"You are uneducable," Chiun spit. "Did you not hear the words he spoke to us?"

"To us?" Remo said. "Not that Sun Source stuff?"

"The same."

"Chiun, that's a coincidence. He can't know that Sinanju is called the Sun Source, too. His name is Sun. They just cooked up some silly Madison Avenue twist on his name—that's all."

"I must make a pilgrimage to see this holy man," Chiun proclaimed. He rose like steam from the floor, smoothing out the skirts of his scarlet kimono.

"Holy my ass," Remo said, also standing. "He's a scam artist, Chiun. Worse than that. He's a bad scam artist. You can't have fallen for that pap."

"You will telephone Smith in the morning," Chiun instructed, ignoring Remo's complaints. "Have him consult his oracles to learn the location of the holy one. I must meet with the wise and all-knowing Reverend Sun."

With that, Chiun turned abruptly and left the room. Remo heard his bedroom door close a moment later.

Alone in the living room, Remo shook his head wearily. "I can't believe it," he sighed. "Not even home for an hour and I already miss Germany."

Picking up their empty rice bowls, he skulked morosely back to the kitchen.

11

One of his first acts in office had been to stop vagrants from frightening drivers at intersections.

The city homeless had somehow gotten it into their heads to stagger up to cars stopped at traffic lights and spit on their windshields. They would then wipe the slimy ooze away with a filthy rag and hold out a grimy hand for a gratuity. Frightened drivers would hand over money, fearing reprisal if they did not.

It was extortion, plain and simple. In a crazed bow to the lords of political correctness, the city of New York had looked the other way for years. That practice changed the minute Randolph Gillotti was elected mayor.

The panhandlers were arrested in a clean sweep.

Homeless activists screamed. Television reporters screamed. Hollywood celebrities screamed. Everyone screamed but Randolph Gillotti. As mayor of the greatest city in the world, he didn't have time to scream.

He had attacked the Mob at the Jacob Javits

Center, forcing out illegal activities. He had flooded sections of New York with police, dramatically reducing certain types of street crime. Briefly, he had even scored points with the right-bashing media by endorsing a candidate for governor who was not of his own political party. And that was only in his first term.

Hated by men on both sides of the political aisle, loved by as many on either side, Randolph Gillotti was the king of controversy in a city that thrived on conflict.

However, on this day, as the mayor of New York fidgeted in his seat behind his city-hall desk in lower Manhattan, Randolph Gillotti felt like anything other than controversy.

The Loonies were back in town.

It seemed like only yesterday when the crackpot cultists were harassing everyone at airports around the country. But after the Reverend Sun's run-in with the IRS, they had all but disappeared. Gillotti—like most reasonable Americans—hoped that they were gone for good. It turned out that they had only been dormant all this time.

The return of the Loonies to active life meant a fresh headache for the mayor of New York.

He frowned as he looked over the latest manpower reports sent by the police commissioner's office on the event Sun had scheduled for noon today.

It was ridiculous. The expenditure of time and

manpower was absolutely crazy. Insane beyond belief. The cost to the city was astronomical. And worst of all, it was not anything that could possibly be twisted into good press.

A mass wedding. According to the documents forwarded by the Washington headquarters of the Grand Unification Church—as Sun's bogus religion was officially called—there would be nearly fifteen hundred couples tying the knot today.

Gillotti was not unlike most good New Yorkers. Most days he blamed the Yankee organization for everything—from the weather to the potholes in the Bronx. But today, it really *was* their fault. The Yankee people were the ones who had rented their stadium out to the crackpot cult leader and his tambourine-banging minions.

The leather padding beneath him crackled as Gillotti tossed the police reports aside. Moaning wearily, he dug at his eyes with the palms of his hands. As if responding to his cue, his desk intercom buzzed efficiently.

"Governor Princippi to see you, Mr. Mayor," his secretary announced.

Gillotti removed his hands from his eyes. Briefly, he considered letting the former Massachusetts governor stew in his outer office for an hour or two, but decided against it. Better to get this whatever-it-was-about meeting over with.

"Send him in," Gillotti lisped tiredly.

Princippi was ushered into the room a moment

later. After exchanging polite handshakes, the ex-governor took a seat in front of the mayor's desk. Principi noted with distaste that the mayor had not bothered to put on a jacket for the meeting. His Honor sat in shirtsleeves, hands cradled on his broad polished desk.

"What can I do for you, Mike?" Gillotti asked. "May I call you Mike?" he added. His smile was that of a cartoon squirrel, so, too, his sibilant *S*-filled speech.

"I suppose," Principi said, clearly unhappy with the familiarity. "May I call you Randy?"

"My people tell me you said this was urgent, Mike," the mayor said, dodging the question. "What's up?"

The tone was set. Though Principi frowned, he pressed on. "You know about the Sunnie ceremony today." It was a statement, not a question.

"The *Loonie* ceremony, yes," the mayor said. "A bunch of middle-class whack-job kids trying to get even with their parents for not buying them that Porsche when they turned sweet sixteen. Frankly, Mike, I'm surprised to see you mixed up in all this."

Principi cleared his throat. "Be that as it may, the Reverend Sun has sent me here as his emissary."

"Is that a step up or down from running for President?" Gillotti laughed. "Sorry," he said instantly, raising an apologetic hand. "We've all got to make a buck somehow."

Princippi's bushy eyebrows furrowed. His embarrassment at the infomercial he had cut for Sun was rapidly turning to annoyance. "You know about the ad," he said flatly.

Gillotti leaned back in his chair. "Yeah, I've heard something about it. Brainwashing wasn't good enough for Sun. He's branched out into fortune-telling, right?"

"In a sense," Princippi agreed. "But he doesn't just see the future. He sees the past and present, as well."

"What is he," the mayor scoffed, "some kind of Korean Magic Eight Ball?"

"It's not a question of whether you believe it or not," Princippi said with a displeased frown. "It's the truth. As much as I hate to admit it."

"Come on, Mike. Don't tell me you buy that bullshit?" the mayor taunted.

Princippi forged ahead. "Can we get back on topic? The *ceremony?*" he pressed.

Gillotti sighed. "What is it, Mike? Cops? You've got a ton of them. Uniforms on foot in the stands and on the field. I've even got you horses in the parking lot. It may bankrupt the city of New York, but you can go back and tell that half-crazy millionaire boss of yours that his ass is safe for his marriage-a-thon, or whatever the hell you Loonies call those sham wedding things."

Princippi pursed his lips. "You are correct," he admitted, thinly hiding his displeasure. "This is about the police."

"I figured as much."

"However, the specific numbers faxed to Sunnie headquarters are unacceptable to Reverend Sun."

"Geez, come on," Gillotti complained, his lisp becoming more pronounced. "You've been around a few crowds in your life, Mike. You know we can't have an equal cop-to-spectator ratio. I can't believe he'd send you here to try and strong-arm me. You go back and tell that old fraud he doesn't get a single blue-suit more than the commissioner has allocated."

Princippi smiled. It was an oily expression devoid of mirth. "You don't understand," he said evenly, "we do not want more police. We want less. Specifically, none."

Gillotti had been readying another mild diatribe but paused in midbreath. He blinked once. "Come again?"

"Sunnie security can handle the day's events. Reverend Sun wishes for this to be a private ceremony. A police presence will only interfere with the solemnness of the occasion."

"Private?" Gillotti said, dully. "With three thousand candy brides and grooms propped on top of the cake?"

"This is what Reverend Sun wishes."

"No way," Gillotti said. "If something goes

wrong, Sun will be the first one screaming bloody murder.''

"Nothing will go wrong," Princippi assured him.

"Who told you that?" Gillotti snorted. "Your buddy the soothsayer? Tell him I am not letting a bunch of frolicking, robe-wearing, head-shaving psychos loose in the Bronx without an armed escort. The cops are there,'' he added firmly. "Whether the Loonie leader wants them there or not.''

Gillotti crossed his arms determinedly. On the far side of the mayor's desk, Mike Princippi allowed himself a small smile. This one genuine.

"I can't tell you how he gets his powers of divination," the former governor said. "But they really are remarkable. Always right on the money. And speaking of money, he told me a little something this morning about the way you financed your first campaign for mayor.''

A tiny squeak came from the mayor's chair. His eyes were dead, unreadable. "I conform to all of the rules of New York's election commission," he said.

"Of course you do."

"The finances are all out there for everyone to see. Even you. And I resent you coming into this office proxying for a thief like Sun and suggesting that anything I've done isn't aboveboard. This meeting is over.''

Rather than buzz his secretary, Mayor Gillotti stood abruptly. Sweeping around the desk, he stepped briskly across the wide room, flinging open the door. In the outer office, the eyes of aides and secretaries looked up at the mayor in surprise.

Back near Gillotti's desk, Princippi stood. Slowly, he stepped across the room to the door.

The mayor's jaw was firmly set. He intended to say not another word to the former governor.

As he stepped past the mayor, Princippi paused, as if considering something. All at once, he whispered a few quick words, too soft for anyone in the outer room to hear.

Although no one outside heard what was said, they all witnessed their boss's reaction. Mayor Randolph Gillotti's eyes grew wide in shock and anger. But he did not turn away.

When he slammed the office door violently a moment later, Mike Princippi was still inside.

12

"Where are all the cops?" Remo asked. As he walked, he was glancing around the grimy parking lot of New York's Yankee Stadium. He didn't see a single blue uniform.

"Perhaps they have journeyed inside for an audience with His Holiness," Chiun suggested, strolling beside him.

"This guy's not the pope, for crying out loud," Remo griped.

"Perish the thought," Chiun said, horrified. "Seer Sun must guard against papist influence. I will advise him so when he honors me with an audience."

Not wanting to get into another pointless Charlemagne–Church of Rome argument, Remo bit his tongue.

At Chiun's insistence, he had called Smith that morning to find the location of the Reverend Man Hyung Sun. Relieved that they had returned from Germany without further incident, Smith had readily supplied the information, warning only that they should keep a low profile. When the CURE director asked why they were looking for Sun, Remo artfully dodged Smith's question by hanging up the phone.

So here he was, strolling across the parking lot of Yankee Stadium amid a sea of pink-robed Loonies. Remo looked with displeasure at the cult members' costumes.

"Don't they get cold wearing those dresses?" he asked.

"Must you take pains to display your ignorance?" the Master of Sinanju sighed.

"What, you're saying they aren't dresses?" Remo said.

Chiun inspected a cluster of Sunnies as they walked past. "The white section is a simple robe," he said. "I detect Roman influence, although in Rome white togas were strictly worn by those running for political office."

"I thought everyone wore a white robe back then."

"That is why you are only Apprentice Reigning Master," Chiun replied. He nodded to a Loonie. "The length of these robes is far too great. Only on state occasions would high officers wear ankle-length tunics."

"What about the pink wraps?" Remo asked.

"Indian sari," Chiun answered. "Although worn entirely incorrectly. A Hindu woman drapes her sari over the left shoulder, a Parsi over her right. These cretins have them thrown all higgledy-piggledy, without regard to caste or sect. It is quite disgraceful. I will have to mention this to His Holiness, as well.''

Nearer the stadium, entrance booths had been set up by vendors. As he approached, Remo was surprised to find them staffed not by hot-dog or beer salesmen, but by more pink-and-white-robed Sunnies.

They were walking past one of the open booths when a blank-faced Sunnie vendor called out to Remo.

''Hello, friend. Would you care to test your skill? It is for the good of the Grand Unification Church.''

Remo looked at the rear of the booth. A large corkboard had been fastened to the wooden structure. A few inflated balloons were scattered across the face of the board while still more deflated bits of rubber hung limply from red thumbtacks. The asphalt floor of the booth was littered with the remnants of destroyed balloons.

''Sorry,'' Remo said. ''Not interested.''

''Speak for yourself, paleface,'' Chiun said. He muscled in front of Remo, taking a spot before the counter.

''Three dollars,'' said the smiling Loonie.

''Chiun, let's go,'' Remo insisted.

''Pay the simpleton,'' Chiun said in reply.

Remo knew from experience that it would be

pointless to argue. Grumbling, he dug into his pocket, producing three singles. He handed the bills over to the Loonie. The man laid three darts atop the counter, which Chiun scooped up into his bony hand.

Tapping a lone dart on the fingertips of his right hand, Chiun's arm wound from behind, looking like a cross between a major-league pitcher and a windmill. When his hand reached the release point of the throw, the dart zoomed from his loose fingers with an audible snap.

The metal-tipped projectile flew at supersonic speed across the length of the booth, exploding a bright red balloon into rubbery fragments before burying itself deep into the surface of the board.

Before the popped cork from the first dart was settling to the ground behind the booth, the second dart was airborne.

This missile passed through a balloon at the lower left of the booth and continued on into the next kiosk. The last anyone saw of it, the dart was heading out toward the Major Deegan Expressway and the Harlem River beyond.

"Watch this, Remo," Chiun cried. "Wheeee!" The third dart was loosed.

Chiun seemed to have lost control of the final missile. Instead of heading directly at the board, the dart fired up to the top of the booth, where it snapped off a metal securing clasp with the report of a rifle shot. The ricochet carried it down to where it clattered amid an explosion of tiny sparks against another small piece of metal attached to a side beam.

A few rusty flakes of metal fluttered to the whitewashed railing below.

The new trajectory of the dart brought it at an angle across the face of the corkboard. As the Loonie barker watched in amazement, the dart wiped out a line of seven fat balloons in a series of rapid-fire pops. In a wink, it had buried itself up to its plastic feathers into the cold tar floor of the booth.

Before the booth, Chiun clapped his hands in glee. "I destroyed nine of the orbs, Remo," he announced proudly. He turned to the vendor. "What do I win?"

"Win?" asked the Loonie vendor. He was still looking in shock at the remnants of his balloons.

"Uh-oh," Remo said.

"My prize," Chiun insisted, still beaming. "It must surely be magnificent for one who has performed as I."

Before the baffled vendor could explain that the only prize was the knowledge that Chiun's three-dollar gift would go to the Grand Unification Church, a voice piped in behind them. Luckily for the vendor, for the interruption allowed him to keep his head.

"It is," the voice proclaimed warmly.

When they turned around, they came face-to-face with yet another pink-robed Loonie.

Remo glanced around. There was no one else in the immediate vicinity. The man appeared to be talking to them.

"My name is Roseflower," explained the Loonie. He smiled a disconcerting, Valium grin. "I have been sent to bestow on you a most valuable treasure."

Remo groaned at the word.

Chiun clapped his hands again. "You see, Remo?" he chirped happily. To the Loonie, he said, "What is my reward?"

"A personal audience with the Reverend Man Hyung Sun himself," Roseflower smiled, nodding.

Chiun could scarcely contain his joy.

"What's behind door number two?" Remo asked, just before Chiun elbowed him in the ribs.

13

The brides wore white. All fifteen hundred of them.

The giggling women were stretched out in zig-zagging lines and clusters that extended from the edge of the dugouts behind home plate to the product-endorsing billboards on the outfield wall.

The grooms wore white, as well. Unlike their brides-to-be, the men still wore their pink saris. Blue sashes knotted around their waists distinguished them from the other male Sunnie disciples inside Yankee Stadium.

A groom had been assigned to each bride that morning. In most cases, the men and women had never met before.

Roseflower led Remo and Chiun down the stands behind the home-base line.

"You mean these are all arranged marriages?" Remo asked as they climbed down the steps. He looked out across the sea of faces awaiting the start of the marriage ceremony.

"That's right," the Sunnie said.

Remo laughed. "I hope you're planning on renting out Shea Stadium for the mass divorce," he said.

"Actually, in those parts of the world where arranged marriage is the custom, divorce is low to the point of being nonexistent," Roseflower explained.

"Baloney," Remo said.

"It is true," the Master of Sinanju said with a nod.

Remo frowned. "Yeah, well, that's probably because you'd get your eyes gouged out by a witchdoctor judge if you even mentioned it," he grumbled.

The stands had been opened onto the field to allow mingling among the Reverend Sun's followers. Roseflower led Remo and Chiun down into the periphery of the crowd.

"Where is the Holy One?" Chiun asked as they walked along just outside the first base line.

"He is preparing himself for the ceremony," Roseflower said. "Your meeting will take place afterward. I thought you might wish to get a better view of the service. This is a good spot, I think."

The Sunnie stopped, still smiling, a few yards away from first base.

Remo looked around. A platform had been set up in the middle of the diamond near the pitcher's mound. It rose high enough above the heads of the many gathered bride-and-groom sets that it was visible from anywhere on the ground.

A few Sunnies were making last-minute preparations atop the stage. Women arranged flowers of yellow and white. The men tested the public-address system on the floral-painted podium. When Remo glanced back at their escort, Roseflower was smiling blandly at the proceedings.

Remo cleared his throat guiltily. "You know, this probably isn't the best time to tell you this, Rosebud," Remo said. He shot a glance at Chiun. "But I don't think we're who you think we are."

The Master of Sinanju scowled. "Of course we are," he insisted. Hazel eyes flamed. "Remo, hold your tongue."

"Chiun, maybe he's supposed to meet somebody important."

"Who is more important that I?" the old Korean demanded.

"I *was* sent for you," Roseflower interjected.

"No," Remo insisted. "It couldn't be us. No one even knows we're here."

"The Reverend Sun does. He knows all."

Remo raised a skeptical eyebrow. "Forgive me if this insults one of the basic tenets of your religious faith, but bulldookey."

"I do not understand," Roseflower said, his bland Midwest face clouding.

"Hokum. Bunk. Crap. Bullshit," Remo elaborated. "I don't believe in any of this fortune-teller malarkey."

Chiun grabbed Roseflower by the arm, steering him away from his pupil. "Do not listen to the heretic. If he blasphemes, it is merely the product of latent Catholicism. Perhaps Good Seer Sun might perform an exorcism," he suggested, shooting a hateful glance at Remo.

"I am confused. Are you not of the Sun Source?" Roseflower asked.

"Yes," Chiun said quickly.

"Ye-es," Remo hedged. "But not the way you mean it."

"See how he qualifies? It is a nasty habit learned at the feet of wimple-wearing dowagers."

Remo rolled his eyes. "What time are the nuptials?" he asked, surrendering to the two men.

His question was answered by a cheer from the crowd.

The roar started suddenly, at a point beyond the platform. It swept rapidly across the packed stadium like a thundering tidal wave.

Pale arms draped in white rose wildly into the air. Trailing pink ends of saris flapped liked flags caught in a crazed wind as the frantic screaming grew.

And the chanting began.

It was low at first, shouted only by a few Sunnies planted at strategic points in the crowd.

"Sun! Sun! Sun! Sun!"

Others around the few screaming men took up the cry. It spread like wildfire. Inarticulate cheering was soon overshadowed by the single, shouted word.

"Sun! Sun! Sun!"

Clapping gleefully, Roseflower joined the chorus of chanting voices. Veins bulged on his reddening neck as he screamed the name of the Sunnie cult leader.

Remo shot a look at the Master of Sinanju.

Chiun had not joined in with the crowd. His hands were tucked inside the voluminous sleeves of his sea-green kimono. Yet even though he did not cheer, his face belied his elation. Hazel eyes danced merrily as he stood on tiptoe, trying to catch a first glimpse of the Reverend Sun.

None of them had to wait long.

All at once, the head of the Korean cult figure began to rise slowly and majestically above the crowd. It was a perfect fluid motion. Sun did not mount the stage in the jerky fashion of someone climbing stairs.

A few dozen yards away from the cult leader, Remo's finely tuned ears picked up the sound of gears grinding over the crowd noise. Sun stood on a small elevator platform.

The shoulders appeared, then the rest of the torso. Sun wore his usual business suit. A white alb was pulled over the conservative blue jacket.

The robe was open in a wide V-shape that extended down to the gathered waist.

"Sun! Sun! *Sun!*"

The screaming grew more intense. The Sunnie leader reveled in the accolades of his wild-eyed disciples. He raised fat hands in a gesture of triumph above his head.

Everyone in the stadium had gotten to their feet. Men and women in the stands stood cheering, as well, their voices raised along with those on the field waiting to be married.

To Remo, it was like being in the middle of someone else's mad dream. He looked around at the sea of zombielike faces. Grinning, beaming. Screaming.

Even for someone like Remo, who had seen much that was alarming and horrifying in his life, standing in the midst of the crowd of frenzied Sunnie disciples was a truly terrifying experience. It was not a fear of injury or death. Remo had been trained beyond both of those childlike things. The frightening characteristic of the Sunnies was their blind devotion to a man whom the rational world knew to be a fraud.

At that moment—as he gazed out upon the sea of rabidly devoted disciples—Remo Williams knew that these demented followers would kill for their leader. Man Hyung Sun need only give the order.

"Friends in the Sun!"

The Reverend Sun's voice boomed out over his screaming flock. Flapping pink saris continued to wave victoriously as the Sunnie throng grew hushed.

"We are gathered here today for a most joyous occasion!"

The brides and bridegrooms cheered as one. Almost three thousand voices rattled across the stadium.

"We must remember that this occasion," Sun continued when the crowd had quieted once more, "while joyful—is also one most solemn!"

Remo sidled up to the Master of Sinanju. "Don't get in my way for the bouquet, Little Father," Remo warned beneath the continuing amplified voice of Sun.

"Must you make a mockery of even sacred ceremonies?" Chiun asked. He was still standing on tiptoes, trying to see Sun more clearly.

"Come on," Remo said. "This is about as sacred as one of Liz Taylor's weddings. In fact, she's probably here somewhere. Don't you find this all a little bit over-the-top?"

"It is not my place to question the wisdom of a holy man," the Master of Sinanju replied.

"I'll take that as a yes."

Sun was still speaking. Feedback squealed occasionally from the tinny speaker system as he continued with the mass wedding ceremony.

As the cult leader was lecturing his followers on

the solemnity of the vows they would take this day, Remo began to notice an odd movement taking shape within the crowd.

He wasn't quite sure how he became aware of the men. It was as if some sort of internal trip wire had been struck.

When his unconscious mind steered his conscious mind to the strange intruders, he saw that there were six of them.

No.

Seven…eight. Eight in all.

They wore white robes minus the blue sashes of the rest of the grooms. But these men had no brides next to them. These were not the only differences between the new arrivals and the grooms, however. These men were armed.

"Chiun," Remo said, his voice low.

"I know," the Master of Sinanju replied, his face stern.

"Eight?"

Chiun shook his head. "Nine. Beyond the stage." He nodded beyond Sun.

The ninth man in white was just threading through the crowd of couples. Like the others Remo had seen, he was moving in the direction of the stage. By the way he walked, it was obvious he had some sort of weapon hidden beneath the folds of his flowing white garment.

"Catch up with you on the other side," Remo said.

Nodding, Chiun split away from him. The elderly Korean moved swiftly toward the right, across the first-base line and onto the crowded infield.

Remo had already moved off in the other direction. He cut a path directly for the first man in white.

"...must appreciate the importance of the church in every aspect of your lives together. There is no individual. There is no couple. There is only Sun...." the cult leader was proclaiming from the stage. His voice boomed out across the stadium.

"Don't *we* have an inflated sense of self?" Remo muttered sarcastically to himself as he slid between pairs of beaming Sunnie brides and grooms.

The nearest moving robe had vanished in the sea of couples. Remo allowed his instincts to guide him through the knot of people. On automatic, his body brought him in a direct line to intercept the would-be assassin.

Passing a thick cluster of people, Remo came out several yards away from the stage. On the other side of the crowd within the crowd, the first white-robed man emerged.

He was Korean. Remo spotted it straight off. The man's sleeves were wider than those of the other Sunnies. In the next moment, Remo realized why.

A gun slid expertly down the length of the

sleeve and into the killer's waiting hand. A rustling at the chest of the robe, and the other hand, which had been concealing the gun, slipped back down the other baggy sleeve.

It was a K-50M. A North Vietnamese knockoff of a Russian Tokarev.

Remo flew over to the man.

The free hand snapped a banana clip into place. Turning toward the stage, the Korean assassin brought his gun barrel up and around, aiming at the fleshy face of Man Hyung Sun.

He would have fired—indeed, he tried to. But something had gone suddenly and inexplicably wrong with his weapon.

It took a second for the killer to realize what was wrong. His gun would not fire without ammunition.

"Looking for this?" Remo asked sweetly. He was standing between the killer and the stage. In his hand was the banana clip from the Tokarev knockoff.

The would-be assassin's eyes grew wide in shock when he saw the stranger standing before him with his gun's magazine. Quickly, his free hand disappeared back up the sleeve, fumbling for a replacement clip. His grasping fingers had just wrapped around one in the pouch at his waist when Remo surprised him by returning the original. However, the way it came back was not the same way it had left.

"Yum, yum, yum," Remo said as he stuffed the curving clip down the man's throat. "Eat up. Bananas are a good source of carbohydrates. They give you that extra burst of killing energy."

The man wiggled and fought. To no avail. Remo jammed the clip down past his epiglottis, blocking the air flow to and from his lungs. Suddenly, respiration became a far more important thing to the assassin than shooting the Reverend Sun. Face turning purple, he sank to his knees, clawing at the rectangular piece of metal that jutted from his open mouth.

To Remo's surprise, the Sunnies in the immediate vicinity did not appear concerned in the least at the display of violence. The faces of those who saw Remo cram the magazine down the Korean's throat held looks of utter indifference. Most of the people around did not even bother to look his way. They simply continued to stare up at their leader, faces rhapsodic.

"Wonder if lobotomies come free with the blood tests," Remo said, shaking his head in disbelief.

He left the killer to choke to death in the grass. Remo dived into the crowd in search of the next assassin.

CHIUN WAS STILL FAR AWAY from the stage when he came upon the first set of killers.

The Master of Sinanju noted with only minor

interest that they were both Koreans. Assuming they were agents of some rival religious sect, he forged ahead.

The two flat-faced men had not even gotten close enough for an unobstructed shot at Sun before Chiun whirled in between them.

Guns were still hidden in the sleeves of their robes. With a move that seemed casual, Chiun sent a single index finger into the baggy cloth at the side of one man. He caught the hollow muzzle of the weapon with his fingertip. Instantly, the gun rocketed up like a missile fired from an underground silo.

The stock had been braced inside the man's armpit. On its path skyward, it wrenched through the shoulder socket with a tearing snap. Arm and gun both plopped from the hollow sleeve. Chiun stifled the man's scream with a toe to the throat. Continuing the move, he brought the heel of his foot into the jaw of the second man.

The killer's head twisted wildly around with the snap of dry, uncooked pasta. Both bodies fell simultaneously.

At the moment they dropped, another armed man sprang from the crowd a few feet away.

Eyes opened wide as the killer saw the tiny dervish whirl out from between his dead comrades. The man tried to fumble his gun free from his robe as the wizened Asian flew over to meet him.

It was no contest.

The barrel had barely emerged from the sleeve before Chiun was before him.

Hand flat, the Master of Sinanju slapped the killer's forehead so hard his eyes sprang loose, popping twin sacs of viscous fluid from bloody sockets. Inside his skull as the dead man fell, his brain quivered like so much gray jelly.

Chiun did not give the corpse a second glance. A remorseless wraith in green, the Master of Sinanju moved on.

REMO DROPPED THE BODY from his outstretched hand. Mouth hanging slack in death, it tumbled atop the other two.

That was four assassins for him so far. There were at least that many in the other direction.

He was much closer to the stage now.

Sun was as oblivious to the threat beneath him as his followers.

"...cannot allow the forces of evil to crush our future. *I* am your future. *I* am the future of the world...."

The cult leader continued to shout into the protesting microphone. In spite of the briskness of the day, his face was coated in a sheen of sweat.

Remo turned from Sun. He looped around the stage, coming up on the far side. This was ridiculous. There should have been police here. He hadn't seen one uniformed officer since arriving at the stadium.

He had no idea how many Chiun might have gotten so far. The crowd in the infield was too thick to see farther than the dozen or so people jammed in any given area. Remo had seen three assassins cutting through the throng on the right. If Chiun had gotten only those, that left two more. At least.

The killers had been weaving and ducking through the vast collection of Sunnies. By this point, the final two Koreans would not be anywhere near the places Remo had first seen them.

He moved swiftly, slipping like a shadow between groups of robed cult members.

Out, look. Around, duck, look again.

No one.

The stage loomed high on his right. He was so close now he could no longer see the Reverend Sun. The cult leader's voice continued to roar out stridently across his throng of faithful as Remo swept around to the rear of the platform.

Nothing. More blissfully ignorant couples. A line of Sunnies stood on the rear of the platform above, backs to the crowd.

He must have missed them on the other side.

Remo spun on his heel and was about to double back when he caught a sudden flash of movement from around the far side of the high-backed stage.

White robe. Asian features.

Yet another Korean assassin.

Remo didn't give much thought to the man's

nationality. He was nothing more than a threat to be neutralized.

Spinning back, Remo raced along the rear wall of the platform toward the lone killer. He was not even halfway there before he knew he would be too late.

The gun was already out and up. Clip in place. Finger caressed the crooked trigger. The explosive rattle of automatic-weapons fire drowned out the electronic bellow of Man Hyung Sun.

Hot lead blasted the backs of the men lined along the rear of the platform. Flesh exploded into flecks of crimson-streaked pulp as the bullets ripped through the Sunnies clustered on the platform.

Like too real ducks in a macabre shooting gallery, the men began toppling over. Some fell face forward onto the stage. Still more dropped in lifeless heaps to the grassy field behind the platform.

The killer had a look of demonic possession in his eyes as he continued firing upward. Round after round rattled into the men on the stage, each bullet coming that much closer to the Reverend Man Hyung Sun.

Oddly, there was no screaming.

Remo assumed the reaction from the crowd would be one of terror. The instinct to flee—for self-preservation—would surely surface among the Sunnie multitude. It did not.

The cult members remained mute spectators to

the carnage. The only visible change was that the ones at the rear of the platform seemed a bit more attentive as Remo flashed over to the man with the gun.

The Korean had nearly exhausted the bullets in the clip. He slipped the weapon back to one side, expecting to make a final sweep across the men on stage before the magazine was spent, when he felt an abrupt tug at his hands.

Popping and wrenching sounds flooded the auditory void that a second before had been filled with the persistent clatter of autofire.

The killer looked down for the source of the strange new noise. He found it at his hands. Or rather, where his hands had been.

The hands were gone, as was the gun. Replaced by twin stumps of spurting red blood.

As he looked down in dull amazement at his lifeblood pumping onto the ground, the assassin became briefly aware of his gun. The barrel was pointed back in his direction and was floating gently toward his face.

Wait.

Not floating.

Hurtling.

In fact, zooming in faster than the fastest thing he had ever seen.

The bone-crushing impact of his own weapon a split second later was the last thing the killer would ever feel.

Remo dumped the body with the gun sprouting from its forehead onto the ground. He was picking his way back through the carnage when a voice exploded on the PA system.

"As I have foretold, so it has come to pass!" the booming voice of Man Hyung Sun announced proudly.

Remo could not believe it. Sun was actually going on with the ceremony.

"I am the seer of legend. I augur great things for the chosen few. Revel in the Sun Source, disbelievers! Let Man Hyung Sun be your guide to blessed *pyon ha-da!* Great shall be the rewards for him who joins our righteous cause!"

"Sun! Sun! Sun!"

The crowd began to chant his name once more.

It was almost as if there had not been an attempted assassination a moment before. For all anyone knew, there were still killers lurking amid the crowd.

The Sunnies didn't care. The bodies strewed around the rear of the stage did not matter. They screamed and chanted with religious zeal, eyes wild with righteous fire.

Hands waved pink saris like trophies. As Remo came around to the front of the stage, he fought his way through the waving streams of silk, still searching for the last of the Korean hit squad.

"One has come to deliver us to that which I

have foretold!'' Sun screamed, quieting the frenzied crowd.

Remo stumbled on the last body. It was at the base of the stage. Every bone beneath the robe appeared to have been pounded to dust. Chiun's handiwork.

He glanced around, looking for the Master of Sinanju in the sea of Sunnie faces.

''It is he who saved your sacred leader! He of the Sun Source whose arrival I have presaged!''

There it was again. Sun Source. The most ancient description of Sinanju, known only to a handful of people. For some reason, it angered Remo to hear the cult leader speak the words. Coming from a fraud like Sun, it was almost a desecration.

''He will help lead us to glory!''

Remo half heard the words.

Chiun was nowhere to be seen. From the direction Remo had taken, there was really only one place the old Korean could have gone.

''Speak that we may hear your words, Great Protector!''

A thought struck Remo. It dropped like a lead ball into the pit of his stomach.

Limbs stiff, face unreadable, he turned to the stage.

The wizened form of the Master of Sinanju stood high on the platform next to the Reverend Man Hyung Sun. The cluster of wrinkles on his parchment face bunched into a tight fist of pleasure as Sun twisted the microphone over to Chiun.

"All hail the Sun Source," the Master of Sinanju's squeaky voice boomed out over the public-address system.

As the world spun and twisted and finally dropped out from beneath Remo's feet, the crowd of Sunnie disciples burst into frenzied cheers.

14

The men wore the blue uniform of the New York City Police Department. Hip radios squawking, they forced their way through the crowd of mingling Sunnies to the pile of three bodies lying on the infield of Yankee Stadium.

Remo was gone. He had seen the police arriving at the very end of the mass wedding ceremony and had taken off in the opposite direction with Chiun. The two Masters of Sinanju had left with the Reverend Sun's entourage.

It was a testament to the brainwashing techniques the Sunnie cult employed that the men and women could ignore all the corpses lying around their makeshift chapel.

Chatting among themselves in the postwedding euphoria, they paid little attention as the police slipped the first trio of bodies into black zipper bags.

Oddly enough, there were no homicide detectives on the scene. Stranger still, the police who were present used no gloves when handling the corpses. They merely stuffed the remains into the bags, zipped them up and moved on to the next bodies. They could have been state workers collecting litter at the side of the highway.

Not one question was asked of the Sunnies.

Not one fingerprint was taken.

Not one hair or fiber or blood sample was lifted from any of the bodies, the ground or the stage.

Nothing besides the actual collection of the corpses seemed to interest the police.

It took little time for them to bag up the assassins, as well as the Sunnies who had fallen victim to the single successful gunman.

The nine bodies of the hit squad were placed in the back of an unmarked van. The remains of the more than one dozen slaughtered Sunnie cult members were put in the back of another nondescript vehicle.

Without a single siren or light to herald their way, the trucks took off in different directions.

The bodies of the Sunnie victims turned up over the course of the next two days, scattered in a wide area around the East River near Riker's Island and in Flushing Bay near LaGuardia Airport.

The remains of the Korean hit squad showed up in a completely different place.

15

It was the beginning of his second full day of work back behind his familiar desk at Folcroft Sanitarium, and Harold W. Smith felt like a new man.

The winter sun reflected brightly on Long Island Sound, dappling in shades of white and yellow the waves that lapped at the rotting dock behind the private sanitarium's administrative wing.

Though the calendar had lately crept into December, a substantial snowfall had yet to come. The crispness of the air and lack of icy buildup on the ground erased images of the deep winters of years past. Residents of the Northeast were enjoying the guiltless lie that this was merely an extended autumn. True winter was still far off.

Typing at his desk computer, Smith was basking in the comforting fiction, as well.

For a time the day before yesterday, he had thought he might be having some kind of relapse. Of course, he knew that was not likely. He had been assured that his recovery would be complete.

However, after he had hung up from Remo, he had a creeping, unnerving sensation in his skull.

It was a strange afterimage of his illness. Almost like exploring the spot where a troubling canker sore had been, expecting the pain to still be there.

Of course Smith was nothing if not logical. He knew exactly why he had felt the way he had. But Remo and Chiun had gotten out of Germany without further incident.

According to the latest information he had gotten from the wire service, the police cordon was still in place around the North Korean embassy. They did not know their quarry was long gone. Let the Koreans at the Berlin mission try to explain their way out of it. It was not a CURE affair.

Just to be certain that every loose end was tied up, Smith was in the process of checking the records of Kim Jong Il's personal jet.

His gnarled fingers ached as he drummed them swiftly and precisely against the surface of his desk. Buried beneath the lip of the onyx slab, alphanumeric keys lit up amber when struck. Dancing fireflies entombed in a sea of black.

While he was convalescing, Smith had gotten used to typing on his small laptop. The sensation was different with the high-tech keyboard on his desk. His body was not as adaptable as it had once been. It would take a little time for his fingers to get used to the different sensation.

Smith soon learned that the aircraft had touched

down in North Korea the previous day. That meant that the Master of Sinanju's share of the Nibelungen Hoard would be halfway to his village by now. Away from the world for centuries—perhaps aeons—to come.

The CURE director breathed a sigh of relief on learning the news. The Hoard would not be a threat to world commerce in Harold Smith's lifetime. And for Smith, that was the best he could hope to accomplish.

As he was exiting the record of flight-log data, Smith's computer system emitted a small electronic beep. It was a signal that the massive mainframes in the basement beneath him had dredged something of interest from the vast stream of facts and curiosities coursing endlessly along the invisible information stream that was the World Wide Web.

Closing out his current application, Smith brought up a window containing the information.

It was a news story from nearby New York City. Eight bullet-riddled bodies had washed up from the East River. Although the features had been carefully mutilated to make identification impossible, police were willing to admit that the victims all appeared to be rather young—ranging from their early twenties to midthirties.

It was being treated as a mystery. The deceased were white males. They did not appear to be victims of a gangland slaying, nor was there evidence of drugs. There had been no missing persons reports filed.

Until new evidence came to light, the men had each been given a John Doe classification.

Smith wondered briefly if this might not be the work of some new serial killer. If it was, it did not fit any pattern Smith knew of.

He decided that an explanation would most likely present itself eventually. Smith was about to close out the file when the blue contact desk phone rang. He left the story on his computer as he turned his attention to the telephone.

"Yes, Remo," Smith said efficiently.

"Smitty, I figured I'd better let you know about the bodies before those damned computers of yours flagged the story," Remo's familiar voice announced glumly.

"What bodies?" Smith asked, sitting up in his chair. He became instantly aware of his surgery scar. He felt gingerly at it with his gray fingertips as he spoke.

"The ones Chiun and I whacked at the Loonie wedding yesterday," Remo explained. "I know you've got some screwy program that recognizes mine and Chiun's techniques. Before you go apeshit, we are not freelancing."

"That is comforting to know," Smith said dryly. "However, I have received no such information."

"Really?" Remo said, surprised. "I figured

those machines of yours would have read the police reports by now.''

"Perhaps we should begin at the beginning," Smith said. "Who did you, er, remove?"

"Nine Korean killers," Remo said. "They were armed to the teeth and tried to bump off Man Hyung Sun himself.''

"There was an assassination attempt against Sun?" Smith asked. It was his turn to be surprised.

"You didn't hear about that, either?" Remo asked.

"No, I did not."

"Gee, maybe it's time for an upgrade or a lube job or something," Remo suggested. "Your computers are slipping.''

"That is not possible," Smith insisted. But even as he denied the possibility that the Folcroft Four could fail, Smith was diving into the system.

He quickly found the reports on the mass Sunnie wedding ceremony. There was nothing to indicate that it had not gone off without a hitch, so to speak.

"Remo, the stories I am reading recount a rather dull ceremony," Smith said, puzzled.

"Whoever wrote that wasn't there," Remo said. "Come to think of it," he added, "I don't remember seeing anyone who looked like a reporter there.''

"I think I see why," Smith said, scanning the lines of text on his computer screen. "All of these stories appear to be pretty much identical to one another. Typical for reporters who have written their stories from either a pool source or a press release.''

''You're saying the Sunnies kept the assassination attempt under their hats?'' Remo asked.

''So it would seem.''

''That doesn't make sense. Sun doesn't seem like the kind of guy who would hide from something that might give him positive press.''

''No, that does not seem to be in keeping with the character of the Sunnie leader,'' Smith agreed.

''You knew he had a new psychic infomercial on,'' Remo said. It was not a question.

''I have heard as much,'' Smith replied crisply. ''It is my understanding that former presidential candidate Michael Princippi is a featured performer.'' He did not attempt to hide the distaste in his tone. ''Apparently, he has sunk even lower since his dealings with Mark Kaspar and the Truth Church.''

Remo stiffened at the reference. ''Don't even mention that, Smitty,'' he complained. ''Those ghosts are all behind us, so let's just forget about it.'' He took a deep breath, banishing thoughts of a more painful time. ''Anyway, it seems crazy that Sun wouldn't want to capitalize on some screwballs trying to kill him on the same week he goes national with some new scheme.''

''I am at a loss to explain it, as well,'' Smith admitted. ''You say these men you eliminated were Korean. Did you think to question any of them?''

"There wasn't time," Remo explained.

"That is unfortunate. Sun is a fervent anti-Communist who has at different times been accused of involvement in illegal activity against both North and South Korea. It is possible that one of the governments on either side of the Thirty-eighth Parallel sent agents to dispose of him for some reason. Why they would choose to do so at this time, I would not begin to speculate."

"Maybe they just don't like weddings," Remo suggested.

"Yes," Smith said humorlessly. "In any event, I will be on the alert for any report concerning the Korean deaths. If there is any new information available, I will let you know. You are at home, presumably."

"Not exactly," Remo hedged. Before Smith could press further, he changed the subject. "By the way, Smitty, the other weird thing about the whole mess is that there weren't any police there during the assassination attempt."

"Did Sun not wish them inside the stadium during the ceremony?" Smith asked.

"In or outside," Remo explained. "There weren't any cops around anywhere. More than twenty bodies raining down all around us, and not even a beat cop with a billy club to give me and Chiun a hand."

"Twenty?" Smith asked, gray face creasing in tart displeasure. "You said there were only nine."

"Oh," Remo said. "I guess I forgot to mention the Sunnies who were killed."

"Yes, you did," Smith said aridly.

"There were about fourteen of them," Remo explained. "One of the hit men got off a couple of rounds before I could get to him."

Smith's pinched face grew troubled. "And they did not report that, either?" he said. "How is it possible they could have kept it sec—?" Smith paused, a sudden realization dawning on him. Typing swiftly, he brought back up on his computer screen the original story that the mainframes had collected.

"Remo," the CURE director said flatly when he was again scanning the familiar lines of text, "I am looking at an Associated Press story out of New York that concerns a number of unidentified bodies that have washed up along the banks of the East River this morning. All eight victims died of gunshot wounds."

"They can't be the ones, Smitty," Remo said. "The police collected the bodies."

"You said there were no police," Smith said slowly.

"They showed up after."

Smith considered. "One moment, please." The aching in his fingers long-forgotten, Smith rapidly accessed a stealth program that allowed him to slip into the computerized homicide records of the NYPD. "There is no evidence of any bodies being removed from the Sunnie ceremony," he said after only a quick perusal of the files. Leaving that aspect of the police system, he logged in to another area.

"That's impossible," Remo insisted while Smith worked. "I saw them myself."

"No," Smith said firmly. "You did not." He had stopped typing. "Whoever you saw was not with the police. There are no records of any officers being placed on duty near Yankee Stadium during the wedding ceremony. Nor were any summoned there for any type of disturbance."

"They were phonies?" Remo asked.

"So it would seem."

"So you think the bodies in the East River are who? The hit squad or the Loonies?"

"It seems that the ones who have washed up so far would be with the Grand Unification Church. All young white males. But there have only been eight in all. Your Korean assassins might still be out there. I will alert the authorities to begin conducting searches along beaches and in the waters between the Triborough and Bronx-Whitestone Bridges. The bodies collected thus far have been tightly concentrated roughly at the midpoint of this area."

"I don't know, Smitty," Remo said doubtfully. "If they dumped twenty-three bodies into the river at once, doesn't it seem like at least one of the eight corpses that have turned up so far would be one of the killers?''

"Possibly," Smith conceded. "But not necessarily. We will learn more when the Korean bodies are recovered."

"I'm kind of curious to know who they were," Remo said.

"As am I," Smith agreed. "I do not enjoy the prospect of assassination squads running loose on American soil. I will contact you when any new information presents itself." Smith was typing as he spoke. "I asked you before if you were at home, but I do not believe you answered."

"Yeah, you did, didn't you?" Remo said.

Instead of a reply to his query, Smith heard the familiar flat buzz of a dial tone.

16

The first government agent to peer into the mysterious box from America threw up. He pressed his hands tightly against his mouth as brown rice launched from between his tense fingers.

"What is wrong with you?" demanded the security agent assigned to watch his colleague. For suspicion rather than security, there were always at least two men in each detail. The second agent's face was angry.

The first agent was vomiting so hard it was impossible for him to speak. He merely turned away at the question, shaking his head as he continued to retch uncontrollably.

The second agent scowled. As he sidestepped both the still vomiting agent and the pile of clotted rice—thick with stomach fluids—gathering at the man's feet, the second North Korean official peered inside the cardboard case.

His lunch immediately joined that of his comrade on the cold concrete floor.

They vomited and vomited until there was nothing left but air. For several long, painful minutes, they continued to dry heave.

The Democratic People's Republic of Korea was starving yet again. Food was being strictly rationed, and every meal was meager.

When they were through vomiting, rather than leave the former contents of their stomachs for the cleaning staff to take home to divide among the members of their starving families, the two men got down on their hands and knees. Like dogs, they began scooping up and eating their own vomit. Only when they had licked the floor clean did they leave the room, careful not to peer at the ghastly contents of the innocuous open box.

THE HEAD OF THE People's Bureau of Revolutionary Struggle was immediately summoned to the locked airport room. He arrived from his Pyongyang office by official car twenty minutes later.

As he entered the small secure room, he noted with disdain the stench of stomach fluids.

The two security agents accompanied him inside. They hung back by the door, faces ashen, as the PBRS head strode over to the cardboard box.

The head of North Korean intelligence did not have the same response to the box's contents as his subordinates.

"When did this arrive?" he asked, hooded eyes peering inside.

"An hour ago," was the reply from one of the sickly men.

"Directly from America?"

"America? No. It came from the South."

"With a message from America," the intelligence head said leadingly.

The men glanced at each other, puzzled. "None that we know of," one admitted.

"Hmm."

For a few moments, the older man merely stared into the box, tipping his head to see inside from different angles. But all at once, to the horror of the two men across the room, the director of PBRS reached inside the box. He used both hands, shoulders making a shrugging motion as he clasped the object contained within.

He lifted it out into the wan fluorescent light of the drab little room located off the main Pyongyang terminal.

For the second time within a half hour, the first security agent's lunch spewed out onto the floor.

The other man had braced himself. Covering his nose and mouth, he managed to keep his rice down, though his stomach knotted in waves of churning acid fire. He swallowed the clump of rice that had gathered in his throat.

Across the room, the director of the People's Bureau of Revolutionary Struggle turned the object over in his hands. He was like a woman in a market carefully appraising a large melon. Except melons did not have noses.

The severed head had distinctly Korean features. But it was somewhat desiccated, even though it had been encased in some kind of plastic shrink-wrap.

The wrapping twisted the nose to one side and flattened the eyes even further than nature had. Deep maroon pools of blood had gathered, mostly dry now, at the bottom of the tight bag. Through the congealed blood, the director could make out jagged tears in the flesh of the neck. The object employed to remove the head had not been particularly sharp.

Without warning, the director tossed the severed head to the subordinate who had yet to throw up in his presence.

"Have this taken to the PBRS forensics laboratory immediately," he ordered.

There were eight other boxes just like it stacked neatly beside the first. They had yet to be opened.

"Do not open these," the PBRS director commanded. "I will hold the two of you responsible if they are damaged in any way. Take them to the lab, as well."

As the director marched from the room, the security agent holding the tightly wrapped package only nodded. To open his mouth would be to release a mouthful of vomit onto the upturned face of the head in his hands.

ONCE THE SHRINK-WRAP had been cut away and the frozen-in-death faces had been forced back into some semblance of normalcy, their nation of origin became more evident.

The faces were certainly Korean. But were they from the North or the South? Perhaps they were not even from divided Korea at all. They could merely be foreign nationals of Korean ancestry.

Fortunately, the forensic experts did not have to rely solely on the heads. Aiding the laboratory investigation was the fact that a small case had been packed inside each box. The first was discovered in the original container amid a pile of white foam packing.

Fingers. Packed like fresh Cuban cigars.

They were lined up between plastic dividers. Two rows of five, one atop the other.

Fingerprints taken from the detached digits were matched against official government records. When suspected matches were found, file photographs were compared to the severed heads.

The identities were soon confirmed. The nine heads with their attendant fingers had belonged to agents from the North Korean delegation to the United Nations.

Further proof came while the lab was completing its work. A phone call from the UN consulate in New York reported that several PBRS agents had gone missing.

The head of the People's Bureau of Revolutionary Struggle learned of the telephone call while he was still reading the lab's findings. It was all the proof he needed to request an urgent audience with the Leader for Life of Korea, Kim Jong Il.

The Supreme Commander of North Korea was in his basement office in the presidential palace when the head of his secret intelligence force was ushered in.

Framed posters of successful American films were crammed together around all four walls. Wherever faces appeared on the long subway prints, the graphics had been altered to give the actors Asian features. The head of PBRS walked briskly past a bloodred poster on which a Korean Captain Kirk and Mr. Spock looked out disdainfully across the vast office.

Premier Kim Jong Il sat in a blue director's chair in front of a special wide-screen projection TV in the corner of the enormous office. Fuzzy images raced around the large screen.

"Can you believe this?" the premier demanded once the security agent had traversed the office. His face was a scowl.

"You have heard?" the intelligence director asked, surprise in his sharp voice.

"Heard? What kind of stupid question is that? Of course I've heard. I just can't believe it."

Though the situation was grave, the PBRS director allowed a small amount of relief. There were times—more of them than he cared to think of—

when the North Korean premier was less than interested in state business.

The director did not worry at the moment that there was an obvious leak in his own department. He would deal with that later. All that mattered now was that the premier knew of the problem and understood its gravity.

"This is terrible," Kim Jong Il wailed.

"Yes, it is," agreed the director.

"The worst thing that ever happened," the Korean Leader for Life moaned.

"I am heartened by your appreciation of the situation."

"I could have done twice the box office of this," Kim Jong Il lamented.

The security chief paused. "Excuse me, O Premier?"

"The box office," Kim Jong Il said. "They pulled in 230 mil, domestic. For what? A bunch of flying cows and a few lousy wind-machine effects. Moo, blow. Moo, blow. Crap, crap, crap. And the story? Pee-yew. I could come up with a better outline sitting on the can."

For a moment, the security director thought that the premier had finally succumbed to madness; however, all at once he noticed the action on the screen behind Kim Jong Il. The premier had been in the middle of watching a two-year-old American movie when the PBRS director came in. The heir to the throne of Kim Il Sung had a passion for movies that no one in his country understood.

"I see," the security director said slowly.

"I mean, stink-o-rama," Kim Jong Il insisted. "They've got a sequel coming out to this piece of crap, don't they? I wouldn't use the print to wipe my ass."

"There is a problem," the security chief said.

"Don't tell me—tell editing," the Leader for Life of Korea said, waving his hand in a dismissive gesture. He stuck a fat fist into a large cardboard tub propped between his knees. Buttered popcorn spilled to the floor as he shoveled some of the puffy white snack into his mouth.

"Not with the film, my premier," the security chief said evenly.

"Don't bet the ranch on that, Charlie," replied the North Korean leader, his mocking laugh muffled.

"It is with the Americans."

Kim Jong Il paused in midchew. "What about them?" he asked, damp popcorn spilling from his mouth.

"Some of our agents in the field have been eliminated."

"Eliminated? What do you mean, eliminated? That's dead, right?"

"That is correct, Premier."

Kim Jong Il shrugged. "And?" he asked.

"The bodies were brutalized, Premier. The

heads and fingers were removed and sent to us. Most likely for identification purposes."

"Chopped off?" the premier asked.

"Yes, my leader."

Kim Jong Il considered for a moment, chewing languidly at his popcorn. "Cool," he said eventually.

"Premier?"

"I mean, cool as a visual. Great scene for a movie. A head in a bag. I can see the camera panning slowly up on it. What's in it? the audience wonders. Tension building. Eerie music." He framed his hands into a makeshift camera lens as he stole up to an imaginary sack.

"Forgive me, Premier, but I believe that this is something far more serious than a scene in a film. Agents have died. *Real* agents."

Sitting before the security man, Kim Jong Il dropped his hands. "Don't get huffy with me, buddy," he warned. "I know what you're talking about. I was just trying to visualize."

"Of course, my leader," the security man said, bowing.

"So what's the deal? Are the Americans pissed at us for some reason again?"

"I do not know, Premier," said the security director. "Their President could not be weaker. He has allowed our nuclear program to continue unchecked. Perhaps there are elements in his government concerned with our having atomic capability. This could be their doing.''

"A warning, you mean," Kim Jong Il said.

"It is possible.''

The premier considered. "You're sure these are our boys, not some sort of *Manchurian Candidate* impostors?''

"There is no doubt.''

Kim Jong Il exhaled loudly. He placed his nearly empty popcorn container on the floor. "How about the injuries to the necks?'' he asked.

"Premier?''

"You said the heads were cut off. Cut off how? Like a knife, like a sword, like magic—how?''

The security man seemed puzzled by the last method the premier mentioned. How could a head be removed by magic?

"A blunt object was used," he said. "There was more tearing than slicing. Our forensic experts say that toward the end, the heads were ripped free.''

Kim Jong Il shook his head. "It's not who I think it is," he said firmly. "If it was one of them, they'd have made it look cleaner than a bowl of Boraxo.''

"I do not understand," the security chief said.

"Be thankful you don't," the premier said pitifully. "It's cost me about a billion bucks in jet fuel to keep them happy over the past couple of months." He considered. "But this isn't their style.

If they weren't happy with the way I handled their cargo, I'd be dead before I even knew it."

"No one could get to you," the security chief said, chest puffing out in pride.

Kim Jong Il only laughed.

"So what do you think?" the Premier asked a moment later. He was wiping tears of mirth from his eyes. "Are the Americans playing some kind of game with us, or what?"

"I honestly do not know, premier. However, I would recommend retribution for these killings. We cannot allow any government to imagine weakness on our part."

"Leave our spies to spy in peace, is that what you're saying?" the premier asked. He did not wait for an answer. "Look, do what you think you have to to get ready for a counterattack. But don't—I repeat—do not set anything in motion until you okay it with me. Is that clear?"

"Yes, Great Leader." The security chief turned to go.

Frowning, Kim Jong Il leaned back in his Hollywood director's chair. "Oh, wait a second," he called after the head of the People's Bureau of Revolutionary Struggle.

The PBRS head turned, thinking something important had been forgotten.

Kim Jong Il was holding his cardboard popcorn container.

"Be a pal and get somebody to pop me up another batch," he said. He waggled the box of unpopped kernels.

17

The banks of buzzing switchboards had been set up in what had once been the grand ballroom of the East Hampton, New York, estate of the Reverend Man Hyung Sun.

Cubicles with portable partitions concealed row upon row of telephone psychics. Remo had to admit, it was quite an operation.

He had returned here with Chiun after the mass wedding ceremony two days earlier. While the Master of Sinanju was in conference with the Reverend Sun, Remo had been forced to tour the grounds alone. He had grown bored with the gaggle of devoted Loonies working the grounds, and so had wandered into this large room.

Walking through the lines of switchboard operators, Remo paused near one in particular. She was a huge woman in a paisley muumuu. Beads and shark teeth had been tamed and coaxed onto several long cords around her thick neck. Giant looping gold earrings with extra dangling crystals hung from meaty earlobes.

Every light on her switchboard blinked crazily. For each light, a hopeless, foolish caller waited for remunerated guidance from a total stranger. As Remo watched, the woman plugged into one of the jacks beneath a blinking green light.

"Sun Source Psychic Network," the woman announced. "I am Dame Lady Mystique, your personal conduit to Reverend Sun." She chewed gum as she listened to the problem of the caller at the other end of the line. "Yeah," the woman said, flipping absently through a catalog that rested before her switchboard, "I got a real strong feeling about that, honey. Two, seven, eight, fourteen, twenty-one and twenty-nine. You get all that? Okay, play those and good fortune will come your way someday soon." She hung up on the caller, flipping instantly to another line. "Sun Source Psychic Network," she repeated to her newest customer.

Disgusted, Remo left Dame Lady Mystique to bilk her latest rube.

As he walked past many of the other paid soothsayers—all engaged in chattering conversations about love, fortune and career—Remo came to one solid conclusion. The success of these psychic lines was a direct descendant of the televangelists of years gone by.

It made sense. As organized religion had become more concerned about worldly rather than spiritual matters, the fundamentalist TV evangelists had swept in to offer spiritual guidance to feckless spirits. Once those charlatans had been discredited in the scandals of the 1980s, something else was needed to fill the pseudospiritual void. Psychic infomercials and hotlines were the obvious successors.

People called up and, after spending a great deal of costly time on hold, spoke briefly with someone who gave them nothing but feeble hope for a better future. And from what Remo could tell of the psychics' end of the conversations, the callers seemed satisfied.

He wasn't certain why, but watching the crazy psychics talking to their foolish callers gave Remo a strange hollow sensation in the pit of his stomach. All at once, he decided that he had had enough of this place.

Scowling, Remo headed briskly for the big doors of the former ballroom.

At the door, Remo almost ran into a pink-and-white-robed Loonie who was coming in from the sumptuous main foyer. It was Roseflower, the same Sunnie who had led Remo and Chiun into Yankee Stadium two days earlier.

"Oh, hello," the cult member said, surprised for a moment to see someone who was neither a Sunnie nor a psychic in the great mansion of the Reverend Sun. "Are you enjoying your stay with us?"

"No," Remo replied tersely. He was about to go around the Sunnie when he paused. "I thought

Sun was the one who claimed he was the fortune-teller?'' he asked, turning.

Roseflower nodded. ''Reverend Sun is a seer,'' he agreed.

''Then what's with all these other fakes?'' Remo said. He jerked a thumb over his shoulder. Beneath the arching skylights and crystal chandeliers, telephone psychics continued to dispense wisdom for a dollar the first minute, four-fifty each additional minute.

''They are Seer Sun's helpers,'' Roseflower explained.

''You mean like street-corner Santas helping out around the holidays,'' Remo said sarcastically.

''That is not far from the truth,'' Roseflower admitted with a nod. ''There is such a great demand for guidance that no one actually expects to get through to the Reverend Sun. He dispenses his psychic energy to these chosen few.''

''Your chosen few could fill the Meadowlands.''

''There are many who desire to know their future. Our supply of psychics must meet that demand.''

''I've never heard a con job put in such capitalistic terms before,'' Remo said blandly.

''The truth is not a con, Mr. Williams,'' Roseflower said placidly.

Remo was taken aback. He could count the number of people who knew his real name on one hand and still have fingers left over. Remo had been framed for murder years before and sentenced to die in an electric chair that did not work. For all intents and purposes, Remo Williams had died on that day. Since then, though he kept his first name, his surname had been an endless series of aliases. He was surprised to hear his real name spoken by a grinning Sunnie cult member.

"Chiun told you my name," Remo said levelly, recovering from his initial confusion.

"No," Roseflower insisted, beaming. "It was told to me by His Super Oneness, the Reverend Sun."

"Crapola," Remo said. "He doesn't know anything his accountant doesn't tell him."

"Not true. He *can* see the future," Roseflower insisted.

"That old fraud couldn't see the *past* with a crystal ball, a Ouija board, a bucket of tea leaves and a mile-high stack of past-dated issues of that newspaper of his," Remo said, annoyance registering in his voice.

"Believe as you wish." Roseflower shrugged.

"Good. I believe he's a flimflam artist," Remo said.

"That is your prerogative," said the Sunnie. "But know that you and the old one are destined for much more with the Sun Source. You have formed a grand karmic link with His Greatness."

"Yeah? Well I'm about to break that link," Remo muttered.

Sidestepping Roseflower, Remo strode purposefully toward the huge curving staircase in the mansion's main foyer.

THE GLASS-ENCLOSED balcony looked out over the rolling rear lawns of the East Hampton estate.

Sitting cross-legged on the floor, the Master of Sinanju basked in the warmth of late-morning sunlight flowing in through the many panes before him. Rectangles of bright yellow stretched out into the bedroom behind him.

Swarms of Sunnies worked in the brisk winter air on the back lawn. Some raked at the brown grass. Others trimmed shoots from topiary shrubs, fashioned into animal shapes. Farther away, still more were operating a mechanical device used to aerate the soil.

Chiun watched them all, yet did not really see them.

The old Korean was deep in thought.

He had had several meetings with the Reverend Sun in the past forty-eight hours. Each one left him more puzzled.

Like Chiun, Sun had been born in Korea but had spent many years in America. He confided to the Master of Sinanju that he shared Chiun's longing to return to the land of his birth. In these things, they were alike. But the similarities soon ended.

Sun's religion was somewhat Christian—at least in its proclamations. At first, Chiun had been horrified to learn this. Sun had explained that he was a Presbyterian minister who had fallen away from the organized church.

The Master of Sinanju had no idea how he would explain this to Remo. The product of a nun-controlled orphanage, the boy had terrible Christian leanings already. His defense of the carpenter and his sect was shameful. He reveled in so-called worthy traits such as honesty and generosity. His pro-Christian leanings were even evident in his defense of Charlemagne. In short, Remo was a great disappointment when it came to his papal-centric worldview. It would only make matters worse when he found out that the Reverend Sun held views somewhat similar to his own.

Chiun's relief was great, therefore, when he learned that Sun had largely renounced his earlier beliefs upon founding the Grand Unification Church. In fact, the new religion had little in common with the Protestant Christian church or its pontiff-tangled roots. But it would still be a tricky matter to get around with Remo.

Chiun was sitting on his balcony, half watching the Sunnie workmen and trying to find a way to properly sugarcoat Sun's early Christianity when he heard the familiar confident glide of Remo's feet on the hallway carpet.

Chiun had not come up with a solution to his vexing problem. His only hope was that it would not come up.

A moment later, a knock came on the door.

"Enter," Chiun called.

The big door pushed open. "Geez Louise, it stinks in here," Remo complained the moment he stepped into the room. As he walked across the bedroom, his features were crumpled in lines of disgust.

"Do not look at me," Chiun said dully.

Remo sank down on the balcony floor next to the Master of Sinanju. "It's that after-shave of Sun's," Remo griped. "The whole upstairs reeks. I take it by the stench in here he's been to see you?"

Chiun nodded. He continued to look out at the robed men scattered around the lawn.

"Did he thank you for saving his fanny yet?"

"Every breath the Holy One draws is thanks enough," the Master of Sinanju replied.

"He didn't thank me, either," Remo said dryly. "Which is just as well, if you ask me. I couldn't get within ten feet of him with all that foo-foo juice he splashes on."

"Do not be impertinent with Reverend Sun," Chiun warned ominously. "His oracular wisdom is vast. Great are the things he presages."

"Yeah, I bet he sees a big fat Swiss bank account in his future," Remo muttered contemptuously.

"Cannot a holy man be concerned with keeping

a roof over his head and food in his belly?'' Chiun asked.

"Have you looked around this joint? It's more than just a roof—it's a frigging palace. And as far as food goes, Reverend Sun doesn't look like he's missing too many meals.''

"Ours is not to question the Seer.''

"Baloney,'' Remo said. "And what's the story with this 'reverend' crap? Isn't that a Christian term?''

Chiun's eyes opened wider. "It is a Latin term,'' he said evasively. "Adopted by clergy who debase its true meaning. Tell me,'' Chiun added, steering the subject away from Christianity, "do you not wish to know why we are here?''

"We're not. At least *I'm* not much longer.''

"That is up to you,'' Chiun sniffed. "But you must surely be curious to know what inspired me to seek out Sun.''

"You didn't talk on the trip down to New York.'' Remo shrugged. "I assumed you still didn't want to talk about it.''

"I did not,'' Chiun admitted. "However, you have forced it out of me.'' The Master of Sinanju leaned forward. When he spoke, he pitched his voice in a conspiratorial whisper. "It is *pyon hada,*'' he intoned.

Chiun leaned back, smiling broadly.

"Sun said that on TV and at the rally,'' Remo said, nodding. "I don't know those words.''

"You would not," Chiun admitted. "It has no meaning to the lesser races. Whites and blacks, as well as many Asians, are unaware of it. You are aware, Remo, of the true story of creation?"

"You mean from Genesis? Adam and Eve and the Garden?"

Chiun waved a disgusted hand. "Do not annoy me with fairy stories," he complained. "I speak of the story of the true Creator." He settled into an instructive pose. "Before the beginning of time, the one who made man formed a likeness of himself from mud and baked it in his celestial oven. Of course, being Creator, he had much on his mind. When he returned, he found that he had left his creation to bake too long. 'Woe to me,' he lamented. 'I have charred this work of my genius.' This, Remo, is how the blacks came to be."

Remo had heard this story before. In his earliest days of training, Chiun used to recount many of his favorite racist stories. Mostly to instruct Remo on how inferior he was to Chiun. However, he could not remember the Master of Sinanju ever relating this story with such passion.

"Wait a minute," Remo broke in. "Didn't you tell me a while back that this was crap? What about Tangun?"

"Tangun established the first Chosun dynasty of Korea," Chiun said impatiently. "He was not the first man. Listen." He continued with his story. "The Creator determined not to repeat his initial error. Into the oven he placed a second image of himself. But in his desire not to create another disaster, he made an even worse mistake than before. This creation he undercooked. 'How horrible this day is!' he cried. 'For in my haste I have created a white man!'

"Only in his third attempt did the Creator finally accomplish what he had set out to do," Chiun went on. "He baked his next creation to perfection, and when it was cooked to the proper shade, out of his oven sprang a yellow man. Afterward he refined this to Koreans and further refined this to people from Sinanju. The process did not achieve perfection until he refined the people of Sinanju into the perfection of a single entity—the Master of Sinanju. My ancestor." Chiun smiled proudly.

Remo nodded. "I haven't heard you tell that one in a long time," he said.

"It is wrong to burden the inferior races with the tale of their defective origin," Chiun said seriously. "I have learned this in America, and this is why I have been silent on this subject for lo these many years."

Remo—who thought Chiun had been anything but silent on the matter of race—shook his head. "I don't understand," he said. "What does this have to do with Sun?"

"*Pyon ha-da,*" Chiun insisted. "It is the end of your long wait. I am so happy for you!" Unable to contain his joy, he threw his arms around his pupil.

Remo was not prepared for such a physical expression of happiness from the Master of Sinanju. He endured the hug, leaning uncomfortably away once Chiun released him.

"So what is *pyon ha-da?*" Remo asked uneasily.

"It is the time foretold in which he who made all finally corrects the errors of his creation."

Remo was still at a loss. Something intensely weird was going on here. Chiun's being happy, for one. The old Korean generally had an emotional range that ran the gamut from annoyed to full-out rage.

Even more out of character, the Master of Sinanju had also taken up with a bogus cult leader. And why was Chiun's story of the creation resurfacing after all these years?

As the old Korean beamed joyfully at him from his simple reed mat, a thought suddenly struck Remo.

"No," Remo said hollowly.

Chiun's smile broadened. "Yes."

"No way."

"Yes way," said Chiun, nodding.

"You actually think this kook Sun is going to wave some magic wand and turn the whole world population into Koreans?" he exploded.

"Of course not," Chiun said placidly. "Sun is but the prophet of *pyon ha-da*. He sees the future as it has been designed by the Creator. It is the Creator who will change everyone into Koreans.''

''Are you out of your freaking mind!?'' Remo demanded, hopping to his feet.

''Do not fight it, Remo,'' Chiun said, his soothing voice sounding for all the world like a Sunnie cult member. ''Be happy that *pyon ha-da* has come in our lifetimes. No longer will I be forced to come up with creative ways to explain your paleness in the histories of Sinanju.''

''I'm not pale, Chiun—I'm white,'' Remo snapped. ''And I'm going to stay that way no matter what kind of bullshit that lunatic Sun feeds you.''

''Do as you wish,'' Chiun said, shrugging gently. ''It will come to pass whether you desire it or not.''

''Well, if it does it's going to have to come looking for me, because I'm not staying one more second in this loony bin.''

With that, he spun on his heel and stomped loudly across the room. The door slammed shut with a viciousness that rattled the big mansion to its very foundation.

After Remo had gone, Chiun breathed deeply, exhaling a thoughtful puff of air.

Remo was quick to anger. He had always been that way. It came from a sense of inferiority. Luckily for both of them, that would all soon change.

Smiling contentedly, the Master of Sinanju turned his attention back to the sprawling lawns below his balcony.

18

Ensign Howell McKimsom could hardly remember the intensive brainwashing sessions. What he could remember he would hardly have termed "brainwashing." If he had been permitted to talk about it, he would have more accurately called it "divine enlightenment." But he had been instructed not to talk about it with anyone.

Not with his friends.

Not with his family.

Not even with his shipmates aboard the USS *Courage*.

It was a shame, for Ensign McKimsom really wanted to share his conversion with his fellow sailors. It was part of the Sunnie indoctrination that made the faithful want to go out and preach to the world the greatness of the Reverend Man Hyung Sun. But Ensign McKimsom had also been instructed in the matter of obedience. He had been told not to talk; therefore, he would not talk. Ensign McKimsom was nothing if not faithful.

He was sitting calmly in the weapons room of

his U.S. Navy destroyer as it cruised the waters of the Yellow Sea off Inchon on the western coast of South Korea.

As he went methodically through the prelaunch routine, he thought it was a shame he could not talk to any of his shipmates about the Sunnie faith.

At first he had been skeptical. When members of the pink-robed cult had thrown a bag over his head while he was on shore leave and dragged him into their waiting car several weeks ago, Ensign McKimsom had actually been resistant.

He had grown since then.

There were others of the faith on board. They had been brought into the fold much as he had. But there were only a few. Just enough to carry out the special mission. They had been clearly instructed not to attempt to convert the rest, lest their true mission be revealed.

Ensign Howell McKimsom sighed as he thought of all the potential faithful that would not be reached because of his inability to speak the truth.

Oh, well. It was all Sun's will.

All at once, the preprogrammed flight plan of the missile system he was reviewing changed drastically. In a heartbeat, the intended target moved 131 miles south.

Sitting up, McKimsom double-checked the green text on his monitor. There would be no room for error.

Everything checked out. The inertial guidance

system would keep the missile true during its brief trip over water.

Smiling, he began initiating the system.

"Mr. McKimsom, what are you doing?"

The voice was sharp. Directly behind him.

McKimsom turned. He found himself looking up into the angry face of his commanding officer.

Howell McKimsom had been instructed what to do at every phase of the operation and in every possible eventuality. He had been given a specific order on how to deal with this precise situation.

Using his body to conceal his hand, Ensign McKimsom reached into one of the big pockets of his Navy-issue trousers. Removing the automatic he had stuffed inside his pants at the beginning of his watch, McKimsom turned calmly to the CO. Face serene, he quickly placed the warm gun barrel against the man's beefy chin and—before the commander even knew what was happening—he calmly pulled the trigger.

The sudden explosion within the confines of the weapons room was overwhelmed by the roar up on deck.

Even as the CO fell—his brains a gray frappé splattered against the gunmetal gray walls—McKimsom had initiated the launch.

Above, men ran screaming as the fiery burst of flame behind the rising 3200-pound Tomahawk missile scattered like the erupting fires of Hell across the deck.

In the confusion, Ensign Howell McKimsom had fought his way on deck. He was in time to see the tail fins of the slender missile level off above the Yellow Sea. He watched with pride as it soared across the choppy waves.

Screaming, the missile roared inland.

McKimsom did not live to see the ultimate explosion. By then he had turned his handgun on himself, accepting a slug of hot lead in his brain for the Reverend Man Hyung Sun.

WHEN IT SOARED OVERLAND, the Terrain Contour Matching system of the Tomahawk kicked in. The TERCOM guidance system faithfully followed the digitized topographical map input into its computerized brain.

Instead of heading up into North Korea, the missile remained south of the Thirty-eighth Parallel. In a horror scenario that the United States Navy never even thought to imagine, the entire flight of the missile into friendly territory took less than one minute.

There was no time to call a warning.

No time to evacuate.

No time for the victims to even scream.

When the missile fired from the USS *Courage* exploded on the grounds of Seoul National University forty-two seconds later, the shock waves were felt halfway around the world.

19

The bombing in Seoul was only minutes old, and Harold W. Smith was trying to make some kind of sense out of the reports he was receiving.

It was clear what had happened initially. A United States destroyer had fired a Tomahawk cruise missile against the capital of South Korea.

An entire building on the campus of Seoul National University had been utterly destroyed. Fortunately, it was early in the academic day, and the building was not yet filled to capacity. But that was hardly a comfort. There had been fatalities. And the U.S. was responsible.

Preliminary reports put the death toll at nearly two hundred, but Smith knew that there was no real way of gauging the number of students and faculty killed so soon. He was not optimistic. Doubtless, the actual number would rise as rescuers began to dig through the rubble.

As Smith typed away at his keyboard, the muted sound of CURE's White House line buzzed inside his desk. Continuing to type with one hand, he reached down, pulling the cherry-red phone from his desk drawer.

"Yes, Mr. President," Smith said crisply.

"Smith, what the hell is going on?" the familiar hoarse voice of the President of the United States rasped.

"You are calling, no doubt, in reference to the situation in South Korea."

"It's the damnedest thing, isn't it, Smith," the President said. "Who'd have thought the two Koreas would be such a problem spot?"

"Your nine immediate predecessors might have had some inkling," Smith said dryly.

Smith had a personal dislike for this President that he tried hard to subdue. After all, it was not his duty to second-guess the wisdom of the American people. But the CURE director could not help but long for a return of any one of the seven other presidents he had served.

"They did?" the President asked. "It doesn't surprise me. Those old farts were always worried about everything that didn't matter. So what's the deal?"

Smith started to speak when a female voice broke in behind the President. Whatever she whispered made the President snort with laughter. Smith heard the chief executive cover the mouthpiece as he whispered back.

"Keep it down, will you?" the President asked. "Okay, Smith, what can you tell me?"

"Who is that?" Smith demanded.

"Oh. Who?" asked the President innocently. A woman giggled somewhere in the nearby background.

"Mr. President, need I caution you again on matters of security? Please ask your wife to leave the room."

"Um, she's not here," the President said, voice almost distant. The giggling again, this time muffled in a pillow.

"I will terminate this call if your wife does not excuse herself," Smith said seriously.

"Okay, okay," the President said. "Honey, you better get out of here. There's some heavy Commander in Chief stuff going on." There was a rustling of sheets, and then the sound of a door clicking shut.

Only when the labored breathing of the President of the United States was the only sound in the room did Smith speak once more.

"Mr. President, we have had this conversation before," Smith said, weary of having to explain yet again the importance of keeping CURE secure. "It is unacceptable for the First Lady to be anywhere near the dedicated line when we are discussing sensitive matters."

The President cleared his throat, embarrassed. "She wasn't. The, um, ball and chain's in California," his hoarse voice said sheepishly. "She's got appointments with a couple of lawyers out there."

"Then who—?" Smith paused. "Oh." It was his turn to clear his throat. Smith rapidly changed the subject. "As you must already know, the U.S.S. *Courage* fired a cruise missile at South Korea approximately twenty minutes ago."

"Yeah, I just found out," the President said. "South Korea? Are they the ones who like us, or not?"

"They like us, Mr. President," Smith said, his lemony voice weary. "At least they did until today. I have heard that already there are organized protestors in the streets of Seoul demanding the withdrawal of U.S. troops from Korean soil and our ships from their territorial waters."

"Aren't they out a little soon?" the President asked.

"My thinking exactly," Smith replied. "It almost seems as if they knew there was an attack coming."

"Is that possible?"

"Sadly, yes. Our armed forces have been infiltrated by foreign spies in the past. Perhaps most significantly to these events, there was the 1996 incident concerning the South Korean who was a naturalized U.S. citizen. He was a U.S. intelligence officer who was caught passing classified information on to the Republic of Korea."

"You think whoever did this was a buddy of his?"

"I will not speculate one way or the other,"

Smith said. "It is merely one of the possibilities I am investigating. It could well be an isolated incident. As it stands now, we do not yet know how many were involved in the firing of the Tomahawk. There are reports of deaths aboard the *Courage*."

"Maybe they were attacked by the Koreans," the President speculated. "They might have been defending themselves."

"Hardly," Smith said. "If my information is accurate, the dead aboard the naval vessel committed suicide."

"Wowee," the President said. "You know, that's part of the reason I despise the military so much. All those guns and rockets and everything. I'd be happier if we could take all that war stuff and dump it in the ocean. Of course, the veep would have my flabby ass if I did. Ecology and all."

"Yes," Smith said, his voice flat. "In any event, there has been another item from the Koreas that has come across my desk this morning. Nine individuals in the North with tenuous ties to the Central Intelligence Agency were murdered this morning. Their decapitated bodies were discovered near the British embassy a few hours before the missile attack."

"Yuck," the President said. "What's that got to do with anything?"

"Perhaps nothing. However, one of my people recently, er, dispatched nine men in New York whom I later learned were North Korean agents. Their bodies were taken by individuals I have yet to trace who were dressed in the uniforms of New York City police officers. Apparently, they were brought somewhere to be mutilated. Their headless and handless corpses were found on a garbage scow in the East River."

"This is gross as all get-out," the President complained. "Just get to the point."

"It is possible that the murders in North Korea are a retaliation for the decapitated bodies found here. The cruise-missile launch following so closely on the heels of both events could signify a link to some larger scheme."

"Like what?" the President asked.

"I am not certain. But it might interest you to know that the same protestors I told you about earlier are calling for reunification talks to begin with the North."

"Is that bad?"

"*Dire* is the word I would use. A unified Korea would doubtless favor the political system of the North. If reunification goes as some expect, we would have the first significant Communist expansion in two decades. In addition, we would lose an important strategic ally in the region. As you no doubt are aware, as far as our military is concerned, relations with Japan are not particularly strong at present."

"Really?" the President of the United States asked.

Smith sighed. "I intend to send my people in to the Koreas," he said. "The Masters of Sinanju are undisputed experts of the Korean political scene, and have been since time immemorial. Since it is his homeland, Master Chiun is infinitely suited to dealing with the current tensions."

"Whatever you say, Smith," the President said. He sounded distracted. "I told you to stay out," he whispered hoarsely.

Over the phone, Smith heard a door creak shut. He closed his eyes patiently. "I will keep you apprised of any new developments," he said.

While he was hanging up the phone, he heard the same woman's voice as before. It was obvious now that it was not the First Lady. She was singing "Happy Birthday" in a husky whisper. Smith hung up the receiver as the President of the United States guffawed with delight.

20

The plain was endless.

There was sky, but it was washed in blood. Like the atmosphere of a planet in the sphere of a red giant sun.

The red Martian landscape stretched out limitlessly in all directions. At some hazy point in the far-distant horizon, the red of the sky swept over the red of the land, creating a muddied seam of blood.

Man Hyung Sun watched the horizon and smiled.

He had visited this place in his mind before. Many times in the past several days. But he had seen it prior to that. In both daydreams and nightmares when he thought he was going mad.

It was not madness. It was real. And *unreal*.

This thing had been calling to him for months. It knew of destiny. It knew his future. It had even given him some directions on a subconscious level for almost a year prior to this current cycle of events.

Mike Princippi had known of it. He had encountered the thing in America's West. But he had chosen to ignore the sweet, vaporous song. He had forced the images from his mind and had given away the vessel. It had taken Man Hyung Sun much time to search out the former governor in his mind. The thoughts drawing him to this place had not been clear until very recently. Now they seemed so obvious.

The figure was where it had been. Clothed in a haze of yellow fog, it sat upon the endless flat plain. The head and eyes of a man looked up as Sun approached.

"I am weak," the strange, otherworldly figure lamented when Sun crouched down beside it. Puffs of yellow smoke danced around the ethereal shape like thin clouds scudding across a clear sky.

It was the same complaint as always. Sun smiled comfortingly. "You cannot know true weakness," he assured the figure. "For to be truly weak is to be Man. And you are not Man."

The creature thought for a moment. "No," it admitted eventually. "But I am not what I once was. My master has fled to the place of the gods. I am a shadow of his greater self, a fraction of that which he is. Without his energy, I am doomed. Soon I will be condemned to nothingness."

Sun knew that the spirit of this nether region was weak. From what he had gleaned of previous conversations, a battle had taken place at some time in the past. The creature in the smoke had not fared well. Nor had its master, who had abandoned this part of himself to the limitless red plain.

"Your plan goes well," Sun offered consolingly. "The land of my birth is reeling on both sides of the division."

"This I know," said the creature, a great weariness in its voice. It did not get up from the ground. It continued to sit—as eternal as the land and sky around it.

"There will be political upheaval from these events. The United States—the Greece of this era—needs a presence in the South to show strength against the North. That foothold appears to be slipping."

"This, too, is known to me," said the fragile creature. "It is as I have designed it to be. To remedy the situation, they will send my young enemy first."

"What of the old one?" Sun asked.

The strange being shook its head. Puffs of yellow smoke escaped from its neck, falling back into the larger cloud. "The Master will remain behind for now. Only the night tiger of Sinanju will go. I have foreseen it."

Sun knew enough not to dispute the creature's oracular abilities. "It is as you say," he conceded. "Is there something you require of me?"

"Their emperor has attempted to contact the Master. So far the old one has not deigned to speak with him, but his soul is more restless than he admits. His attitude could soon change. Keep him with you so that they do not communicate.''

"Can you not see his future, O Prophet?" Sun asked, puzzled.

"I see much," agreed the creature. It exhaled ancient puffs of sickly yellow. "But it is as mud. The clarity is gone. It is…difficult for me."

"But *my* future," Sun stressed. "That is clear to you."

"Yes," the being admitted. It seemed drained.

Sun smiled. "I will do as you say. I have another taping today. The old one can accompany me."

Before him, the creature sighed deeply. Its breathing was ragged. "I am not what I once was. Prophesying fatigues me. Leave me now to my waning days."

Although the being shook a substantial hand at Sun, the cult leader lagged. "Um, if you could…?" he asked.

The creature looked up tiredly. Sun still squatted beside it. Its eyes closed, and it nodded in understanding.

Reaching out two humanlike hands, the being pressed its palms against either side of Sun's head.

The explosion of yellow was blinding, brilliant.

The vision came at once.

He was as a king. Riding a cloud from the heavens. The vast domain of Korea stretched out beneath his feet. Beyond it, the world lay waiting.

His future.

The flash of yellow consumed him with a shocking abruptness. Sun shuddered, gasping for breath. He blinked madly, chasing the dancing yellow spots from before his eyes.

As the brightness faded, Sun looked around.

He was back in his closet. Hangers hung from wooden rods beyond the thin film of yellow smoke.

Between his ankles was the strange urn with the Greek carving along its sides. The same urn that had been in the possession of Mike Princippi and given away. The urn he had had his Sunnie followers remove from the Boston Museum of Rare Arts.

The yellow smoke rose in uncertain puffs from the damp powder within the ancient stone vessel. The stink of sulfur clung to every corner of the room.

Sun struggled to regain his breath. He looked down at the powder in the urn.

"Would it be disrespectful to say that that was one hell of a rush?" he enthused as he stood.

He drew the damp towel from around his neck, tossing it on the floor near a humidifier. Sweating, Man Hyung Sun left the small fetid room.

21

The drive from New York to Massachusetts did not help to diminish Remo's sour mood.

When he stepped through the front door of the condominium he shared with the Master of Sinanju, he heard the telephone ringing at the rear of the house. Scowling, Remo walked back to the kitchen.

"What do you want?" Remo asked, picking up the receiver.

"Remo? Smith. Thank goodness I was finally able to reach you."

"Been trying long?" Remo asked with sarcastic sweetness.

"Yes," Smith replied, unaware of the sarcasm. "When I could not reach you at home, I traced your call back to Sun's mansion, but you and Chiun had already left. I trust you already know about the situation in Korea."

"You're too trusting," Remo said. "And Chiun didn't leave. He's still with the Reverend Sun."

"Oh? He did not come to the phone."

"Probably busy passing around the collection plate," Remo said. "So what's with Korea?"

Smith explained the situation both north and south of the Thirty-eighth Parallel. As he regurgitated the raw data, he quickly told Remo of the headless Korean bodies discovered that day and their connection to North Korea, which Smith had established through that nation's New York UN mission.

"I need for you and Chiun to fly to South Korea immediately. If there is some kind of sinister force behind this, I want you on the ground ready for quick action. I've arranged military transport for the two of you."

"Better cancel one of those tickets," Remo said.

"Why?"

"Chiun won't be coming."

"I *need* him," Smith stressed. "It may become necessary to stabilize the situation in North Korea, as well. Chiun has a knack for dealing with government leaders. Particularly in his homeland."

"And I don't?" Remo asked.

Smith's hesitation spoke volumes. "Er, if you are saying that Chiun is at the Sun mansion, perhaps I could try to reach him there again," he said vaguely.

"He's not going anywhere," Remo insisted, his tone betraying his offense. "He's sitting in his room waiting for the human race to jaundice."

"I do not understand."

"Join the club."

"This is a vital situation," Smith urged.

"Chiun's found something that's more vital. Take my word on this one, Smitty—you aren't moving him an inch."

Smith considered for a long moment. "You may go alone," he said finally, clearly unhappy with the situation. "But remember that South Korea is still an ally. Try your best to be diplomatic."

"Blah, blah, blah," Remo said.

"The North is an even trickier situation," Smith pressed on. "They look for any opportunity to drive a wedge between the United States and the South. Try not to give them any ammunition."

"Gee, you want me to make sure I wear clean underwear in case I get in an accident, Mom?" Remo asked.

Smith continued, undaunted. "It is not yet known if the nine informants killed in the North are a tit-for-tat for the nine you removed here. It is important that we do not act unilaterally until we are certain of our facts."

"Yammer, yammer, yammer," Remo sighed. "Stop worrying, Smitty. Just get me on the right plane, and everything will work out for the best. Trust me. I can be very diplomatic."

Another deafeningly loud pause.

"Are you absolutely certain Chiun is not available?" Smith asked, his voice strained.

THE MASTER OF SINANJU heard the heavy footfalls in the hallway outside his room. They certainly did not belong to Remo. His pupil's confident glide had moved in the opposite direction hours before. He was too stubborn to return.

No, these were footsteps Chiun had come to recognize clearly in his short stay at the East Hampton estate.

"Enter, Most Holy One!" Chiun called even before his visitor had a chance to knock.

Man Hyung Sun stuck his head around the doorway.

Chiun smelled the after-shave lotion even before he had opened the door. Remo was right about that, at least. The stink about the Reverend Sun was strong. Almost overpowering.

"Am I disturbing you?" Sun asked.

"A visit from a holy man can never be a disturbance," the Master of Sinanju replied from his lotus position on the glass-enclosed balcony.

He had turned his back to the lawn. The setting sun had fallen from the bleak winter sky. It was being swallowed up by the distant black trees.

As Sun came across the room, Chiun did something that he rarely did. Even for Smith, whom he called Emperor and for whom he rarely displayed anything short of obsequiousness.

Chiun rose from the floor.

When Sun stepped onto the balcony, the two

men exchanged polite bows. Not deferential. But certainly respectful.

As Sun found a seat on one of the Western chairs on the balcony, Chiun sank back to the floor.

"Your son is no longer here," Sun said.

Chiun shook his head sadly. The puffs of hair over his ears shook with deep sorrow. "Lamentably, no," he said. "He does not believe in *pyon ha-da*. The boy is young still, with skin of improper hue. My fear was always that by flittering around in a shell of ivory, he would not know the true beauty of the world."

Sun nodded. "It must be awful for you to squander your wisdom on a white," he agreed.

Chiun bristled slightly. "Remo is a fine pupil," he explained. "His mongrel lineage is not his fault. Indeed, I have confirmed that which I always suspected. There is some Korean blood within him. Dissipated over the years, of course. But in his heart, he has always been Korean."

"I meant no offense, Master of Sinanju," Sun apologized, bowing his head as he did so.

Chiun nodded in return. "*Pyon ha-da* will change all," Chiun said, his happiness returning. "No longer will my son with a Korean soul be painted the shade of sickness and death. My joy for him is without measure." The parchment skin at his eyes squeezed to vellum knots of delight. "Tell me, O Seer Sun, when is the blessed moment to take place?"

"Soon," Sun said absently. "Quite soon. Tell me, does your son intend to return?"

"Remo?" Chiun asked. "I do not know. He leaves, he comes back. Who can keep track of children these days? Can you not see, O Seer?"

Sun smiled. "I see much, but not all," he admitted. He stood from his chair. "I have a commercial to tape in New Jersey today. I would be pleased if you would accompany me."

"It would be my privilege."

Smiling, the Master of Sinanju rose from the balcony floor once more.

As Chiun walked beside Sun to the door, he was careful to stay as far as was politely possible from the range of the cult leader's wretched perfume. Unbeknownst to him, the powerful sulfur stench of the ancient Greek urn clung just beneath the thick fragrance.

Had Chiun recognized the sulfur smell, he would have slain Sun on the spot and flown to Remo's side. But he did not. Instead, he stepped placidly and guilelessly from the room in the company of the man who had been chosen by the ancient spirit of the urn to slay both Masters of Sinanju.

The big door shut with echoing finality.

HE KNEW WHEN THEY BROUGHT him through the police cordon at the Berlin embassy that his life was over.

After the high-speed chase with police and the subsequent crash at the North Korean mission, the Communist government needed a scapegoat. Rim Kun Soe had been chosen to fulfill that role.

He had sullenly accepted the blame for the chase that had resulted in several injuries—some severe. Face a tight mask, he had voiced regret over the death of the Burg police officer whose bloody, battered body had been returned to German authorities.

There had been two people in the cab, the police had argued. Where was the other man?

A dummy, was the explanation. They were a new thing from America for single travelers intending to lend the impression of more than one person. In his love of all things Western, Rim Kun Soe had purchased one of these. They had even produced one of the dummies for authorities.

It was another insult heaped atop the pile.

Rim Kun Soe hated the West and everything that remotely resembled the bourgeois American culture. He would have just as soon been dragged from his car and beaten to death on one of the lawless streets of America itself as buy one of their artificial people for protection.

But he had accepted the added indignity like the good Public Security Ministry officer he was.

Fortunately for him, he was not turned over to German authorities. This was not due to any loyalty on the part of the North Korean government.

It was merely feared by those in the ministry that his recollection of events would not match the reality of the American who had really been driving the truck.

He was in Germany as a diplomat and therefore enjoyed the protection of extraterritoriality. He was exempt from the laws of his host state, so the police could do nothing to Rim Kun Soe as he was hustled through the line of officers and reporters onto the first plane home.

Back in North Korea, he had been reprimanded by the ministry he served. Somehow they had decided that he was responsible for the debacle concerning the American and the aged Master of Sinanju. Even though he had been following the orders of his superior, even though Kim Jong Il himself had turned over use of his jet to the two smugglers, Rim Kun Soe had borne the brunt of the punishment.

He had not yet been relieved of duty, but that was certainly coming. There might even be a show trial. Prison, perhaps. Maybe worse.

Until that time, he had been given minor security work at the airport in Pyongyang. According to whispers of those in the know, there had been several mysterious packages delivered on a mail flight from the South two days before, and as a result security had been tightened greatly.

Shipments that had been flown into the country were not leaving as they should. Slow under ordinary circumstances, the movement from the airport was practically nonexistent. Earlier that morning, the security officer had realized just how slowly things were moving from the airport when he spied some familiar crates in a back room. They were no longer his problem, he decided. Let someone else take the blame.

In the vast storeroom off the main concourse, there was a bottleneck of government luggage and mail—government officials being the only ones with access to travel and some, albeit censored, communication with the outside world.

After several hours at work in the back rooms of the airport, Rim Kun Soe had been turned over to a detail that was inspecting the suitcases. It was the greatest indignity he had endured in his entire career. Searching through the dirty undergarments of stupid diplomats.

The security officer was not exercising much care as he fumbled through the cheap suitcase of a support staffer from the North Korean mission to Hanoi.

While he worked, Soe was forced to endure the endless prattling of a pair of very junior officers with the People's Bureau of Revolutionary Struggle. They appeared to be obsessed with food.

"Were you able to eat today?" one asked as he swept an electronic device over a pair of trousers.

"Some," admitted his partner.

"I, as well. It has not been easy."

The other nodded. He wore a sickly expression.

As a member of the Public Security Ministry while at home and particularly during his brief stay in Germany, Rim Kun Soe had always been able to eat his fill. However, returning as he had in disgrace, he did not enjoy the privileges he once had. Back home in Pyongyang, he had been dropped into the middle of another one of the interminable food shortages the North Korean government specialized in.

Somehow, the men he now worked with seemed to have been affected by more than the famine.

"I think about it at night," the first said. "How he pulled it from the box and threw it to you. Last night, my meal came up in my sleep. I was awakened by the sound of my wife eating it off the blanket."

The other nodded. "I have told my wife I will turn her and the children out if I find them eating my vomit," he said knowingly. "Strength is the only way to deal with them."

"Mmm," said the other in bland agreement.

The conversation went on like this for much of Rim Kun Soe's day. It was humiliating for one who had had so much in his political career to deal with wretches like these two.

His only relief to the embarrassing tedium came when the hip radio of one of the two men he was with squawked to life.

"Security Officer Hyok," the first man announced into the mouthpiece, his breath reeking of stomach acid.

There followed a steady stream of Korean so frantic as to be unrecognizable from Soe's position across the big room.

The security man blanched when he heard the report over the radio. When the voice was through issuing orders, the man stuffed the radio away, quickly drawing his side arm.

"What is it?" his partner asked.

"We are needed on the tarmac," said the first. "Right away. You," he commanded to Soe. "There is an emergency. Come with us."

Soe was grateful for the break in the tedium. He pulled his automatic free and, with the others, made his way out of the building and into the pale sunlight of Pyongyang Airport.

They reached the tarmac at a run, finding many security personnel already there. As Soe looked around, he realized that this was probably the entire airport detachment.

There were hundreds of men standing around. All were looking skyward. Many jeeps lined the periphery field beside the long runway.

"What is it?" Security Officer Hyok asked when he and the others ran into the crowd.

"A plane," said a ranking officer of the PBRS. "From the South."

"Why has it not been shot down?" Soe demanded.

The ranking officer looked angrily at the brazen security man. "It has requested asylum."

The plane was in sight. A fat dot in the white-washed sky, it moved remorselessly closer. It was attended by a number of smaller specks. Like flies around a larger animal. North Korean fighter jets.

Soe wheeled to the officer. "Shoot it down any-way," he insisted. "It could be loaded with chem-ical or biological weapons. Worse, it could carry a nuclear payload. Who knows what technology the fool Americans have given our capitalist cousins? They have been jealous and fearful of the people's nuclear program for years. This could be their reckless attempt to finish us all."

Though the officer looked blandly at Soe, venom roiled beneath the surface of his well-fed face. "Are you not Rim Kun Soe, the disgraced lackey running dog of the capitalist-loving Master of Sin-anju?"

Soe stiffened. "I am no one's dog, you ignorant son of a mongrel!" he snapped.

The officer did not hesitate. He sent a balled fist directly into the face of Rim Kun Soe.

As Soe reeled back, nose gushing blood, the man ordered the two agents who had accompanied the dishonored Public Security Ministry represen-tative onto the tarmac to take hold of him. In-stantly, Soe felt his arms being pinned behind his back.

Then the officer turned back to the plane.

It was much closer now. As Soe bled onto his uniform, the entire group of gathered agents watched the plane touch down.

It hit with a squeal of smoking rubber. The plane rapidly decelerated. As it slowed to a stop, a wheeled staircase was rolled out beneath the main exit door, which was now open. The engines died.

The Korean military jets that had acted as escort roared back and forth across the airport as the first gunmen raced up the steps and on board the now silent plane.

There were several tense moments when nothing happened.

All at once, a man stepped out onto the upper platform of the staircase. He had his hands atop his head, fingers intertwined.

For a moment, the security personnel assumed that this was one of the men from the South requesting asylum. This mistaken impression lasted only until they realized that it was one of their own security men whom they had sent aboard to secure the plane.

Several others followed. All were in the same pose. None carried the rifles they had brought aboard with them.

"What is this?" the officer demanded when the first man had climbed down the steps. "Where are your weapons?"

"He took them," the soldier admitted.

"Who?"

"The one who did this." The man tugged at his arms. Though it appeared as if he was trying to move them, they did not budge. The fingers remained locked atop his black hair.

"Lower your arms," the officer commanded, disgusted.

"We cannot," said the soldier.

The others were straining behind him. They appeared to be having the same difficulty as the first.

The officer grew angry. He grabbed the lead soldier's arm at the elbow and yanked. It did not budge. Surprised, he pulled harder. The arms remained locked in place. It was as if they were glued to his head.

The officer finally gave up. "How many are aboard?" he demanded, scowling.

"Only one man," said the soldier.

"One?" asked a stunned voice from behind the officer.

The soldiers all looked in the same direction. Rim Kun Soe stood behind the officer. Wet blood streaked down his suddenly fearful, cold face. He appeared to know something that the others did not. His expression was more uneasy than it had been when he suspected the plane might be carrying a nuclear payload.

The officer did not have time to waste on an insubordinate agent like Soe. He turned back to the soldiers.

"The flight crew?"

"Are still in the cockpit, I assume."

"You assume," he spit. The man glanced at Soe one last time. He drew his side arm. "You," he said, spreading his arm to the next batch of soldiers in line. "Come with me."

The officer himself led the next charge into the belly of the mysterious plane. When he came out a few minutes later, his face was almost as red as Rim Kun Soe's. However, it was not blood that turned his skin to scarlet. It was embarrassment.

The man's hands were locked atop his head. His weapon was nowhere to be seen.

He was also not alone.

"Man, I forgot what a desolate lump of ice this country is," Remo Williams complained from his position behind the officer.

On the ground, Soe attempted to back away. The two agents held him fast. "No," he said, his voice small.

As one, hundreds of weapons suddenly trained on the doorway of the 747, in spite of the presence of their commanding officer. Bolts clicked like so many metal crickets as the handguns and rifles were cocked.

"Do not move!" shouted a junior officer.

"Hold your fire!" screamed the officer with Remo. "Hold your fire! He is friendly!"

Remo waved to demonstrate this. "Hiya!" he called to the crowd of soldiers.

This did nothing to convince the men to lower

their weapons. However, they did not wish to go against their commanding officer. Three hundred gun barrels tracked the two men down the stairs to the runway.

"If you know what's good for you, you'll get them to lower their weapons," Remo cautioned the officer.

Apparently, Remo had done something more than merely freezing the soldier's hands atop his head while they were on board the plane. His red face grew more ruddy as he screamed out to the soldiers.

"I will personally see to it that every soldier who does not stand down this moment will spend the rest of his miserable days rotting in a People's prison!" he screamed over the gusting wind.

They hesitated at first. After all, sometimes there was rice in the People's prisons.

"With no food!" the officer screamed.

The guns were not only lowered; they were dropped, *flung*. They clattered loudly and crazily to the frozen tarmac.

"That's better," Remo said, glancing around. His eyes alighted on Soe.

The former Berlin embassy man had been trying to sink back into the crowd. Remo bounded over to him.

"Hey, I know you!" Remo said, beaming in recognition. He slapped a hand on Soe's shoulder. "He'll be my driver."

"Please—" Soe begged of the officer.

"Fine," the officer said.

As Soe watched the last hope of salvaging his career drain away, a jeep was brought forward. He was pushed in behind the steering wheel. Remo took the seat next to him.

Rim Kun Soe wished he still had his gun with him. If he had, he would have ended his life right then and there. Particularly at the next words that issued from the filthy American's capitalist mouth.

"Which way to the presidential palace?" Remo asked, smiling.

22

Mike Princippi suspected that it would someday come to this. He had known it since he'd collected the stone urn from the ruins of that cult in Wyoming a year ago.

It was a stupid, stupid move. He should have left the urn where it had been buried. The cult lay in ruins. The secret would have remained buried along with the urn.

The whole affair was a time in his life that was best forgotten. Some people had said that about his failed run for the presidency. But if they only knew about that urn, they would have conceded that the national embarrassment of losing the election was a bright spot in the biography of Michael "the Prince" Princippi compared to the terrible days he had spent in the vicinity of that ancient stone artifact.

He didn't know much about the history of it. Just that it had been found at an archaeological dig in Delphi and brought to America. Most recently, he had owned the urn for a brief time, finally turning it over to a local Boston museum when the strange dreams he was having refused to subside.

And now the Reverend Man Hyung Sun owned it. It was a chilling prospect.

Principi was generally a practical man. The only mystical matters he had ever trucked in were those pertaining to the Massachusetts budget when he was governor. As far as anything otherworldly was concerned, he didn't believe a word of it. But the urn had changed his mind.

The powder contained in that ancient piece of carved rock possessed a force greater than he had ever imagined.

The being within the urn was a fragment of the ancient god Apollo. The Pythia, as it was called, was the oracular force behind the famous temple at Delphi. Indeed, it was for this creature who imparted knowledge of the future that the word *oracle* was given.

The Pythia saw the future. People had died for it. Most recently at the museum in Boston where it had been stored. And Mike Principi had known about it.

It would be the end of his political career if this ever got out. Worse. Prison, possibly. Who knew what else?

Principi thought of this as he got out of his battered old Volkswagen in the parking lot of the Channel 8 studio in Passaic.

Sun's limo was already there, as were several

Sunnie vans. The tambourine-rattling nuts were probably scattered all over the studio like a flock of bald flamingos.

Mike Princippi was locked in with these people. Whether he liked it or not.

He knew that Sun was aware of matters unknown to the rest of the world, with the Pythia on his side. Sun knew that Princippi had been involved with the Pythia before. Although the former governor had not been in it as deep as the others at the Wyoming cult, he had been there. Sun had the goods on him.

But there was some hope.

The ashes were the strength of the Pythia, Princippi reasoned. If he could keep his mind completely blank and get close enough to the yellow dust, he might be able to get rid of it. Maybe flush it down a toilet or something.

He hadn't really thought about it at Sun's Manhattan apartment. At the estate in the Hamptons, he had not yet been able to get close enough. When he did, he would get rid of them. Once and for all. Sun would be left with an empty stone pot.

The rest would be hearsay. A crazy cult leader accusing a respected ex-presidential candidate of insane behavior.

Ultimately, it might be a smudge on his record. Maybe not, however. In this day and age of political scandals, from blatant lies to cover-up and blind public acceptance of it all, who knew? The only certain thing was, the longer the dust remained collected in that accursed urn, the deeper grew the hole Mike Princippi found himself in.

The former governor kept his thoughts buried as he strolled into the studio building. As he had expected, he found Sun on the set of his latest infomercial.

The head of the Sunnie cult sat on a sofa on the new set. Roseflower stood nearby. Princippi smiled weakly at the bodyguard as he walked over to the cult leader.

Another old Asian was with Sun on the set. He sat cross-legged on the floor at the feet of the Sunnie leader.

The stranger wore a traditional kimono and had skin the texture of sunbaked leather stretched to the cracking point. As hooded eyes sized up the approaching Princippi, his features curled into wrinkles of distaste.

"Hi," Princippi said, nodding to the Master of Sinanju. "You a Sunnie or something?"

"Or something," Chiun sniffed in reply. The look of disgusted condemnation never left his face.

"Uh, yeah," Princippi said. He turned his attention to Sun. "How soon are we starting?"

"Ten minutes," a harried voice announced behind him.

Princippi nearly jumped out of his skin. He spun. Dan Bergdorf stood behind him.

"What!" Princippi demanded. He realized only

when he saw the stunned look on the face of the infomercial's executive producer that he had yelled the word. He glanced nervously over his shoulder at Sun. The cult leader was not even looking at him. "I'm sorry," he apologized to Dan. "You startled me. What did you say?"

"We start in ten minutes," the executive producer said. "You have the new script?"

"Me? No. No, I don't."

Dan grabbed a script from a passing stage manager. "Go over this first," he pleaded. "Cold reads on the first take *never* work."

"But that's. the way we did it last time," Princippi argued.

"I *know*." Turning, Dan left the former governor clasping his new script in his moist hands.

Princippi looked back at Sun. "Um." He shrugged uncertainly. "Are you going back to the mansion anytime soon?" Princippi asked nervously. He tried to force a smile.

Sun looked up from the script he had been reading. "No," he replied. "Our work here will take some time. Why?"

"No reason," the former governor said. "It's just that I—I left my coat there. Maybe. Anyway, I thought maybe I could take a look around and see." Princippi pretended an idea had suddenly occurred to him. It was worse than the acting he had displayed in the first Sunnie infomercial. "Say, I have an idea," he said, snapping his fingers. "Why don't I go back. Sort of on my own. I could look for it myself. No need to bother you."

"Yes, that would be fine," Sun agreed.

Princippi beamed. He began backing away. "Great, I'll just—"

"There is a small matter...." Sun began. His eyes were dead as he stared at the former governor.

Princippi felt his stomach turn to water.

He knew. Of course. He *must* know. He had the urn.

Sun knew of his intentions, knew that he planned to dispose of the powder in the urn. He never should have come up with the scheme to begin with. Never should have thought to go against the sinister force of the Pythia.

"You must wait until *after* we have completed this day's taping," Sun finished. He returned his attention to his script.

That was it. Mike Princippi felt as if he were dancing on air.

"Of course," he gushed. "When we're done here. After. I'll go there after. Alone. Or with you with me. But you can stay here. Whatever. Doesn't matter to me." As he stepped anxiously backward, he nearly knocked over a camera. Stumbling over the wires, he continued to babble until he was halfway across the studio.

Once Princippi was out of earshot, Chiun turned to Sun.

"He is lying," he offered blandly.

From his spot on the couch, Sun glanced down at the Master of Sinanju. "This I know," he replied in the same flat tone. "For can I not divine the future?"

"He also intends to do you harm." Chiun frowned. "But he does not give off the signals of one who means to make use of conventional weapons." He tipped his head as Princippi vanished from sight. "This is most puzzling."

Sun seemed surprised. "You can gauge a threat simply by looking at someone?"

Chiun nodded. "A man's body tells much that is otherwise hidden. That Greek's is a mystery to me, however. It is almost as if he intends to do you harm without doing harm to you. How could this be?"

"Who can understand the Greeks?" Sun asked with a shrug.

Chiun accepted this. "Indeed," he said. "In *pyon ha-da*, we will none of us have to deal with the maze that is the mind of non-Koreans."

"It will truly be a glorious day," Sun echoed. He returned to his script. As he read, he wondered absently what the best time would be to kill the treacherous Michael Princippi.

WORD OF THE RETURN of the Master of Sinanju's white son to Korean soil was greeted with concern in the People's Palace in Pyongyang.

News of the incident at the airport spread like

wildfire through the capital of Communist North Korea. Although he was seen speeding through the streets in the company of a disgraced Public Security Ministry officer, none of the forces on the ground were brave enough to intercept him.

Kim Jong Il sat in his secure basement office in the presidential palace. Waiting.

The room was four stories down in solid bedrock. To reach it, one had to travel in an elevator like a pneumatic tube that was accessible to only the elite of the nation. Soldiers were stationed in the two hallways that led out and around to the elevator in a labyrinthine design known to only eight people in the country. The soldiers had been led in blindfolded. Only when they were in place were the cloths removed from their eyes.

Briefly, the premier had considered stationing guards at his secret entrance, as well. He dismissed the idea almost immediately. His father, the late president Kim Il Sung, had ordered the escape tunnel to be dug. Afterward, he had had the workmen shot. The only person alive who knew of the tunnel was Kim Jong Il, who preferred to keep it that way. At the first sign of trouble from the hallway outside, he would slip through the secret panel and flee to safety.

While he sat sweating into his People's uniform, he stared off into space. The large-screen TV before him played a wide-screen laser-disc version of

The Empire Strikes Back. He saw the film without watching.

One boot tapped relentlessly at the polished granite floor.

Retaliation had been a mistake, he now realized. He never should have let the People's Bureau of Revolutionary Struggle director talk him into it. The Master of Sinanju and his heir worked for the Americans. Even though there had been no explanation, the heads that had been mailed to North Korea were a sign of something. But what?

If the last report of the American's whereabouts was accurate, the premier might only have a few moments left to decipher the cryptic message. Otherwise, it might very well be *his* head that next wound up boxed for shipping.

The premier pressed both hands tightly against his throat as he tried desperately to think what the message had meant. His Adam's apple fought past his clutching fingers as he gulped in fear.

For Kim Jong Il, the third act was about to begin. And no one had bothered to give him a script.

PYONGYANG WAS A GHOST town.

Remo saw soldiers while he drove. They peeked out like frightened specters from doorways and windows. But no one made a move toward him as his jeep roared down the wide, empty streets.

The People's Palace loomed big and ugly before

them. Remo ordered Rim Kun Soe to stop at the huge stone staircase before the massive building.

"Let's go," Remo said, climbing down from the jeep. He put one foot on the first broad step.

"You would dare enter the presidential palace, American capitalist cur?" Soe asked, astonished and angry at once.

"If this is where that rat Kim Jong Il lives, I guess so, Soe," Remo replied. "Hurry up."

Soe crossed his arms. "I will not," he insisted. "You will have to kill me first."

"As tempting as that may be, I need you as my passkey."

"I have no key to the palace, fool."

Remo smiled. "You *are* the key."

He reached over and dragged Soe across the seat, dropping the Korean onto the sidewalk.

Soe looked up, face a mask of seething fury. "I should have killed you in Berlin," he sneered.

"I wish you had," Remo sighed. "It would have saved us both a whole lot of grief."

Grabbing the Public Security Ministry officer by the scruff of the neck, Remo headed up the abandoned steps of the great People's Palace.

HE HEARD THE STEADY pop-pop-pop of automatic-weapons fire from beyond the great steel door. It was still far away. Echoing along the labyrinthine halls.

Kim Jong Il chewed the inside of his mouth as

he waited. He had always felt safe in this stronghold. If he escaped through his secret entrance, would he become a greater target once he reached the surface?

The bedrock in which his office was secreted absorbed a great deal of sound. Vacillating, he strained to hear how close the gunfire actually was.

Sudden silence.

The guards had stopped firing. That meant only one of two things. They had either failed or succeeded.

A fresh round of gunfire much closer to his sealed door gave him the terrifying answer.

"Impossible!" the premier hissed.

Somehow, the Master of Sinanju's protégé had found his way through the maze. He was right outside the closed door of Kim Jong Il's inner sanctum.

Escape was now no longer a question. It was imperative. Leaving his television to display images of Darth Vader to an empty chair, the premier hustled over to a single framed poster on the wall next to his bar.

The artwork depicted Arnold Schwarzenegger straddling a motorcycle. The sunglasses that had appeared on the actor in the original picture had been airbrushed out. The Asian eyes that had been painted in stared menacingly down at the North Korean premier as he grabbed at the edge of the frame.

The frame swung away with a single tug, revealing a long corridor beyond it. Kim Jong Il was just picking one foot up over the threshold of the secret doorway when a terrible pounding began to echo through the basement room.

The gunfire had stopped. All that was left was the incessant pounding. Frozen in place, the premier watched as the metal door buckled beneath some great external pressure.

Kim Jong Il came to his senses all at once. He was just lifting his other foot inside the panel when the main door to the room gave way completely. It collapsed inward in a hail of crumbling concrete and tinkling metal shards.

The thing that had been used to batter in the door fell in after it. The battering ram groaned.

As he stood in the open door to his secret corridor, the premier's shocked gaze raked Rim Kun Soe. As he lay dazed on the broken door, the security agent's head bled profusely. His eyes rolled in their sockets, settling unsteadily on Kim Jong Il.

"Traitor!" the premier screamed. His eyes went wide as Remo stepped into the room behind Soe.

Yelling in fear, the premier desperately dragged the secret door shut behind him. He almost got it closed.

Tugging on the interior handle, he found that it would not go the final inch. The door would be impossible to seal if it was not closed. All at once,

Kim Jong Il noticed a set of fingers wrapped around the side.

His heart caught in his throat. With both hands, he dragged at the door. To no avail. Even though he pulled with all his might, the premier felt the door being dragged inexorably open. In a moment, he was face-to-face with the frightful visage of the Master of Sinanju's son.

"Remember me?" Remo asked sweetly.

Grabbing the Leader for Life of North Korea by the throat, Remo tossed him back into the basement office. Kim Jong Il landed in a heap near his crumpled basement door. Near him, Rim Kun Soe groaned.

"This is your doing!" the premier screamed. Scrabbling across the debris, he grabbed the security man around the throat. He began strangling Soe, banging his injured head against the steel door. The former embassy agent took the abuse with dull incomprehension.

Remo had to drag Kim Jong Il off Soe.

"Knock it off," he growled.

The premier wheeled on Remo. "So, do you intend to kill me?" he demanded.

"No, O Great Leader," Soe replied from the floor. He was still on the floor, trying to shake the ringing sound from his head. It sounded like a supper gong.

"I wasn't talking to you," Kim Jong Il snapped.

"No, I'm not going to kill you," Remo said. "Yet."

"What's the meaning off all this, then?" the premier asked. "Geez-O-man, you wrecked the place." He looked out through the open basement door. He spied several pairs of army-issue boots jutting into view. None were moving.

"We need to talk," Remo said.

"Is that all? Couldn't you have made an appointment?"

"Your thugs killed nine people suspected of being agents for America," Remo pressed on. "I'm here to find out what the hell is going on."

The premier frowned. "So, that *is* what this is about."

"That is what what is about?" Soe asked, dazed.

"Shut up," Kim Jong Il ordered. He turned to Remo. "I didn't want to do it at first," he begged. "They talked me into it. And anyway, I didn't think you or your old man were involved in this."

"Involved in what?" Remo asked. "I'm just here to make sure you people don't run around killing everyone on this benighted peninsula who ever accepted a handful of rice from some dopey CIA spook."

"So you don't know?" Kim Jong Il asked suspiciously.

"Know what, my premier?" Soe asked.

"Know what?" Remo asked, shooting a sour look at Soe.

Kim Jong Il nodded seriously to Remo. "Perhaps you should come with me," he said.

THE MORGUE WAS out-of-date by fifty years according to Western standards.

Premier Kim Jong Il himself led Remo into the chilly, windowless room. Bulbs flickered on in fixtures suspended from the ceiling.

"We are not as closed a society as some think. We allow some mail to enter our country from the South," the premier explained as they walked across the room. "These arrived on a flight several days ago."

They were at a row of drawers along a side wall. Kim Jong Il grabbed on to the handle and pulled the long sliding drawer into the room.

It was a standard morgue slab. But instead of the usual body that would be lying in the refrigerated interior, there were three separate large objects.

Remo looked down at the trio of severed heads. Ten fingers were arranged around each, like spokes on a wheel.

"I know you've got another famine going here," Remo said evenly. "Don't tell me your pathologists ate the rest."

"This is all we received in the mail from the

South," the premier said. "Presumably from America originally. There are six more like these."

"Six?" Remo asked. Leaning, he squinted at the weirdly swollen face of the nearest man.

"Yes," Kim Jong Il replied. "We assumed it was a sign from your intelligence community. However, I allowed my people to convince me that it couldn't have come from you, since the heads were torn off in such a savage manner."

"You're right there," Remo admitted. "But this is definitely one of the guys we killed."

The premier blanched. "You did this?" he asked.

"Not the decapitation part," Remo said. "That's a mess. But see that?" He pointed to a tiny waning-moon-shaped incision in the nearest forehead. Blackened blood collected in the narrow sliver. "That's obviously Chiun's handiwork."

Kim Jong Il gulped. "The Master of Sinanju?" he asked. His tone betrayed his fear.

"The one and only," Remo said. He was frowning. "This is really wacky," he said, straightening up. "Smith said only the Koreans' bodies turned up. I just figured it was some ritual and the rest of them got eaten by fish or washed out to sea or something."

"Smith who?" Kim Jong Il asked.

Remo looked over at him, shaken from his thoughts.

"These guys were spies," he said, indicating the

heads lying on the cold metal bed. "They were trying to kill someone, so Chiun and I whacked them."

"Impossible," the premier insisted. "They were stationed at the New York mission. The PBRS assures me that they were given no activation orders."

"Be that as it may, they were pretty active last I saw," Remo said. "The United States government had nothing to do with sending these parts over here. In fact, I'd guess it was probably someone trying to provoke something between our countries."

"Who?"

Remo did not reply. Instead, he reached out and grabbed a cluster of nerves behind the North Korean Leader for Life's right ear. He squeezed.

Kim Jong Il's eyes looked as if they were going to spring out of his head. He tried to scream, but the only sound that escaped his throat was a strangled chirp.

"Never mind. Just don't kill any more spies or even suspected spies," Remo instructed. "You got that?"

Kim Jong Il nodded. Frantically. Painfully. His eyes watered in agony.

All at once, Remo released him. The relief was blessed, instantaneous. He gulped in a deep gust of air.

"There," Remo said, as if finishing up. "Now,

as long as you can keep the rest of your ducks in a row, we won't have any more problems.''

"No problems," Kim Jong Il insisted, rubbing his ear. "None at all."

"Right," Remo said levelly.

He looked down at the heads one last time. Who had shipped them here? The bogus New York police? The Loonies? Whoever it was, Remo was pretty sure whose orders they had been following. He'd have a word or two with the Reverend Sun as soon as he returned to the States. But first, he had another duty to attend to.

Remo shoved the drawer shut. "By the way, I hijacked a South Korean plane in England," Remo said.

"I heard," Kim Jong Il replied, still feeling behind his ear. Surprisingly, there was no blood. "It is being detained at the airport."

"Let it leave unharmed," Remo instructed.

"It'll be as you wish," Kim Jong Il agreed.

Remo looked around, trying to think if there was anything else he had to do. "I guess that's it," he said with a satisfied nod. "Unless you can think of anything."

"No," the premier said, shaking his head desperately. He tried to force a smile. "Not that I can think of," he added, with hollow joviality.

Remo smiled back. Sincerely. "Great," he said. "That's settled. I guess we're through."

They began walking to the morgue door. Remo

could only think of Smith and the doubts the CURE director had had about sending him to the Koreas alone. His smile broadened.

"So I'm not a diplomat, huh?" he asked the premier.

"No, you are not," Rim Kun Soe's weak voice called from the outer room.

23

The woman looked as if she had cornered the silicone market in her chest. Though she jumped energetically, there was very little jiggle as she gushed her enthusiasm for her latest project.

"I don't, like, *do* endorsements," she babbled happily. "But when my agent called me about this one I, like, went totally and completely wild for the idea."

"Totally," agreed the young man next to her. He looked as if he spent eighteen hours a day at the gym and another fifteen at the dentist.

The pair were soap-opera actors who had been linked romantically in real life. Their affair had been the product of months of negotiations between their respective people. Neither his boyfriend nor her girlfriend was terribly happy with the business arrangement.

"I was just wondering," she said. "I was up for a movie part the other day. I think I did really, really good and all. Do you think they'll call back?"

The Reverend Man Hyung Sun looked blandly at the woman. "No," he said.

"No?" she asked, crestfallen. "Oh." Though she was deeply disappointed, neither she nor her costar made a move to leave.

Chiun was standing at Sun's elbow near the studio door. "Do you wish me to dispose of these empty-headed ones, O Holy Seer?" the Master of Sinanju offered in a loud whisper.

He did not have to.

"Okay, we're done here," Dan Bergdorf said, sweeping in from the set. The executive producer shepherded the pair of soap-opera actors away from his featured performer.

The two of them had been hired by Bergdorf for the latest Sunnie fortune-teller commercial. Soap stars had instant face recognition from the types of people who called psychic lines. These two were the flavor of the month.

"You're going to get a lot of callers telling you they phoned in because of Cassandra and Cleft," Bergdorf warned as he came back over to Sun, using the actors' TV names.

Roseflower was walking briskly behind him.

"As long as they call," Sun replied flatly. "We go now," he said to the Master of Sinanju.

Chiun allowed the cult leader's assistant to guide them out to the limousine. He got in the back seat with Sun while Roseflower climbed in behind the wheel. They were out of the Channel 8 parking lot and on the highway back to New York in a matter of minutes.

They had driven in silence for almost twenty minutes before the Master of Sinanju spoke. "Something puzzles me, Great Mystic," Chiun said.

"A question is the first step to knowledge," Sun intoned seriously.

Chiun resisted the urge to accuse the Sunnie leader of sounding like a Chinese fortune cookie. After all, he was the herald of *pyon ha-da*.

"Why must you do these programs?" Chiun asked. "They are demeaning. Beneath one as holy as you."

"You honor me with your words," Sun said. "But know you this," he continued, raising an instructive finger, "even a god must pay the rent."

And at these words, Chiun grew silent. He remained mutely troubled for the entire journey back to the East Hampton, Long Island, estate of Sun.

When they arrived, they found Michael Princippi's ratty old car already parked near the closed garage bays. Roseflower parked the limousine away from the main house.

Chiun and Sun walked together up the gravel pathway to the mansion.

"There are those who would do me harm," Sun said as they climbed the steps.

"They must get through me first, Holy Seer," Chiun said.

"I am pleased you say that," Sun replied. He paused, resting his hand on the door handle. "Such a one is in my home at this very moment. I have foreseen it. As have you, though to a lesser and mere mortal degree."

Chiun's eyes strayed to the battered Volkswagen rusting in the driveway.

"The one called Prince," he said.

Sun nodded. "I fear my life is in danger. You are my only salvation. Will you remove the evil from before me?"

"I live to serve, Holy One," Chiun said, bowing.

Sun returned the gesture, though with regal restraint.

"Then it shall be."

Smiling, Man Hyung Sun pushed the door open.

IT WASN'T THERE!

Princippi had searched for the ancient urn in every room upstairs. He could not find the stone container anywhere.

"He must have read my mind," the former governor muttered as he looked in the bedroom closet of the Reverend Sun for the third time.

It had been at his Manhattan apartment earlier. Sun might have moved it back. Hell, the Hamptons house was so huge it could have been hidden anywhere in any of the dozen buildings. Even on the grounds somewhere.

Princippi was frantic. He had been a party to the murders the first time around. Again, this time. It could ruin his life—any future career he might have—if that urn wound up in the wrong hands.

He looked around desperately at the big empty closet. Four walls. One mirror. A few hangers. Nothing more.

His heart thudded like mad. He felt his stomach twisting and churning anxiously. His bladder felt as if it were going to burst.

Bladder!

"Bathroom!" Princippi cried.

Running, tripping, he ran into the master bath.

It was huge. Whirlpool. Sauna. A tub seemingly as big as an Olympic pool.

Princippi dived at cabinets and closets, throwing towels and toiletries onto the tiled floor. His knees ached as he skidded to a stop in front of a pair of closed louvered doors. Hands shaking, he fumbled them open.

Nothing. Controls for the hot tub. No sign of the Delphic urn.

His head twisted around. He felt dizzy. Lightheaded.

The bathroom was a mess. Junk was strewed everywhere.

No urn.

No urn anywhere.

The entire estate to search.

No time.

He didn't know how long Sun would remain at the studio. The cult leader had told him he planned to stay behind for several more hours, but he might change his mind.

Mike Princippi desperately wanted to go to the bathroom. It felt as if he was about to wet his pants. He looked longingly at the toilet across the field of scattered debris.

No time.

Head reeling, he raced from the bathroom.

The bedroom suite was still empty. Run. Escape. Hide somewhere. Anywhere. Anywhere *he* would not think to look.

Blood drumming frantically in his ears, Princippi ran through the bedroom and out into the upstairs hallway...

...directly into the Reverend Man Hyung Sun!

Princippi skidded to a stop. "I, uh... Hi!" He was sweating profusely. His ears rang like twin deafening gongs. "I was, uh, I was just going."

The ex-governor attempted to sidestep Sun but was stopped by a frail hand that seemed to come out of nowhere.

Chiun stepped out from behind the cult leader. His hand was pressed firmly against Princippi's chest. It was as if the former presidential candidate had slammed into a solid brick wall. Chiun's face was cold.

"You thought I would not know of your treachery?" Sun demanded. "How could you be so foolish?'' There was almost a pitying expression in his angry eyes. Princippi caught a hint of the yellow fire in his pupils.

With his back to Sun, the Master of Sinanju did not glimpse the hint of demonic possession. He continued to stare—eyes glinting cold like midnight glaciers—at the former Massachusetts governor.

''I-it wasn't...'' Princippi stammered.

The flickering yellow fire in Sun's eyes. The accusatory tone. Chiun's icy, level gaze. It was all too much for him. He shook his head helplessly.

''Some are too weak, even for *pyon ha-da*,'' Sun said to Chiun. ''This is such a one. All the gods together could not make this Greekling a true Korean.''

''Huh?'' Mike Princippi asked.

''Kill him,'' Sun commanded.

Princippi's eyes went wide. ''No,'' he said. A spark of hope dawned. He wheeled to Chiun. ''The urn. Ask him about the Delphic urn,'' the ex-governor pleaded.

His own voice sounded far away. It took him a second to realize why.

He had not spoken the words at all. They were heard only by him in his own mind. He knew this because one needed a throat, tongue and a working larynx in order to articulate sounds. Most of the aforementioned list had somehow inexplicably been ripped from the person of Mike Princippi.

Much of his neck lay in a pile on the carpet before Man Hyung Sun's bedroom. The Prince wondered briefly how they had gotten there and—all at once—he stopped wondering. To wonder, the only thing one really needed was a functioning brain, but the late Mike Princippi no longer had that particular item.

The former governor and presidential candidate slumped to the floor on top of the tattered bloody strips of his own throat. Even as he fell, Chiun was tucking his slender killing fingernails back into the folds of his kimono.

The Reverend Man Hyung Sun looked down at the body of Mike Princippi. He nodded, impressed at the swiftness of the attack. The yellow fire of possession no longer burned in his eyes as he turned to Chiun.

"You are quite skilled," he said, nodding his approval.

"I am honored you think so, Holy One," Chiun said with a pleased bow.

Sun smiled at the body. "Do you think you could teach me to move thusly?"

Chiun returned the smile. "It would be my pleasure, Seer of *pyon ha-da*," he said. His hazel eyes burned with quiet pride.

"WHAT KIND OF IDIOT is this premier of yours?" Remo demanded.

Rim Kun Soe sat behind the wheel of Remo's

borrowed jeep. They were parked on the tarmac at Pyongyang Airport looking out at an empty field. It seemed as if even the security people were in hiding.

"You did not tell him to keep the plane here for you," Soe pointed out. His head ached where Remo had used it to bash down Kim Jong Il's door. He had washed off most of the blood and applied a few bandages at the morgue.

"Did so," Remo challenged.

"You only told him to let it leave unharmed," Soe insisted. "You did not say to make certain you were aboard."

"Since when are you the Commie court stenographer?" Remo complained.

"I heard what I heard," Soe said. "If you wish to steal a plane from here, I would be pleased. If only to get you out of my company and to get my own execution over with faster."

"No deal," Remo said. "If your planes are built like everything else around here, it'd crash and burn before we even taxied from the terminal. The only plane in this country I trust is Kim Jong Il's and that jet's gotten too many miles on it for my liking lately." He frowned.

"Then you stay," Soe said.

"Not very bloody likely. How far a drive is it to Seoul?" Remo asked wearily.

"Approximately 130 miles. Through heavily fortified zones."

Remo sank back into his seat. "So what are you waiting for? Start driving," he ordered, crossing his arms.

Though it was suicidal for them to try to breach the security of both Koreas, Soe knew better than to argue. With a jounce of tires, the jeep took off across the vacant, windswept runway.

U.S. ARMY FORCES along the demilitarized zone between North and South Korea had been on high alert ever since the Tomahawk incident two days before.

Tensions were higher than at any time in Colonel Nick DeSouza's entire military career. And that was saying a lot. Since before Colonel DeSouza was born, the two Koreas had always seemed poised on the verge of war. Sometimes things were better; sometimes they were worse. But it was always a very real threat.

In recent years, the student demonstrators in the South had upped the ante for the Americans stationed along the DMZ. There had been protests—many violent—from the young in the lower half of the Korean Peninsula. Their press for a unified Korea would effectively push out foreign troops from the region, allowing the entire nation to be swept away in a tidal wave of soldiers from the North.

Almost fifty years of efforts to keep the Communists at bay would be for naught if the idiot students had their way. And after the bombing of the college in Seoul, things had only gotten worse.

Colonel DeSouza had no idea what *that* had been all about. The United States government had apologized for the mishap. The South Korean government had been understandably unforgiving. Given the circumstances, DeSouza didn't think he'd be very forgiving, either.

Yes, sorry about blowing up your university, and all. Hope you're not too upset.

Upset? Us? Not at all. It'd take more than one measly little cruise missile to bother us. A dozen, *maybe*. One? Forget about it.

DeSouza thought they were lucky that the whole damned population south of the DMZ hadn't overrun their position by now.

So there it was. Hostiles to the north. More hostiles to the south. And the United States Army plopped down right in the middle.

"Par for the course," DeSouza muttered as he ambled along the craggy southern lip of the Bridge of No Return.

The bridge was a narrow iron affair that separated the two Koreas. If there was ever a ground invasion from the north, it would start through this slender corridor.

As DeSouza sipped tepid coffee from a tin mug, he thought wryly that the assault they had always anticipated might come from a direction none of them had ever expected. The south.

Even as he thought it, he heard the sound of an engine whining somewhere distant.

He looked over his shoulder.

In the distance, he saw the encampment where the latest student demonstrators from the South had parked themselves after the bombing. There was activity around the camp, but no vehicles moving out of it. With a sick feeling, he realized that the sound was coming from the other side of the bridge.

"Perfect," Colonel DeSouza complained, flinging his coffee away.

A truck was parked in perpetuity in the middle of the Bridge of No Return. Its engine was left running so that if an invasion from the north ever materialized, it could be used to bottle up the bridge so that enemy forces would have a harder time in their push south.

DeSouza jogged partway out on the bridge, listening to the sound he had heard over the rumble of the big truck.

Jeep. Definitely a jeep. But if it was an invasion force, Kim Jong Il would have to have packed a couple of thousand troops onto that one jeep, because as far as Colonel DeSouza could tell, there was just the one vehicle.

A moment later, he realized that he had been right. A lone jeep bounced into view. Two men in the front seat. That was all that was visible from this end of the bridge.

Colonel DeSouza had been ready to shout orders to his men, thinking that the North was using the opportunity of crisis with the South to drive a wedge between the U.S. and its host nation. But as the jeep slowed to a stop on the far side of the bridge, he wasn't sure what to do.

A lone man got out of the passenger's side. DeSouza saw instantly that he wasn't Asian.

Tall. Thin. Dark hair. Possibly Mediterranean features. Definitely not Korean.

The man crouched down on the far side of the jeep, out of sight of DeSouza. After only a moment, the jeep tipped over to that side. The man reappeared. Under his arms, he carried two fat black objects. Whistling, he hustled across the bridge, leaving his jeep and driver behind. When he was close enough, DeSouza saw that he was carrying two of the jeep's tires.

The stranger hurried past the parked American truck with its running engine and over to DeSouza. Suspicious soldiers leveled their weapons but held their fire, awaiting orders from their commanding officer.

"I don't trust that bugger Soe not to run off," Remo complained as he marched up to DeSouza.

"You're an American," the colonel said, unable to mask his surprise.

"As an IRS audit," Remo replied with a tight smile. "Where can I put these? The idiot Koreans already lost a 747 on me. I don't want to lose a jeep, too.''

He held aloft the two tires. DeSouza could see that he was unarmed.

"Who are you?'' the colonel asked. Suspicion finally overcame surprise. His hand felt for his side arm.

"Do you mind, MacArthur?'' Remo groused. In spite of a hundred weapons aimed in his direction, Remo looked around for a place to put the tires. He found a nice spot near the side of the bridge. He dropped the two of them there, turning back to DeSouza.

"I asked you a question,'' the colonel stressed. The gun was now drawn. His face was serious.

"Listen, I've had a lousy day,'' Remo explained. "I had to meet with one of the last Communists in the world outside of Washington and I feel like I need a week-long shower to clean off. Mind if I borrow a jeep?''

That was it. He'd had it with this wacko. Let someone else deal with it. "I'm going to have to detain you,'' DeSouza said firmly.

The colonel was about to gesture to a few of his men with his gun when he suddenly realized that the gun was no longer there. He was waving with an empty hand. Quickly, he looked to the stranger, thinking that he must have disarmed him somehow.

Remo shook his head. "Check your holster," he said.

DeSouza did. His gun was back where he had gotten it. The snap was even attached.

"The way things are going around here, you may need it later," Remo said. "I might be able to stop things from getting any worse if you'll just get me a jeep."

Colonel DeSouza considered for a moment. Finally, he glanced back at his nervous men. "Get this man a jeep!" he shouted. Turning to face Remo, he said, "Are you some kind of spook or something?"

"Or something," Remo said.

The jeep was brought forward. A soldier was even offered as a driver. Remo declined.

"From what I've heard, the South is going to be even dicier than the North," he said as he climbed behind the wheel. "And I'm pretty rough on drivers."

"Good luck," Colonel DeSouza offered.

The stranger—who was obviously CIA or was with some other covert agency—answered in a most enigmatic way.

"I believe in luck about as much as I believe in fortune-tellers," Remo muttered, turning over the engine.

Flooring the jeep, Remo raced away from the Bridge of No Return, down toward the student encampment.

24

He remembered the camp.

Freezing-cold winters that seemed to last forever. Scorching summers that took up the time between blizzards. And no food. He remembered the hunger more than anything.

The prisoners had been forced to work. Many died hollowing the great gun caves in Stone Mountain, which overlooked the DMZ. Still more had perished digging the eight story subbasement complex of the People's Bureau of Revolutionary Struggle, the deep basement bomb shelter of the presidential palace or the labyrinthine undergrounds of government buildings all around Pyongyang.

It seemed that anything the Democratic People's Republic of Korea deemed important was buried so far below the surface that no one without a pickax and a hundred years would ever see it.

Man Hyung Sun had seen it. At least in its rudimentary stages. And he remembered.

He had starved as he wielded his ax beside other

laborers. They chipped away for hours upon hours. Day would come up on their chipping. Night would descend, and still the relentless chip-chip-chip sound would fill the dark shadows.

Only when the cloak of night had been pulled so tightly that even the North Korean soldiers who oversaw their work force recognized the difficulty of the task were the prisoners allowed to shuffle off to their camp. They were awakened before dawn to begin the process anew.

This was how Man Hyung Sun had spent several long years in the early part of his life.

Sun had once been a soldier under the command of Kim Il Sung himself. He had been a favorite of the future president during those dark days when Kim led a Korean unit in the Soviet army during World War II. But when Kim Il Sung had become president of the People's Republic in 1948, the seeds were sown for their eventual falling-out.

Man Hyung Sun had been opposed to the invasion of the South by Kim that led to the Korean War. The president saw his opposition as treachery. His former ally was thrown into prison without any more compassion than one might show an ant underfoot.

Sun lived for several long years in the camp. The work was hard, the food scarce. The hunger? Severe.

There were many times he thought he would die. Many more that he wished he would.

It was only by a miracle that Sun ever escaped.

As the work detail was being led back to the prison one cold dark night, one of the guards got sloppy. His attention was drawn away. Afterward, Sun never could remember why.

A scuffed shoe. A stumbling prisoner. Perhaps one of the emaciated wretches farther along had died. It did not matter. Sun saw his opportunity and took it.

While the guard was looking away, Sun smashed him over the head with a rock. He did not creep up. No stealth was involved. Indeed, he could not have managed it if he had to.

He saw an opportunity and sloppily seized it.

The trip across the frozen wasteland to the DMZ had been arduous and fraught with difficulties. There were soldiers, dogs, mines. Even tanks and planes. Searchlights.

None were looking for him specifically. They were just the regular accoutrements of a Communist dictatorship.

By some miracle, he made it. By an even greater miracle, the Americans had let him across. Man Hyung Sun became a free man on that day. Penniless, starving but free.

Fortunately for him, he already spoke English, having taken many courses at university as a youth. He stayed in the South only a brief time, eventually moving on to America.

His single foolhardy experience opposing Kim

Il Sung notwithstanding, Man Hyung Sun was nothing if not savvy. He soon learned that the Americans had a law that allowed churches to operate without paying taxes.

Sun needed money and food. It was a match made in heaven. He founded the Grand Unification Church in 1956.

It was amazing how easy it was to manipulate the minds of the imbecilic American youth. The first were ordinary converts. He needed to do nothing special to convince them to devote their lives to him. In a land as rich as America, the spoiled, idle children were looking for ways to avenge themselves against their parents for showering them with so much. Sun and his church became the ultimate vengeance.

The culture of sloth was beginning to erode the foundations of the great Western nation in the years immediately following the establishment of his church. America was on the cusp of the 1960s. Man Hyung Sun read the times like a clairvoyant.

During the full blossom of the sixties, his followers were commissioned to bring others into the flock. Whether they wanted to join or not.

Sun had not been a Communist for nothing. He knew all of the advanced brainwashing techniques taught to the North Korean government by their friends the Russians. The new recruits were quickly converted to the Grand Unification Church. In short order, they were in airports all around the country haranguing travelers with flowers, tambourines and words of love from the Reverend Man Hyung Sun.

For more than a decade, parents were reluctant to charge the church with taking their children against their will. Most attributed the new attitude of their offspring to dope, free love, whatever. It was the times, after all. The kids would come around.

They didn't.

Only when the sixties became the seventies did people begin to look more deeply at the "conversion" tactics of the Reverend Sun. He managed to escape criminal prosecution on these charges, but it was during this closer scrutiny that his non-church-related tax irregularities became evident to the federal government.

Sun went back to prison.

It was not as it had been in North Korea. He had more food than he could eat, and he was still able to run his religious empire from inside. Upon his release, he decided to take a more low-key approach to his religion.

Property became very important to Sun. Also his Washington newspaper, which he frequently used as a forum to harass his old friend, now bitter enemy, Kim Il Sung.

It was while working at his newspaper that he began hearing stories of a place out west. Supposedly, for a fee, one could learn the future there.

The service was only available to the very wealthy or the very connected. Actors, businessmen, politicians—all swore by this place.

Something about the story intrigued Sun. It was not on a conscious level. More of a dream trying to push itself into the reality of his daily life.

Sun planned to visit the ranch where the prophesying was alleged to take place, but history was one step ahead of him. There was an explosion at the Truth Church. Along with many deaths. Sun had been too late. Or so he thought.

The day of the explosion at Ranch Ragnarok was the day he began having the visions.

They were bizarre, surreal images. Waking dreams.

There was the great plain. As vast as time and space itself. A sky so red it was as if it had been painted in thick daubs of blood. Ground as bloody as the sky above. And sitting in the center of the lonely battlefield, a single morose figure. A patch of yellow. Beckoning. Always beckoning. Calling out to Man Hyung Sun.

He had been chosen. He did not know why, only that he had been selected above all others.

The spirit was frail. The visions strong at times, weak at others. It took many months to realize what was being communicated to him. During this time, he did as the mysterious, dreamlike figure suggested. More Sunnies were indoctrinated into the faith. The sailors aboard the U.S.S. *Courage*, some New York police officers, some South Korean student protestors, as well as several other individuals—the importance of all of whom was unknown to Sun. He merely did as the spirit commanded. Still, he did not know where to locate this strange force. It took him a great deal of soul-searching to find out.

When he was finally certain, the reverend had dispatched his Sunnie servants to find Michael Princippi and to find the urn of the Pythia the ex-governor had carried away from the ruins of the ranch in Wyoming.

Sun needed only to come in contact with Princippi to know that the former governor had been ignoring the signals being sent to him by the Pythia. The essence of the spirit was strong within the sneaky technocrat. The Pythia had been trying desperately to seek his aid, but Princippi had ignored it. Sun was not like the ex-governor. He had heeded the call.

It was glorious. Once the urn of yellow powder was in his possession, the waking dreams were far more powerful. There was someone else in his mind at all times.

The Pythia was stronger when Sun was near the urn, but once he had accepted the essence of the ancient offshoot of the Greek god Apollo within him, not a moment passed wherein he did not feel the presence lurking within him.

It was fitting. In Greek mythology, Apollo had

driven the chariot of the sun across the sky. His fractured essence had sought out one called Sun.

In his first moment of complete possession, Sun had been given a vision by the Pythia. A gift to reward him for his loyal service. Blessed with the ability to foretell the future, the yellow spirit had let Sun see himself in the very near future. He would be a king. The nation he had fled in ignominy would be his to rule over. There would be no North, no South. It would be complete. Whole. Under the iron fist of Man Hyung Sun.

Sun loved that vision, *lived* for it. It was like a drug to which he had become hopelessly addicted. He longed to see it now, as he stood on that desolate plain in his mind.

THE PYTHIA SLUMPED before him. A strange combination of yellow cloud and human features. Only in this place of unreality could the images be remotely reconciled.

"I grow weaker still," the Pythia lamented. The voice that rattled up the spirit's throat was a pathetic rasp.

"The Greek who ignored your entreaties is no more," Sun offered, as if to cheer up the ancient spirit.

"Do you think I do not know? It is I who told you of his treachery." Squatting in the misery of its own yellow smoke, the Pythia shook its head bitterly. "The time I wasted on that Greek. If my master were here, if my strength were greater, he would not have ignored me. My power was once feared by man. I am a shell of what I once was.''

Sun seemed uncomfortable. ''You are a powerful seer,'' he said. He tried to think of something that would bolster the Pythia's flagging spirits. ''My 900 line is ringing off the hook,'' he offered suddenly.

At this, the Pythia looked up at Sun. There was a scornful expression on its bronzed face.

''Vengeance propels me, though my spirit longs for nothingness,'' the Pythia intoned. ''It is time.''

''For what?'' Sun asked.

''Time to crush my enemies.''

Sun's heart raced. The Pythia had prophesied to him that his time of ascendancy would come immediately on the heels of the final defeat of the men from Sinanju.

''What do you wish for me to do, O Prophet?''

''The young one is already in place. Your minions have done well to draw him into my trap.''

''Thank you, Great Herald,'' Sun said proudly.

''It is time to bring the old one there, as well.''

Sun's face clouded. ''I thought it was your wish to keep them apart.''

''It was. It no longer is. The time has come that we should bring them together.'' The Pythia smiled. ''And set them against one another.''

And as the Pythia went on to describe its plan to the Reverend Sun, the cult leader could not help

but smile, as well. Their deaths—and his future—
were all but assured.

CHIUN WAS SITTING in his balcony sunroom, which
overlooked the grounds of Sun's estate, when the
reverend knocked on his door once more. The
Master of Sinanju bade the cult leader enter.

"I have been meditating," Sun said, sitting
across from Chiun on the balcony.

The Master of Sinanju did not bother to mention
that the all too familiar stench of Sun's after-shave
had preceded him into the room yet again. Every
time Sun meditated, he came back smelling like a
French brothel. His breathing shallow, the old Korean merely nodded.

"I have had a revelation," Sun continued. "It
is time."

Sitting in a lotus position on the floor, Chiun
had not yet opened his eyes. He did so now.

"Time for what?" he asked, not daring to allow
hope to betray his studied tone. The answer sent
his soul soaring.

"*Pyon ha-da* is upon us," Sun said. "As is my
moment of greatness. We must return in haste to
the land of our birth so that I might be allowed to
ascend to my proper place as leader of unified Korea. I wish you to be at my side."

Chiun rose from the floor like a puff of thin
smoke. "It will be my joy to safeguard your holy

life, Seer of *pyon ha-da*," the Master of Sinanju intoned, squeaky voice chiming with undisguised joy. The bow he gave to Man Hyung Sun was reverential.

25

The student activists of the South were more difficult to get through than the whole of the People's Defense Forces of the North from Pyongyang to the demilitarized zone.

In his U.S. Army jeep, Remo Williams had to dodge bricks, bottles, rocks, sticks and just about anything else the "peace-loving" student demonstrators found to throw.

As he was racing through the streets of Seoul, someone hurled a Molotov cocktail onto the hood of his speeding jeep. The bottle crashed with the sound of shattering china, and the gasoline mixture splattered orange flames back across the windshield. Remo drove through the fire.

Riot police were out in full force. White helmets protected heads while thick transparent face shields extended down to bulletproof vests. Kevlar gloves and blast-resistant shields completed the rest of the armor the police had been forced to wear over their jumpsuits.

From the look of the debris field that was the

streets of Seoul, the demonstrations by the students had taken a bad turn during the previous night. Charred cars lined the road, some still sending plumes of acrid smoke into the clear winter-blue sky.

Remo weaved his way through students and police alike, arriving relatively unscathed at the South Korean National Assembly building.

Roving packs of students could be seen wandering between buildings and cars. They looked like the irate villagers out of an old horror movie, determined to rid the local castle of an evil scientist. All they needed were a few pitchforks and some torches to complete the image.

Remo prayed that for now his vehicle would be safe from the students. He didn't plan to leave it there long.

He abandoned the jeep by the side of the road. At a run, Remo flew up the stairs and into the big building.

PRESIDENT KIM DAE JUNG had personally called for the secret emergency meeting of the Kuk Hoe, the National Assembly of the Republic of Korea. All 299 members of the unicameral body were present, as well as every cabinet and high-ranking security officer in the nation. With the number of people crammed inside the assembly hall, the president wondered how long his secret meeting would remain a secret.

The issue before them was one he had not thought to seriously face in his lifetime. Reunification with the North. It had been brought up many times in the past, but it had always been unthinkable to reasonable people. But reason had taken a holiday since the American bombing of Seoul National University.

"The Americans take our relationship for granted!" the ranking member of the Party for Peace and Democracy shouted from behind the podium. "They believe that they can drop bombs on our heads and we will still scurry over to them like dogs beneath their master's table. It is time we demonstrate to the powers of the West that we, too, are a force to be reckoned with. Only a unified Korea can show such strength."

It was the same speech many others had given. From his seat behind the main podium of the parliamentary chamber, the president watched the faces in the crowd.

Only about one-fifth were from the Reunification Democratic Party. These were usually the ones screaming for talks with the North at every perceived slight from the West. But they had remained largely silent this day. Suppressing grins, they had watched others from more conservative parties get up and give the same speeches they had given in the past.

The president had tried to call for calm in the face of this latest crisis. Washington had apologized for the Tomahawk incident. Screaming would not bring the dead back to life. Nor would it rebuild either the destroyed portion of the university or the fragile bridge to the West.

He was shouted down.

The entire nation was spinning out of control. If these supposedly rational elected officials were so frenzied over this issue, there was little hope for the rest of South Korea. Indeed, the rioting overnight in Seoul had been the worst in the president's memory. And he had been an activist and political prisoner years before.

And so he sat, staring into the abyss, helpless to stop his countrymen from taking that last step into madness.

"I cannot help but say that we saw this coming." The ranking delegate of the Reunification Democratic Party had taken the stage. The smugness oozed like snake oil from every pore. "The Americans cannot possibly understand us or our culture. Some of you have had trepidations when we have discussed the inevitable union with our northern cousins. You must all admit now that the North would understand us better than America. The United States bombs us and then they say they are sorry. That might be good enough for our president, but it is not good enough for us."

"What if we say we're really, *really* sorry?" called a voice from the rear of the assembly hall.

Faces shocked, the assembly turned as one to

see who it was who had the audacity to shout out during a floor speech. Their expressions grew even more amazed when they saw that the speaker— though he spoke flawless Korean—was distinctly non-Korean in appearance.

Remo Williams strode up the aisle toward the speaker's stand. At his seat above and behind the podium, the president of South Korea was as alarmed as the members of the National Assembly.

"You see?" shouted the highest-ranking member of the Reunification Democratic Party over the murmurs of the crowd. "Do you see how they feel as if they can just storm in here? We are not an ally—we are but a servant!"

Remo hopped up to the platform. "And you are a whore to your masters in Pyongyang," he said.

The speaker's microphone amplified his words, carrying them back across the National Assembly. There was a gasp from the crowd.

The Reunification Democratic Party member's face turned red with rage. Forgetting all decorum, he lunged at Remo, arms outstretched.

Remo sidestepped the man, grabbing him by the scruff of the neck as he passed by. He hefted him high into the air before the assembly. "See the true servant," he announced in perfectly accented Korean. "People like this want you to surrender your freedom to the idiot son of Kim Il Sung."

A look of disgust creasing his hard face, Remo flung the man to the floor of the assembly.

The president had found a microphone by now. "Who are you?" he demanded of Remo.

Remo looked over at the man. "I am the son of the Master of Sinanju," he announced.

There were gasps from the crowd. Remo heard many of the men whispering "Sinanju" to one another. Good. By the looks he was getting, many of them had heard of the ancient house of assassins.

"I have heard the Master of Sinanju had taken a white as his heir," the president said, nodding. "But I have heard that you work for America."

"That's right."

"Then you are here on behalf of American interests," the president of South Korea pressed.

"I am here in the interest of sanity," Remo replied. "There doesn't seem to be a heck of a lot around here lately."

"How do we know you are truly of Sinanju?" one of the members of the Democratic Justice Party shouted from the assembly floor.

"Yes!" yelled the embarrassed member of the Reunification Democratic Party. "You are not Sinanju! He is CIA!" he cried to his fellow assemblymen.

"A spy!" shrieked another.

The murmuring, which had been more confused than anything else until now, began to grow more hostile. Things were getting out of hand. Remo had to find a way to calm the assembly down.

He glanced around. The nearest thing available

was the podium at which the representatives to the assembly had been taking turns denouncing America and calling for reunification talks with the North.

Slapping his hands to either side of the quarter-ton slab of wood, Remo tossed the big stand up into the air. The National Assembly gasped as the huge stand rose impossibly toward the vaulted ceiling of the chamber.

All at once, the podium reached the crest of its arc, dropping like a lump of lead to the stage. The assembly held its collective breath, expecting the impact to be deafening. But five feet before it was set to crash, its movement was abruptly arrested.

The men and women watched in astonishment. The podium had landed on the tip of Remo's raised index finger.

With his free hand, Remo began spinning the huge podium in place—like a kid in a schoolyard performing a simple basketball trick. As it whirred, the stand began to hum a loud, even purr.

Remo's hand flew faster and faster until the stand was a blur. It eventually moved so fast that it seemed to disappear altogether. That was when the sawdust appeared.

Wooden powder flew off in large clouds with each invisible spin of the podium. If someone had thought to check his watch, he would have seen that it all took no more than forty seconds.

The whirring stopped. The podium reappeared.

It was now only a narrow piece of wood, fatter at the top and bottom. Like an apple that had been eaten to the core. Remo stood in an ankle-deep pile of dark sawdust.

He set the remains of the podium down.

"I am the future Reigning Master of Sinanju," Remo announced to the crowd. "Does anyone still doubt me?"

No one dared dispute his claim. None in the assembly dared to even speak.

"Good," Remo said, satisfied. He glanced around, finding the president. "You," he said, pointing to the terrified Kim Dae Jung. "We've got to talk."

He grabbed the president by the scruff of the neck and hauled him from the room. No one in the astonished assembly attempted to stop him.

"ARE YOU HERE to kill me?" the president asked nervously once the two of them were alone. They were in a private office off the main assembly chamber.

"I could have picked a less public way of doing that, don't you think?" Remo asked blandly.

The president thought about some of the things he had heard about the Masters of Sinanju. If only a handful of them were true, he would not be alive now.

"Then you are not here to kill me," he said. The president breathed a relieved sigh and was immediately annoyed with himself for being so concerned for his own life.

"No," Remo said. "I'm here to figure out what the hell is going on."

"I suspect you know already as much as I do." The president took a seat behind the cluttered desk in the room. He looked old. And tired. "It is madness. All of it."

"We didn't launch the missile on purpose," Remo insisted.

The president waved a dismissive hand. "I know this," he said. "It was a stupid mistake."

"Maybe not," Remo said.

This caught the South Korean leader's attention. "You say it was not deliberate, then you hint it might have been. Which is it?" he asked.

"It's not deliberate on behalf of the U.S. government," Remo explained. "But according to my information, the men who fired the cruise missile into Seoul all committed suicide afterward. That tells me they were protecting someone."

The president shrugged. "A theory," he said.

"What else would it be?" Remo asked.

"I do not know," the president admitted wearily. "It makes sense—I will admit that. But I am tired of making sense to that mob out there." He motioned vaguely in the direction of the assembly hall. "The young cry out for reunification with the North. They do not know what it would be like. Our population is greater, but Kim Jong Il's tanks are stronger. Without the involvement of the United States, we would fall under the treads of the invaders from the North.''

"*Tell* them that, then," Remo argued, his tone exasperated. "Tell them we didn't have anything to do with the bombing, that it was probably part of some bigger scheme and that they'll have a certifiable nut running things around here if they don't smarten up.''

The president looked at him, eyes dead. "You drove to get here, presumably?"

"What's that got to do with anything?" Remo asked. "Yeah, I drove.''

"You saw the conditions in the streets. The student demonstrators have been a problem for us for a long time. Blessed with the ignorance of youth, they refuse to believe the world's harsh realities. But whereas before they were merely an annoyance, they have gained great strength in the wake of the bombing. They have stronger sympathizers now who are powerful in government. Reunification is no longer a dream. I fear it is an eventuality.''

"You're just going to roll over and play dead?"

"What more can I do?" the president asked.

Remo's face was fierce. "You think the students here are weak, blind fools?" he demanded. "I say *you* are. You're the one who should be out there screaming at the top of your lungs against that crackpot Kim. Hell, *he* might be the one behind all of this.''

''Perhaps.'' The president shrugged.

It was the feeble indifference in the move that did it to Remo. The willingness to betray freedom because it was easier than standing up to a tyrant.

Remo's mouth set in a firm line, thin lips pressed into bloodless white strips.

Reaching across the desk, he grabbed the president of South Korea by the front of his shirt. Lifting by a bundle of shirt and tie, he hauled Kim Dae Jung out over the rubble of the desk, toppling an angry shower of papers and envelopes to the floor.

Wordlessly, Remo hauled the president from the cramped office. His eyes were filled with visions of death.

26

The squadron of six North Korean Foxbat fighters intercepted the Reverend Man Hyung Sun's personal jet as it was flying west across the Sea of Japan.

The Sunnie pilot tried to calm the flaring tempers of the MiG-25 pilots, but the military fliers seemed more hostile than usual. As if something had recently ruffled their feathers.

Chiun was sitting in his normal seat above the left wing when he was asked to step into the cockpit by one of Sun's comely stewardesses at the urging of the harried flight crew. Annoyed, the Master of Sinanju hustled up the aisle.

"We're still over international waters," the pilot explained when Chiun stepped into the small cockpit. Sweat dripped down his broad forehead. "I think that's the only reason they haven't shot us down yet."

"I would speak with them," Chiun announced.

"Gladly," the pilot said.

The Sunnie copilot operated the radio while the Master of Sinanju spoke.

Chiun cleared his throat. "Whoresons of Pyongyang harlots—" he began.

"We're dead," moaned the pilot.

"—begone from the skies around this most holy aircraft, or face the awesome wrath of the Master of Sinanju."

The two Foxbats that were visible through the cockpit windows remained locked in place. The twin AA-6 Acrid rockets on the nearest wings of each fighter were reminders that there were four more planes just like them somewhere behind Sun's jet; each was equipped with four of the deadly missiles. One would be enough to blow the unarmed jet from the sky.

The Foxbats matched the speed of the civilian jet, never wavering a fraction. For a few tense moments, not a sound issued from the lead fighter.

Chiun stared over at the port MiG. The pilot's domed head was visible through the cockpit glass. The old Korean stared daggers at the man.

"We're about to pass into North Korean airspace," the copilot announced worriedly after a short time.

As they watched their controls with steadily increasing apprehension, the MiGs remained glued to their positions beside them.

Mere seconds before they were to pass into North Korean airspace, a voice crackled over the radio. The MiG pilot sounded as if he would choke on the message he had been ordered to deliver.

"Proceed, Master of Sinanju. And welcome home."

Only then did Chiun tear his eyes away from the man in the Foxbat. Turning abruptly, he left the bewildered cockpit crew and returned to his seat.

"Is there a problem?" Man Hyung Sun asked. The cult leader had been napping in his seat across from Chiun and had just awakened.

"None, O Holy One," the Master of Sinanju replied.

Chiun settled in to watch the wing. He had heard that sometimes they dropped off during takeoffs and landings.

COLONEL NICK DESOUZA couldn't believe his eyes. The CIA spook who had crossed the DMZ only a few hours before had not only made it safely through the gangs of student rioters running amok through South Korea, but was already returning. And he was not alone.

DeSouza thought he recognized the Korean passenger as the battered jeep bounced back into view up the road to the old iron bridge.

"It's a little worse for wear," Remo said as the jeep skidded to a stop. There were various dings all around the vehicle. One of the front windshield panels had been shattered at the corner. The telltale burn marks of Molotov cocktails were all around the hood and sides.

"You signed the insurance form. It's your problem, not mine," DeSouza deadpanned as Remo hopped down to the ground.

"Things still quiet?" Remo asked.

"The kids haven't attacked yet, if that's what you mean," the colonel said. "No troop movements out of the North, either, according to intelligence."

"A silent coup," Remo commented dryly.

Glancing past the idling truck on the Bridge of No Return, he noted that Rim Kun Soe still sat morosely on the opposite side of the bridge. Remo was certain that, left to his own devices, the Korean security officer would have hightailed it out of there by now.

Trotting, Remo went over and collected his North Korean jeep tires from their resting spot on the southern side of the bridge.

"Let's go," Remo said to his passenger.

The South Korean president had yet to get down from the American Army jeep.

"I will not," Kim Dae Jung announced.

"Wrong time to grow a backbone, pal," Remo said.

He dropped each of the tires one at a time, giving them a nudge with his toe the moment they hit the road. They each took off like a shot, rolling straight across the bridge and into the nose of the listing North Korean jeep.

Soe popped out of the driver's seat in a heartbeat, racing around to collect one of the tires. He vanished around the far side of the distant jeep.

"I give Soe one minute to reattach those wheels and bag out on us," Remo said to the president. "You either walk, or I carry you."

"That's the president of South Korea," Colonel DeSouza announced with the shock of sudden recognition. He had come in behind Remo.

"Your point being…?" Remo asked blandly.

"I have been kidnapped," the president said to the Army colonel. "This fool intends to deliver me into the hands of the North."

"I'm trying to defuse this bomb before the whole place goes up around our ears," Remo promised.

DeSouza seemed uncertain as to what he should do. He shot a glance at his men. They had not raised their weapons at Remo's appearance this time. Many of them stood at a distance, faces curious. The colonel could give them the order to fire at any time.

Remo sensed the military man's internal conflict.

"You've been carrying their water for how long?" Remo asked. "And you see how they're treating you. Who are you going to believe, me or him?"

"As president of your host country, I demand you defend me against this crazy man," Kim Dae Jung insisted.

DeSouza glanced from the president to Remo. He then looked out across the Bridge of No Return.

"You'd better hurry," the colonel said to Remo, eyes flat. He backed away from the jeep. "Your driver's already working on the second tire."

THE GREAT LEADER FOR LIFE of North Korea, Kim Jong Il, stood on the freezing tarmac. Wind whipped the flaps of the fur-lined Red Army–issue hat that was pulled tightly down over his ears.

All around him, men stood protectively. There were generals and foot soldiers and men from the government. All freezing and huddled in on themselves, afraid to stamp their feet against the cold.

The jet had appeared a few minutes before. It faded up out of the milky white winter sky like a reverse dissolve in one of his precious Hollywood movies.

Korean Foxbat fighters remained at a respectful distance from the civilian craft.

It was humiliating. To have two planes violate North Korean airspace twice in the same day was unthinkable under almost any circumstances. Unpardonable under all but one.

Two, actually.

The first was gone, thank God. That white one always gave Kim Jong Il the screaming meemies.

The second had just touched down at the far end of the runway.

The premier thought it best to meet personally with the Master of Sinanju, considering the fact that it was he who was responsible for the deaths of some of the North Korean agents in New York. Although it was not authorized by Kim Jong Il's government, the dead agents had apparently gone off on some sort of murderous rampage that had put them in the path of the men from Sinanju. The premier wanted to make it absolutely clear that there was no animosity between his regime and Sinanju. That was why he was here.

There was also a part of him that thought a face-to-face meeting with the old one might help with the young one. The Reigning Master of Sinanju was frightening and quick to anger, but he was also occasionally deferential—at least on the surface. The young one was not like that at all, and was therefore all the more frightening. Kim Jong Il reasoned that if he got on the good side of the father, the son might like him more.

The premier's ruddy face was hopeful as he watched the cluster of aircraft swarming toward him.

As the MiGs soared off, the private jet raced over toward the premier's party, slowing quickly. It rolled to a stop near the Great and Wonderful Leader for Life.

Even as the engines were powering down, the

rear door of the aircraft popped open. The short staircase descended, dropping neatly against the rough asphalt.

Kim Jong Il smiled so broadly he thought his frozen face would crack. He did not want to provoke even a hint of anger in the Master of Sinanju.

The soldiers and functionaries around him smiled, as well. They were one big, happy Communist reception party.

As the premier and his group watched, a man stepped down from the plane.

The Leader for Life blinked. For a moment, the frozen smile remained locked in place.

The man was not the Master of Sinanju. Even through his surprise, Kim Jong Il thought he recognized him. The face was from a time far away. He could not quite place...

His smile melted into a scowl of recognition.

Kim knew him all too well. He was a traitor to the Democratic People's Republic of Korea. The man's newspaper regularly insulted the Great Leader from the cowardly safety of the United States.

All thoughts of the Master of Sinanju were gone. Kim Jong Il turned to his troops, aiming a fat finger in the direction of the traitorous Man Hyung Sun.

His order crackled as clear as the frigid winter air around them.

"Shoot him!" screamed the Leader for Life of North Korea.

REMO HAD NO LUCK at the presidential palace. According to the premier's frightened underlings, Kim Jong Il had left suddenly for the airport. No one knew why.

He was forced to drag his untrustworthy little band back out into his borrowed North Korean army jeep. As they rode through the streets of Pyongyang to the airport, Kim Dae Jung hid behind the back of Remo's seat.

"It is not safe for me here," the president of South Korea said nervously.

"It's a hell of a lot safer here than in your own streets right now," Remo replied.

"No, this filth is correct," Soe said from behind the jeep's wheel. "Though he has a Korean face, he is no more than a capitalist running dog lackey of the pig West."

"Is that all with hyphens?" Remo asked.

"What?" asked Soe.

"Just shut up and drive," Remo suggested.

"I would kill him if I had the chance," Soe persisted.

"You won't get the chance." Remo sighed.

"I have to go to the bathroom," the president of South Korea whined.

"You should have thought of that before we crossed the Thirty-eighth Parallel," Remo said.

"I will kill you the first chance I get," Soe said over his shoulder to the president.

"What part of 'shut up' don't you understand?" Remo snapped.

They drove in silence for a few long moments.

"I am not saying that I *will* kill him," Soe said to Remo suddenly, "but if he were to die by accident—"

Remo bounced Soe's head off the dashboard. After that, the security officer remained quiet.

They were still a good distance from the airport when Remo spied the private jet soaring in, attended by the squadron of North Korean fighters.

"There's a familiar sight," he said, brow furrowing in concern.

"That is not your lost plane," Soe pointed out.

"No, but it's the same setup. Why would a bunch of Korean jets follow another plane without shooting it down?"

"Perhaps it is Kim Jong Il's. Is he scheduled to go abroad?" the South Korean president asked hopefully.

"No," Remo said. "And if you'd get up off the floor you'd see that it's landing, not taking off." He shook his head after another moment's consideration. "I can think of only one reason why they'd be taking a hands-off approach like that."

"What?" Soe asked.

Remo glanced at the driver. "Do you really want to know?" he said.

Soe judged Remo's wry tone. The security officer glanced at the cluster of planes soaring in toward the airport, still far across the dreary North Korean capital. He suddenly realized why Kim Jong Il had gone to the airport.

Remo could tell by the look on his face that Soe had figured out who was on board the plane. "You better hope for your sake that last shipment of gold made it back safely."

He was so intent on watching the landing plane that he didn't comment on the look of instant, horrible fear that blossomed on the face of Rim Kun Soe.

THEIR HESITATION HAD saved all of their lives.

The soldiers were about to fire at Man Hyung Sun, as per the order of their Glorious Leader for Life, when another figure appeared from the open door of the jet.

Chiun's face was severe. The trails of his golden kimono flapped wildly in the bitter wind.

"Hold!" the Master of Sinanju commanded.

The men were taken aback by the harshness of the command. Their weapons were raised to Sun, but they were looking beyond the cult leader at the wizened form of the Master of Sinanju. Kim Jong Il saw Chiun, as well.

"Hold your fire! For God's sake, hold your fire!" the premier screeched.

The North Korean leader took off his great furry hat and began jumping between his troops, swatting down gun barrels that were still hesitating in the air.

The troops soon got the point. Those who had not lowered their guns at once soon put theirs down, as well. Greatly relieved, Kim slapped his hat back on his head, slightly askew. He instantly thought better of the move, ripping the hat off once more. He held it politely in both hands as he went to greet the Master of Sinanju.

"Welcome home, O glorious and awesome Master of Sinanju—he of lightning hands and eagle eye. Whatever your son has told you, don't believe it," he blurted out, quickly adding, "unless it's good. Hah-hah." He forced a chuckle to take the edge off things.

"Greetings, first son of Kim Il Sung," Chiun replied. He bowed respectfully.

Kim returned the bow nervously, dropping his hat as he did so. A hundred hands swarmed into view to try to pick it up. The premier kicked or swatted them all away.

"It is a pleasure to meet you," Man Hyung Sun said. He extended a hand to the premier.

"Forgive me, O Awesomeness," Kim said, ignoring the hand. He grabbed up his own hat. "But might I inquire as to why you are in the company of this traitor?"

"Traitor?" Chiun asked bewildered. "This man is no traitor. He is the savior of all Koreans."

"Listen to this wise one, my premier," Sun said, his tone sly.

"No way," the Leader for Life insisted. "Your paper said I had the brain of a duck and the wit of a Kennedy. If that ain't treachery, then I'm Fatty Arbuckle."

"My quarrel was with your father," Sun said smoothly. "If I have transferred any of my feelings for him to you, then I deeply apologize. But he is dead. We are not. Let us inter our past differences with his bones."

"Easy for you to say, Loonie," the premier challenged.

There was a flicker of anger in Sun's eyes. Chiun interceded before the war of words could escalate.

"What is past, let us leave to the past," the Master of Sinanju intoned. "It is for the future that I have returned to the land of my birth in the company of this holy man."

"My ass is holier," Kim Jong Il said. "*And* it smells better. What the hell kind of stink-o-rama cologne are you wearing?" He flapped his hat in front of his face.

Chiun pulled the hat away and swatted the premier over the head with it. Thus cowed, the premier grew silent.

"Heed you this!" the Master of Sinanju shouted to the gathered North Korean soldiers and officials. "Today is the dawning of a new era for all the world!'' He indicated Sun. ''This man is a seer of divine inspiration! He has seen the future. The future of Taehan-min'guk, as well as that of Choson Minchu-Chui Inmin Konghwa-guk! These are but titles! Worthless names that have separated this blessed land for far too many years! This day, we will be one! Together as a united Korea will we face the future! The future of *pyon ha-da!*''

The many hooded eyes of those gathered grew wide at the last words. Even the premier took a shocked step back. He quickly gathered his senses, glancing from Sun to Chiun.

''It is true?'' he asked.

Chiun nodded. He crossed his arms impassively over his bony chest.

''We must prepare for destiny,'' Man Hyung Sun said somberly. His flat face was confident.

The premier seemed unsure what to do for a long moment. The wind continued to blow crazily around him, throwing the trail of his greatcoat out behind him like a desperate drab windsock. At long last, he spoke, his words dull.

''Kim Jong Il is not so foolish to resist the pull of future history,'' the premier said somberly. It was as if he were delivering the eulogy at a dear loved one's funeral.

In a move that would have shocked the world political community, the Leader for Life of North Korea sank slowly to his knees on the frozen tarmac before the traitorous Reverend Man Hyung Sun.

And, just as shocking, behind their leader, hundreds of Korean troops and civilian government agents did the same.

"WHAT IN THE BLAZING heckfurters is this?" Remo Williams asked as his jeep bounced onto the Pyongyang Airport runway.

It was as if they had stumbled into an outdoor Muslim prayer service. Except instead of facing Mecca, the Koreans on the tarmac were facing two very familiar figures.

"If they are praying, perhaps we should come back later," ventured the South Korean president, near Remo's left shoulder. He was peeking over the back seat.

Remo ignored him. "Bring us up in front of that mob," he instructed.

Soe steered the jeep in a straight line toward the aircraft that stood directly before the hundreds of kneeling men. They stopped before the throng.

Remo climbed down next to Chiun.

"What are you doing here?" Remo demanded.

"This is a free country, is it not?" the Master of Sinanju sniffed.

"No, actually, it's not," Remo snarled. He looked down at Kim Jong Il. "What do you think *you're* doing?"

"Paying respect to the herald of *pyon ha-da*," the premier explained.

"*Pyon ha-da?*" The shocked voice came from Remo's jeep. All at once, the president of South Korea climbed out onto the runway. He was joined quickly by Rim Kun Soe. "It is true?"

"The time has come," Kim Jong Il announced from his prostrate position before Sun.

"C'mon," Remo snapped at the dictator. "Don't tell me you believe that crapola?"

"*Pyon ha-da!*" the president of South Korea repeated, his voice a shocked gasp. He began getting to his knees beside the leader of the North.

"Oh, don't even start," Remo growled at him. He grabbed the president under the armpit, hauling him to his feet.

"You cannot fight the inevitable," Man Hyung Sun said seriously.

Remo wheeled on him. "Look, you don't even want to get into this with me, pal," he warned, raising a threatening finger to the cult leader.

"Remo!" Chiun said, aghast. "You will show proper respect for the Messenger of the Korean Age."

"Respect?" Remo scoffed. "He's lucky I don't rip his lungs out and knot them around his frigging neck." He took a step toward Sun.

There was a sudden blur, like a scattering of gold dust in the gale-force wind. All at once, the Master of Sinanju stood protectively before Man

Hyung Sun. His hands were down at his sides. Knots of ivory bone, ready to strike.

Remo took a shocked step back. "What do you think you're doing?" he asked.

Chiun's face was cold. "Guarding the life of the prophet with my own."

Stunned, Remo released his grip on the president of South Korea. The man sank slowly to his knees next to the North Korean premier. Remo hardly noticed.

"I can't believe you're falling for this fraud, Chiun," Remo said, shaking his head in astonishment.

"A fraud is only a fraud to those who disbelieve him," Man Hyung Sun intoned.

Remo ignored the platitude. He was staring into the fiery hazel eyes of the Master of Sinanju. There was not a hint of deception in them. He appeared to be quite serious. Was this the final, fatal look that had been seen by so many of the old Korean's victims?

Chiun seemed poised to strike. And for the life of him, Remo could not tell if he was bluffing.

A few present on that icy runway sensed that there was an epic battle about to commence. Looking up from where they knelt, they spied the two men standing face-to-face. In truth, what was happening was more an epic sizing up.

Remo rotated his thick wrists absently as he looked down at the tiny wisp of a man who had taught him so much. Chiun stared back, face impassive.

Remo was the first to blink.

"The hell with this," he said, stepping back. He waved an angry hand. "You'll see I'm right soon enough."

Stepping away from the Reverend Sun, Remo slumped back against his jeep, arms crossed sullenly across his chest.

Chiun relaxed his stance. Hands slithered up the sleeves of his golden kimono, locking on to opposite wrists.

The Reverend Man Hyung Sun beamed.

"Do we not see the future already?" he proclaimed. "When every face is Korean and every mind and soul equally wise, there will be no more competition. No more fighting. No more conflict. Paradise waits in *pyon ha-da!*"

Sun clapped his hands loudly together. All eyes looked up to him. The cult leader indicated that the men should rise. Soldiers came forward to help the dictator of the North and the democratically elected president of the South to their feet.

"Bring transport!" Sun called. "The future begins in the wounded belly of this divided land!"

Limousines, jeeps and trucks were driven onto the runway. The leaders of the two Koreas climbed into the first limo together as the rest of the men scattered among the remaining vehicles. Sun ducked back inside his jet to collect a package.

While he was gone, the Master of Sinanju approached Remo.

"Are you coming?" Chiun asked, his voice betraying no emotion.

"Yeah, I'll go," Remo said. "But I don't believe in any of this crystal-ball bullshit."

Chiun shook his head. There was not a trace of warmth in his eyes. "It no longer matters what you think," he said seriously. "It is destiny."

Turning away from his pupil, the Master of Sinanju went in search of transport. He did not look back.

27

Spy satellites and reconnaissance planes were the first to see it. The information was radioed back and up along the chain of command until secure phone lines from Washington to Moscow, from London to Beijing, were ringing off the hook. In military war rooms all around the globe, the slow, relentless movement of the caravan toward the Thirty-eighth Parallel was greeted with great apprehension.

And in the lead limousine of the mighty line of army and civilian vehicles, Remo Williams sat brooding. He was also trying to stay out of range of the Reverend Sun's wretched after-shave lotion.

"Is he always like this?" Man Hyung Sun whispered to the Master of Sinanju.

"Sadly, yes," Chiun replied. "It is a trait he picked up from his mother."

"Leave my mother out of this," Remo snapped. "You never even met her."

"Neither have you," Chiun sniffed. He pitched

his voice low again. "He is an orphan," he said
to Sun.

"That's none of his damned business, either,"
Remo said harshly, his eyes betraying his deep anger.

"Perhaps we should leave this one alone for
now," the Reverend Sun suggested. "I fear only
pyon ha-da will turn him from his deeply ingrained
white ways."

"Listen," Remo said, "I'm not picking a fight
with you, Chiun, but there is no way in hell the
entire human race is going to turn Korean overnight."

Chiun nodded. "That is correct."

Remo brightened. "So you agree this is nuts?"

"No," Chiun said. "I merely agree that it will
not occur overnight. Seer Sun has informed me that
pyon ha-da will take place during daylight, so that
the entire population of the world can witness its
moment of flowering perfection."

Remo closed his eyes. "Half the world is dark
at any given time," he said. "How's Houdini
gonna fix that?"

"When the world is Korean, the Creator of all
things will no longer allow night to fall," Chiun
explained. "He only invented darkness to at least
partially mask the shame he felt for his mistake at
the heavenly oven. When there are no more whites
or blacks or other inferiors, there will no longer be
a need for night."

"Remind me to toss out my night-light," Remo deadpanned.

"You need not be so recalcitrant," Sun offered. "Your father in spirit has told me that you already possess some Korean blood."

"Nice of him to share a family secret," Remo said, his voice level. He glanced at Chiun.

"As part Korean already, you will be superior to the others who will only be naturalized Koreans. You will be a leader in the new order."

Remo laughed mockingly. "So even with this big crackpot change of yours, there's still going to be some sort of wacky caste system."

"Order must be maintained," Sun nodded.

"Spoken like a member of the future ruling class," Remo muttered. He turned away from the others, staring out across the bleak Korean countryside.

"Do not pay attention to him, Holy One," Chiun instructed with a frown. He nodded to the cult leader, abruptly changing the subject. "Perhaps this is a good time for our next lesson."

"Very well," Sun agreed.

Remo continued to stare out the window as the two men spoke. He felt the springs in the seat beneath him shift as Man Hyung Sun settled into a more comfortable pose.

"Concentrate here," he heard Chiun say. "This is the center, the beginning of all life. Pull your breath into this white hot spot. Feel it coursing through you.''

Remo started. He spun, looking over at the two men. He was shocked by what he saw.

Chiun was leaning from the seat across from Remo and Sun's. He had his slender fingers pressed into the rounded paunch of the cult leader's abdomen. Sun inhaled deeply. With Chiun's deft manipulation, he pulled breath down into the natural point deep in the pit of his stomach.

Remo glanced wildly up at Chiun, outraged by what he was seeing. "You're teaching this faker Sinanju!" he demanded.

"He expressed an interest," Chiun replied. "Which is more than can be said for you at our first meeting."

"This is crazy," Remo said, furious. "You can't teach that con man Sinanju."

"How dare you?" Chiun flamed. "Who are you to say with whom I can or cannot share my wisdom?"

"I'm the Apprentice Reigning Master," Remo snapped. "That's who. Now knock it off."

Chiun's eyes instantly narrowed into savage slits. For the second time in less than an hour, the tension between the two men was as it had never been at any time in their near three-decade relationship.

For his part, Remo refused to back down. Chiun had always taught him that the art they both plied was a link to ages past. Passed on from Master to Master, Sinanju had woven its invisible deadly thread throughout history. It was a craft and a way of life far too important to be wasted on the likes of the Reverend Man Hyung Sun, no matter if the swindler learned only the basics. To his very marrow, Remo knew that he could never allow the ultimate betrayal of Sinanju to take place, even if the betrayer was his own adopted father.

They stared at one another for a long time across the well of the limousine. Finally, with no words spoken between them, they both broke away, staring out opposite windows.

Man Hyung Sun repressed a smile. "Are we finished?" he asked, one eyebrow raised.

"Yes, we are," Chiun said coldly.

And the way in which he spoke the words told Remo that the old Korean was speaking about more than just a simple breathing exercise.

As he stared out at the dreary Korean countryside that was passing rapidly by the limo, Remo felt a welling hollowness slowly drag away the anger he was feeling. It pulled and pulled until there was no fury left.

When it was gone, there was nothing inside him but a vast emptiness. So great was the sensation of isolation, he found himself longing for the rage. It was as if the blackness of eternity had opened up and swallowed his soul.

It no longer mattered to Remo what happened

here in Korea, or in the rest of the world for that matter. Let the world sort out its own problems. Remo had his own to deal with. In the blink of an eye, his entire life had ended.

28

The wealth of information coming out of both Koreas was matched only by the amount Smith had yet to learn.

He had hooked into the Central Intelligence Agency database at the outset of the latest crisis. The computer monitor buried in his high-tech desk showed him up-to-the-minute satellite images of the movements in the North. Scrolling text from CIA headquarters indicated what the Langley analysis teams were coming up with as explanations for the sudden, bizarre activity.

Smith had his own theory.

Remo.

There were strange reports coming from the South. Only the Reunification Democratic Party was talking, and then only in cryptic statements. From what Smith could gather, there had been some kind of disruption at the National Assembly. Afterward, the president had gone into seclusion.

Somehow, Remo had affected the man. To what end, Smith had no idea.

He had only sent CURE's enforcement arm into Korea to await orders, not to stir up trouble. Smith could only guess that the problem Remo was having with the Master of Sinanju had caused him to act unilaterally in this crisis. And now it looked as if the divided country was ready to erupt because of his actions. Whatever they might be.

Smith had tried to get in touch with the Master of Sinanju at the Sun estate. His hope was that Chiun could stamp out the fuse Remo had set. The CURE director was upset to learn that Chiun had departed with Sun to parts unknown. It was only when he tried to trace the old Korean that Smith, to his horror, had learned that the cult leader, and presumably the Master of Sinanju, had taken Sun's jet to North Korea. They had apparently landed without incident.

And so both Remo and Chiun were likely there. Each with his own hidden agenda. Neither obeying orders from Smith.

It was the worst crisis Smith could think of facing in recent memory, including his dire trip to the hospital. The two Masters of Sinanju were like rogue nuclear warheads, ready to blow the entire Korean Peninsula to kingdom come.

And all Harold W. Smith could do was monitor the increasingly tense situation.

The phone to the White House rang suddenly. Smith was relieved for the distraction.

"Yes, Mr. President?" he asked, cradling the

red phone between his neck and shoulder. He continued to access reports even as he spoke.

"What the hell is going on in Korea, Smith?" demanded the President. He felt confident asking about the country now. Someone had shown him a map, and he was pretty sure he could find where it was without help.

"Unknown at present," Smith said truthfully.

"Didn't you send your people in?"

"Not exactly," Smith hedged.

"What's that supposed to mean? Did you or didn't you?"

Smith stopped typing for a moment. He closed his eyes as he spoke. "As best as I can tell, they are both somewhere on the Korean Peninsula."

"Somewhere?" the President asked. "That's pretty damned vague."

"I cannot get more specific at the moment," Smith said. He quickly changed the direction of the conversation. "But I can tell you a few things. To begin with, the student protestors in the South have grown even stronger since the Tomahawk incident. The streets of the South—and those particularly in Seoul—are no longer safe. The reports I have read detail rioting on a huge scale."

"What about their president? Some of my people are saying that he's gone underground."

"I have heard similar reports, though they are unconfirmed at the present time."

"Whew," the President said. "It sounds like it's falling apart in the South."

"Indeed," Smith echoed. "And it looks as though the North might be capitalizing on the social instability. Even as we speak, a line of vehicles is approaching the border between the countries."

"I've heard," the President told him. "My people are saying it's an invasion force."

"They are wrong," Smith said crisply. "I am looking at highly detailed images right now. While there *are* military vehicles in the convoy, there are also civilian cars. I seriously doubt even Kim Jong Il is insane enough to mount an invasion of the South using limousines."

"There are limos?"

"Yes, Mr. President."

The chief executive sounded more than a little annoyed. "I wonder why my people didn't tell me that," he complained.

"Perhaps they were preparing you for the possibility of invasion," Smith suggested. "However, it is never my intention to deliberately mislead a President. I will give you the facts, and allow you to make a judgment. For good or bad."

"Thanks for not sugarcoating it for me," the President said levelly. It was obvious he was irritated by Smith's contention that he might make a bad decision. "So what do we do about the situation?"

"Nothing."

The President was surprised. "Shouldn't we do something?" he asked. "It won't look good to the world if I just sit on my fanny during all this."

"It is not always necessary, Mr. President, to respond to every little thing that happens in the world. Sometimes, when left alone, things work out on their own."

"So we should take a wait-and-see attitude?"

"Yes," Smith agreed. "But I think none of us need worry about a long wait. Whatever is going on there, things appear to be progressing at a brisk pace."

"Armageddon is supposed to happen fast, isn't it?"

Smith did not respond to the pointless question.

"Our troops along the Thirty-eighth Parallel are on high alert for any eventuality," the CURE director said. "They had been prepared for many years for an assault from the North. The last few days, they have had to worry about the South. Now it appears as if they have to be concerned with both directions. If you are looking for something to do, I would recommend that you have your strategists prepare some sort of withdrawal plan for our men on the ground."

"Retreat?" the President asked.

"The social order of the South is on the verge of collapse. The North will most certainly sweep in to fill the power vacuum. If the Koreas unify under Pyongyang, it goes without saying that our troops will no longer be welcome."

The President sighed. "I'll get on the horn with the Pentagon," he said. "With any luck, your people will be able to iron out this mess before it gets any worse." He broke the connection.

Smith dropped the cherry-red phone to its cradle. He stared for a long time at his computer screen.

The images of the cars were fuzzy. The resolution on the satellite over the Koreas was not particularly great. But it was clear enough.

There were a lot of them, snaking back along the road to the North's capital. But were there enough vehicles for an invasion force?

He had assured the President that it was not possible. That Kim Jong Il was not that crazy. But was he?

Smith realized all at once that he had been looking blankly down at the computer screen for almost ten minutes. He was frozen in place, hand still resting on the open desk drawer with its dedicated White House phone.

Things would work out. For better or worse.

He slammed the desk drawer shut. Spinning away from his computer screen, Smith stared out through the one-way picture window behind his desk at Long Island Sound.

Above the waters, the winter sky was sallow. The weathermen promised snow today. Smith would watch for the first flake to fall. He had nothing better to do.

29

At a signal from Sun's limousine, the convoy containing the leaders of both Koreas paused on its way to the historic reconciliation. The many vehicles slowed to a stop two miles shy of the demilitarized zone.

The hundreds of North Koreans who had followed Sun from Pyongyang swarmed reverentially around the prophet of the Great Korean Age. Soldiers and politicians alike got to their knees on the bitterly cold road, hands raised above their heads in supplication. Sun waded through the mass of humanity like a conquering god.

"Is something wrong, O Seer?" Kim Jong Il asked from a spot near the second limousine. He, too, was kneeling on the ground, alongside the South Korean president.

"I fear so," Man Hyung Sun admitted. "Tell me," he said, turning to the South Korean leader, "how will our journey to the border be interpreted by your people?"

"*Our* people," the president corrected.

"Yes," Sun said, smiling tightly. "This was not an attempt to trick you. There is still a government in place in Seoul. They will have heard of our caravan."

"That is likely," the president admitted with a frown. "They will not be pleased. However, there are other concerns in the South right now. Our streets are dangerous. Unrest and violence run rampant through our capital. I am certain that my kidnapping is also troubling. I suppose it is *possible* that we have not been noticed."

"They know," the Master of Sinanju said. He stood behind Sun, hands tucked inside the sleeves of his kimono.

Remo was the only other person besides Sun and the Master of Sinanju still standing. He remained several yards away from Chiun. As his teacher spoke, he turned away.

"The capitalist troops along the border will be prepared," Kim Jong Il interjected. "Even if the South does not know, they certainly will."

Sun nodded. "Precisely," he said. "It is far too dangerous for us all to proceed, though I know you all wish to share in this glorious moment. Our number must be trimmed to only the most essential, lest we risk destroying all we hope to achieve."

"Can't you see the future?" Remo mocked.

Sun turned to him. "I see," he said, blandly. "And I interpret. It is not my place to tell all."

"Convenient out," Remo snorted. Crossing his arms, he stared off at a frozen rice paddy. As he looked at the barren expanse, he could feel Chiun's eyes boring angry holes into the back of his head.

"The leaders of this divided land should come with me," Sun announced to the crowd. "As should the Master of Sinanju. The rest must stay here."

There was a disappointed groan from those gathered.

Sun raised his hands. "Any slight sadness you feel now will turn to unbridled joy with the coming of *pyon ha-da.*"

With that, the cult leader pushed back through the kneeling throng to the open door of his limousine.

The president of South Korea and the premier of the North followed behind him. Padding silently in the wake of all three men came the Master of Sinanju.

Remo stuffed his hands in his pockets. Sullenly, he left the crowd and wandered over to the waiting car.

When Remo reached the limo and began to climb in, an arm suddenly barred his way.

"You cannot come," Man Hyung Sun announced from the back seat. His eyes were flat.

"Move it or I break it off," Remo warned, indicating the cult leader's arm with a nod.

"Remo!" snapped Chiun. He had been getting

in the other side of the black limousine. His head bobbed above the roof now as he stared furiously at his pupil.

"I mean it, pal," Remo said to Sun, his voice perfectly level. "If you don't want to go through the rest of your life with one wing, you'll move. Now."

This was the last straw for Chiun. The old Korean flapped around the rear of the car, coming up beside Remo.

"Forgive this one, Great Seer," Chiun spit. "He is a fool."

"Better a fool than a stooge," Remo countered. Chiun bridled at the insult.

"This is a holy moment," Sun interjected. "It is not open for disbelievers."

"I don't know what kind of half-assed, get-rich-quick scheme you've cooked up," Remo said. "But there's no way you're going without me."

Remo felt Chiun move in closer. His steady voice chilled Remo to the icy center of his barren soul.

"Leave," the old Korean commanded.

Slowly, like the deliberate movement of a glacier through a mountain-rimmed valley, Remo turned to his teacher.

"Make me."

The challenge was given. Remo did not need to wait to see what Chiun's response would be.

Stepping sideways, the Master of Sinanju moved

away from Sun and the limousine, keeping Remo in sight at all times. He circled until he felt that he was a safe distance from the man he had sworn to protect.

Careful to keep up his guard, Remo matched Chiun's moves, becoming the mirror image of his teacher. As they danced around one another, the limo melted farther and farther away.

The crowd of Koreans broke out around them, forming a concentric circle outside the much smaller center that was the two combatants. Even the two Korean leaders scampered back out of the waiting car to watch the inevitable fight. Only Sun did not trail them.

"You are a blasphemer," Chiun hissed as he circled Remo.

Remo shook his head. "He's a liar, Chiun. You know it on some level, I'm sure."

They were far enough away from the limo. Sun had still not followed them.

"He was a confidence man at one time," Chiun agreed hotly. "But are you so blind that you cannot see that is past? People change. The troublemaker Jew you so revere was a carpenter before the onset of celebrity."

"A carpenter isn't a bunco artist," Remo advised.

"No," Chiun admitted. "A bunco artist can sometimes make something of himself."

Still circling and without yet making a single

move toward each other, the two men slid off the road and out onto the frozen mud of the rice paddy. Their curious and expectant entourage followed.

THROUGH THE SMOKY GLASS of the limousine, Sun watched them go. He had clicked the door shut after the crowd moved across the road. Now, as the huge group stepped out onto the broad wasteland, he bent over, collecting something from the floor.

It was the package he had retrieved from his private jet back at Pyongyang airport. Tucking the flat box up under his arm, he slid out the far side of the limo.

Stealing back down the long line of vehicles, he found the first jeep with a set of keys left inside. Climbing in, he glanced over to the field where Remo and Chiun and their crowd of followers stood.

They were far away. Largely blocked by a line of official North Korean government cars.

Smiling, Sun started the jeep. He pulled out on the side of the road opposite the crowd. He drove along the bumpy shoulder to the front of the line, nosing in front of the armor-plated limousine that he had never intended to take to the border.

Driving off, he saw briefly in the wide expanse of the Korean countryside the bloodred arena of his waking dreams. It flickered in like a mirage.

The wounded form of the Pythia hovered at the

periphery of his consciousness. Although its cloak of yellow smoke seemed more faded than ever, there was a sense of satisfaction in the ancient spirit.

"You have done well," the voice in his mind rasped. "All has happened as I have foretold."

As he bounced down the long road to the Thirty-eighth Parallel, Sun felt his heart swell with pride. "And I will rule this united land?" he asked.

"Of course, my vessel," said the vision as it began to slowly fade. "Of course."

And if the demon force did not cloud his mind so completely, Man Hyung Sun might have detected the hollow tone of untruth in the words.

CAPTAIN YUN YONG GUN of the North Korean frigate *Chosun* had been defying orders for the better part of four hours.

The increased student activity in the South had brought some concern to the North. Captain Gun was supposed to be patrolling farther up the Korean Bay near Nampo, where the waters of the Taedong-gang flowed out into the Yellow Sea. It was part of the muscle flexing that had been going on in the North Korean military for the past several days.

Instead of sailing north, the captain of the *Chosun* was loitering farther south, in the North's territorial waters west of Haeju.

There he waited.

He smiled blissfully as the appointed hour approached, oblivious to the stares he was receiving from his men. It did not matter what they thought. Nothing mattered except the wisdom of the great holy man whose followers had shown him the proper path in life. His only regret was that he had not been able to share any of his revelations with the men under his command.

When the time came, Captain Gun ordered his men to begin the prelaunch sequence for two of the Free Rocket Over Ground old Soviet tactical missiles that had been adapted for use aboard the *Chosun.*

As his orders were followed, he fretted that the payloads of the two FROGs were conventional HE warheads and not nuclear. Nuclear would have been more fun. With atomic warheads, he would have been able to see the mushroom clouds from where his ship bobbed in the rough waters of the Yellow Sea.

When all was ready, Captain Yun Yong Gun personally entered the new target sites into the system. When his weapons officer pointed out that one of the sites was within the boundaries of North Korea itself, Gun pulled out his automatic and shot the man between the eyes. In the resulting confusion, the captain fired both missiles.

The frigate *Chosun* felt as if it would rattle apart as the two FROG 7s rumbled from their sleepy nests and arced up into the sky over the great black sea.

Captain Gun did not witness the majestic sight. As the twin infernos of tail fire were clearing the launch tubes on deck, he was already pressing the barrel of his automatic against his own temple.

The sharp explosion from the muzzle of his weapon was muffled by two things: Captain Yun Yong Gun's brains and the sound of the sleek missiles roaring inland.

THINGS HAD GONE FROM BAD to worse to something even worse than worse, and it still looked as if they had yet to hit rock bottom. At least that was Colonel Nick DeSouza's assessment of the Korean crisis.

He had been on the blower with the commander of U.S. forces in the region no more than ten minutes before. There was word out of Washington that the Pentagon was trying to come up with a scheme to clear all service personnel out of the DMZ. Of course, this would require more U.S. forces to be dropped into play. Ninety thousand, according to the report DeSouza had heard.

As was the case of late, the United States would beef up its forces and then lag behind to make sure everyone else was safely away. The UN, the Red Cross—even the damned Girl Scouts if there were any left in Seoul. All of them would be covered by U.S. service personnel. Only when it was strictly American asses that were left on the line would the U.S. ground troops be given the okay to bug out. Of course, by then there would probably be a full-scale ground war raging around them and there would be no escape route left.

Tension was high among the troops as he toured the last line of defense between the North and South. It was no wonder. It looked for all the world as if the DMZ was about to be overrun by both the North *and* the South.

The colonel looked back down the road toward the camp of the student demonstrators. Dusk had started to settle in, and with it came the inevitable bonfires. The figures skulking around the open flames seemed to be moving more purposefully. Or maybe it was his imagination.

"Calm down, Colonel," DeSouza muttered to himself as he tore his eyes away from the huge encampment.

He glanced in the opposite direction, across the Bridge of No Return.

Colonel DeSouza had heard about the convoy that was heading their way from the North. Intelligence claimed that it was probable the force was not hostile. There were too many civilian cars in the line. One report even had two of the bulletproof limos of Kim Jong Il himself at the lead.

DeSouza didn't doubt that there was some kind of force heading his way. What he did not trust was the speculation that it was not hostile.

There was no telling what was going through the mind of the North Korean premier at any given time. Some claimed he was eccentric; others insisted he was insane. Colonel DeSouza fell into the latter category.

Obsessed with motion pictures, Kim Jong Il was probably filming the invasion from the comfort of his limousine. Who knew? Maybe one of the nukes the North was supposed to have been working on sat in the back seat. The car would be driven as far as the demilitarized zone, and *kaboom!*

It could be anything. To try to outguess the Korean premier was to go crazy oneself.

DeSouza felt the frustration of not knowing what was going on, but hid it from his men. His face was blank as he stared beyond the ever running truck parked at the midpoint of the Bridge of No Return.

The faintly rusted bridge was the tenuous link between the two halves of the Korean Peninsula. Whatever was going to happen as far as the North and South were concerned would happen there. Everyone along the DMZ knew it.

As he was staring—seemingly into space—the colonel heard the sound of a whining jeep engine.

The men around him tensed.

DeSouza spun. ''How far away is that convoy?'' he demanded of a subordinate.

''Two miles, Colonel,'' reported the soldier, who had just run up from the command center.

"It was two miles ten minutes ago."

"It's stopped, sir. No forward progress at all in that time."

The colonel turned back around. The jeep sound still persisted. Briefly, DeSouza thought it was the spook returning—the guy he had pegged as CIA. As he watched, the vehicle appeared out of the rugged terrain.

It wasn't the CIA operative. The man behind the wheel was Korean. What's more, he was dressed in the uniform of a South Korean general.

The jeep screeched to a stop at the far side of the bridge. It was still rocking on its shocks when the general popped out. He threw his hands into the air.

"I must cross at once!" he demanded. "An emergency situation has developed!"

"I beg your pardon, sir," DeSouza called, "but who in the hell are you?"

"I am Assistant Minister Bae Park of the Ministry of National Defense of the Republic of Korea and I have important information for my government."

DeSouza shook his head. "Do you have any identification to back up your claim?"

The man stepped onto the bridge. He walked slowly, hands still raised above his head. "Idiot!" he spit. "Is not this uniform identification enough? When I went on my secret mission to the North, I buried it not far from here in the event of just such an emergency. Now I order you to let me pass.''

He was at the idling truck and still coming. The men around DeSouza were tensing, guns trained on the lone intruder. Some looked to the colonel for orders. The rest stared coldly at the general.

''I'm sorry, General, but I can't do that.''

The man was beyond the truck by now. He was nearly over to the other side of the bridge. He stopped only a few yards away from DeSouza.

''The North is about to drop a bomb on your fool head!'' the general screamed.

He stabbed a finger into the darkening north-western sky.

Colonel DeSouza followed the frantic gesture. He saw that a new star had appeared in the sky.

No, two. But they were not stars. With sudden horror, he realized all at once what the swift-moving objects were.

''Incoming!'' DeSouza screamed, racing from the bridge.

The South Korean general was forgotten as the men scrambled for cover. As the rockets from the frigate *Chosun* roared in, the Reverend Man Hyung Sun threw his hands down. Running in his baggy South Korean army general's uniform, he scrambled into an American jeep.

Steering away from the imminent explosion, he raced down the road away from the DMZ.

THE AIR AROUND THEM crackled with electricity. The men who had gathered around as the two Masters of Sinanju squared off felt the hair at the backs of their necks rise from the palpable energy being thrown off by the only human beings on the face of the planet trained to the limits of their physical and mental capacities.

Neither of them had yet struck a blow. It was like some friction-causing dance that would go on and on until the energy level became so unbearable that the built-up power would have to be released.

To the spectators, the younger Master of Sinanju seemed strong and agile, but the old Master exuded a sense of quiet confidence and grace.

At the center of the crowd, Remo washed slowly around the flawlessly artful movements of his mentor.

Chiun had yet to attack. One thing was certain— Remo would be damned if he'd be the one to strike the first blow. If Chiun was so sure of his allegiance to Man Hyung Sun, he would have to be the first to lash out. Only then would Remo defend himself. But so far, Chiun had not fired a fist.

The surge of raw, violent power welling up around them was beginning to throw off Remo's senses. His nervous system was so finely tuned that it could not long take exposure to the kind of unseen dynamic energy that was produced by another Master of Sinanju. It was like putting a magnet next to a compass.

Expecting an attack, they had both cranked up their senses to the limit. When one did not materialize, they still could not tune down their level of preparedness, lest in relaxing either one of them would leave himself open to an assault from the other.

Remo was beginning to sweat. Across the cold plain, he could see beads of perspiration break out on the furrowed parchment forehead of the Master of Sinanju.

They were both beginning to tire.

Remo felt dizzy. He tried to concentrate the awkward sensation away.

Chiun suddenly stumbled over a small stone that was jutting from the frozen mud. He caught his balance quickly, resuming his deliberate circuit around Remo. Though he did not otherwise show it, the point was made. He was feeling as light-headed as Remo.

The parked cars swept up behind Remo as the two men pirouetted around one another. He felt the crowd, more dense at his back toward the road.

Ordinarily, he would have been able to hear and sort every individual heartbeat within the multitude. Here, they were just background noise. A cacophony of thudding.

He circled back around. Chiun was now moving toward the road. They were almost to the point where both of them were parallel to the stretch of desolate roadway when Remo's senses picked up something from the string of army vehicles.

It was an odd sensation. Something concentrated, directed at him.

No. Beyond him now.

As Chiun moved toward the road, Remo realized that whatever had been focussed on him was now aimed at Chiun.

He was straining too hard. It was too difficult to push his senses farther than Chiun. He was about to shift his attention solely back to the Master of Sinanju when he heard a distinct metallic sound. It spurred him to action.

Without warning, Remo lunged at Chiun.

The Master of Sinanju seemed genuinely shocked that Remo would actually attack him. His almond-shaped eyes opened wide as he prepared a defensive blow. But there was no defense to what Remo next did.

Using every ounce of Sinanju-trained strength and energy in its most crude form, Remo flung himself clumsily atop Chiun. The two men toppled in an awkward bundle to the frozen rice paddy.

A lone bullet sang over both their heads.

As the rifle crackled through the wasteland, the fascinated crowd scattered in a panic. The collection of men—including the president and premier—ran for cover behind various vehicles.

"Get off, lummox!" the Master of Sinanju demanded. He batted and pushed Remo off him.

Another shot rang out. Remo threw himself back on top of Chiun, pushing both of their bodies to one side as he did so. The second bullet thudded into the earth where they had been.

"This is inexcusable!" Chiun shrieked. He kicked Remo away, scampering quickly to his feet. "Why do you leap on me like a perverted ox?"

"I was saving your life," Remo growled.

A few more shots rang out. The friction that had been building between them was now broken. With their senses back to normal, the latest volleys were easily avoided by both men.

"You were doing no such thing, for I am about to die of embarrassment. Have I trained you to be Bulk Hogan?"

"I figured you'd thank me. I know you were too far away to sense him."

"I was no such thing," Chiun sniffed. He adjusted his kimono skirts with fussing agitation.

"Whatever," Remo replied, annoyed.

They turned in unison to see who it was who had started taking potshots at them. Remo was not completely surprised to spot Rim Kun Soe bracing a rifle against the hood of a parked North Korean army jeep.

Running, the two of them crossed the distance to Soe before he was able to squeeze off another shot. Remo yanked the gun away from the Public Security Ministry man, cracking it in half. He dropped the two sections to the ground.

"What is the meaning of this!" Chiun demanded.

"He's ticked at you for calling him the son of a Pyongyang whore the whole time we were at the Berlin embassy," Remo supplied for Soe.

"Oh, and am I now to be shot at for speaking the truth?" Chiun asked, jamming his fists against his hips.

"He was also probably trying to keep you from carving him a new belly button for not getting all your gold back to Sinanju." Remo smiled at Soe. "Just because I didn't say anything, it doesn't mean I missed your jaw smacking the dashboard when I mentioned the gold."

Chiun's eyes had grown wide. "This is true?" he cried, his voice rising several octaves.

"It is not my fault," Soe begged. "A government edict froze all incoming freight. I discovered the last shipment in a storage area when I was reassigned to the airport."

The premier of the North and the president of the South had come forward once Remo had disarmed Soe. At the security man's latest revelation, however, Kim Jong Il began to tiptoe slowly backward.

Chiun wheeled on the two leaders. Kim froze.

"Does this pile of dog droppings speak the truth?"

"All deliveries were held up at the airport after the head incident," Kim Jong Il admitted uncomfortably. "I suppose some of your gold *could* have been left behind. But it wasn't my idea," he added quickly, raising his hands in a defensive posture.

"Observe your future, crazed offspring of the corrupt Kim Il Sung."

Chiun raised a finger as he spoke, long nail extended. With a daggerlike thrust, the sharpened nail penetrated the belly of Rim Kun Soe.

The security officer's eyes grew wide in shock as Chiun wrenched upward. The razor-sharp nail sliced from Soe's navel to his sternum. Steaming organs slipped from their resting place, plopping to the frozen ground like heavy water balloons.

Soe's mouth formed a frantic, slow-motion *O*. But even as the intense pain was registering, he was pitching forward. He fell on the viscous bags of his own internal organs. Once he dropped, he did not stir again.

Chiun aimed the killing nail at the body of Soe.

"That is **you** if my gold is not in Sinanju this day," the Master of Sinanju intoned to the North Korean premier.

"I swear it will be done," Kim Jong Il insisted. His eyes were sick as he looked down on the security man's body.

The premier scampered back to his limousine. Throwing his driver out onto the ground, he climbed behind the wheel. Almost as soon as the engine started, the car began making a huge circle through the field next to the road. Straightening out, it zoomed back in the direction of Pyongyang.

"That is that," Chiun said, satisfied. "Now, where were we?" He turned back to Remo.

Remo wasn't paying attention to the old Korean. He was glancing along the line of cars. "Where's Sun?" he asked.

With the excitement over, people had emerged from between the vehicles. Man Hyung Sun was nowhere to be seen.

"He is here," Chiun said. "Perhaps I will not have to throttle you if you agree to beg his forgiveness."

"No, Chiun, really," Remo insisted. "He's not here."

A quick search of the crowd and cars failed to turn up the Reverend Sun.

"That is odd," Chiun said, baffled. "Why would the seer desert us on the eve of *pyon hada?*"

The answer to his question came from a point far above all their heads.

A great whistling sound filled the sky. As the faces of the Korean delegation looked up to the noise, they were horrified to see a flaming object hurtling toward them through the gathering twilight.

The FROG missile tore through the sky at a speed far greater than even a Master of Sinanju could outrun.

As they looked up at the incoming missile, Remo and Chiun both knew with cold certainty that they were standing at ground zero. With nowhere to hide.

30

As they watched the missile streaking in from the north, another bright object snaked up over their heads from the south. It came from somewhere in the direction of the DMZ.

The latest alien celestial object flew in a direct line for the first. Their flight paths intersected high above the line of cars.

The explosion was brilliant. Flaming debris rained down, trailing smoking bright trains in their wake.

Soldiers and government officials ducked for cover inside cars and under trucks as tiny shards of shattered metal dropped all around them.

Remo and Chiun had dived into the safety of the remaining bulletproof limousine. After the explosion, they emerged to survey the wreckage.

"What the heck just happened?" Remo asked.

"The boom device boomed," Chiun said dully.

"No, there was another one," Remo insisted.

"Two booms, one boom—who cares?" Chiun said. He stamped out a small fire at his foot.

"Patriot missiles!" Remo said all at once. "They were deployed along the DMZ a couple of years ago. They must have tracked the incoming missile and shot it down."

The Korean soldiers were beginning to mutter among themselves. As they spoke, they looked in the direction of the South Korean president. None of them seemed pleased.

The president did not appear very comfortable with the attention he was receiving. He ducked behind Remo.

"I guess we know what happened with Sun," Remo announced as he looked at the suspicious soldiers.

"We do?" Chiun asked.

"C'mon, Chiun," Remo said, annoyed. "It's pretty obvious he bagged out on us."

"Perhaps your heresy chased him away."

"Bull," Remo said. "If he knows everything like you say, then he knew the missile was coming. I think he knew 'cause he arranged for it to happen. Either way, he left you here to die, Little Father."

He could see his argument was having an effect. The seeds of doubt had been sown in the old Korean.

Around them, the crowd of North Korean soldiers and government officials was beginning to grow more hostile. In the absence of either their premier or the seer of *pyon ha-da*, they were turning their hostility concerning the missile attack against the closest representative from the South—Kim Dae Jung. None of them seemed to much care that the missile had come from the north.

"Perhaps you are right," Chiun grudgingly conceded, as he eyed the angry crowd. "I am not saying that you are, but *if* you were, what would you do now?"

Remo was looking at the crowd, as well. Nodding, he raised his eyebrows. "Run like hell?" he suggested happily.

"A wise choice," the Master of Sinanju replied.

Bundling up the South Korean president, the two of them jumped into the nearest jeep. Leaving the angry crowd in a cloud of dust, they tore off down the road toward the DMZ.

COLONEL DESOUZA HADN'T been in the Gulf War, so he had never had the privilege of seeing the Patriots in action. Until today.

As he scanned the field of smoking debris along the old iron bridge, he had to admit it. He was impressed.

For the third time that day as he was looking out across the bridge, a jeep drove into view on the other side.

It was the CIA guy. He had returned with the president of South Korea, as well as another man who appeared to be almost as old as the rock-faced mountains above them. Maybe older.

The trio hurried across the bridge.

"Sorry," the young Caucasian announced as the trio ran past DeSouza. "No time for chitchat. You boys keep up the good work."

The colonel said nothing as they climbed into an Army jeep and drove off. They headed down through the field where the protestors had been camping out the past few days. In the wake of the missile attack, the university students were already hightailing it back for Seoul.

When the jeep was long gone, Colonel DeSouza turned back to his men.

"Requisition me a damned tollbooth," he said. "I'll be a millionaire in a week."

Shaking his head, he wandered back through the debris field to his command center.

31

"Where the devil have you been?" Smith demanded over the international line.

"Relax, Smitty," Remo said. He was standing in the main terminal of the airport in Seoul. "You're going to pop your cerebellum again. You've got to get me out of here."

Smith's response was firm. "Out of the question. There is a crisis situation in both Koreas. I need you there."

"Crisis averted," Remo insisted. "I'll tell you all about it if you tell me where Man Hyung Sun is right now."

Smith paused. Remo could hear the CURE director's angry breathing on the other end of the line. Finally, without Smith saying a word, the sound of rapid typing filtered through the receiver.

"Sun's jet landed and took off from the airport in Seoul an hour ago," Smith said momentarily.

"Kim Jong Il must have given permission for it to leave before all this nonsense started," Remo mused.

"About him," Smith pressed. "What is the situation in the North?"

"It's fine. Everything's fine. Kim is pissing his pants over Chiun's gold. He doesn't have time for anything else. Where's Sun's plane heading?"

"This is all irrelevant," Smith complained.

"Where?"

Smith sighed. "Of course he may have logged a false flight plan, but New York seems to be his ultimate destination."

"Great. Get me on a plane to New York."

"Not now," Smith said. "There are still matters to be resolved in the Koreas."

"There aren't any matters left. They're all resolved."

Smith did not sound convinced. "Are you certain?"

"What, are you kidding me?" Remo scoffed, as if insulted. "Didn't you know I can see the future?"

32

Sun arrived back at his East Hampton estate, jet-lagged yet triumphant.

The great force of the Pythia had remained quiescent since he had left North Korea. The spirit had been greatly weakened from its mighty battle a year before. The action of the past few days had not helped. Sun needed exposure to the urn in order to recharge the batteries of the possessing force within him.

His limo driver dropped him at the end of the main driveway near the front door. Roseflower greeted him as he stepped inside the large foyer.

"I heard the bad news, Reverend," his Sunnie assistant said somberly.

"Bad? Are you crazed?" Sun asked, grinning. "Things could not have gone better. Both Kim Jong Il and Kim Dae Jung are dead. My country cries out for a ruler. Pack my belongings. We shall all return to a united Korea this day where I will be crowned king."

"But…" Roseflower seemed perplexed. He held

in his hand the latest edition of Sun's own newspaper. The Sunnie glanced from the headline to his leader, obviously uncertain as to whether or not he should continue.

Sun snatched the paper from his hand.

U.S./South Korea To North: "Bombs. Away!"

The Sunnie leader was instantly confused. He perused the text quickly, his face growing more ashen with each line he read. He had gotten no more than a few paragraphs into the story before flinging the paper at his subordinate. As the different sections tumbled in huge sheets to the floor, Man Hyung Sun was already running up the stairs to his bedroom.

THE AIRPORT TAXI DROPPED Remo and Chiun off outside the high walls of Sun's East Hampton, Long Island, estate.

"Are you all right with this?" Remo asked once the cab had disappeared down the street.

"There is nothing with which to be all right," Chiun sniffed. "You have posed an interesting theory. However, I reserve judgment until we speak with Sun."

Remo noted that the Master of Sinanju no longer referred to the cult leader as Great Seer or by any other title. He didn't mention the lack of honorifics.

They took to the wall, scampering quickly up

and over like a pair of spider monkeys. They were greeted on the other side by an eruption of gunfire.

"Doesn't look like they're too happy to see us, Little Father," Remo said as he danced around a hail of bullets. Sudden pockmarks spit powder from the wall behind him.

Armed Sunnies were fanned out across the lawn. They were lying in their pink robes on a thin coat of freshly fallen snow. The only thing that might have made them more obvious would have been if their bald heads lit up in neon.

Chiun did not respond to Remo's comment. No sooner had the gunfire begun than the Master of Sinanju was off. He swirled into the midst of their attackers, his toes seeking out bald domes. Wherever they landed, there was a hollow *thwak,* as of somebody puncturing a soccer ball. After each *thwak,* another gun would fall silent.

"Aiiee!" screamed the Master of Sinanju as he tore through the Sunnie army.

"If they didn't know we were coming, they do now," Remo commented to the holes in the wall.

He ran after Chiun.

THE SCREAM FROM OUTSIDE chilled Man Hyung Sun to his very marrow. It was the Master of Sinanju. He lived. And he was coming for Sun.

The cult leader was in his bedroom closet. The humidifiers were on, and he had a blanket thrown over both his head and the ancient Greek urn. But although he pulled deeply at the thin yellow smoke that rose like mist from the damp powder, no visions came.

The Pythia was weaker than ever. The fractured essence of Apollo was all but gone. It had not been merely dormant on the flight back to America. It was almost dead.

The gunfire stopped abruptly.

Sun gulped at the yellow smoke, fear gripping his chest.

The Pythia was almost dead. As was he.

PINK-SWATHED BODIES lay strewed across the lawn. Some of the Sunnies fled when they realized the pointlessness of their efforts. Remo and Chiun let them go. Their prize was in the main house.

They crossed a snow-covered terrace and kicked in a set of French doors that opened into the grand ballroom. The psychic-hotline switchboards that had been there two days before were gone. Remo didn't know if they had shut down the tele-scam operation or simply moved to another location. Nor did he care.

The two Masters of Sinanju breezed into the ballroom, crossing the highly polished floor to the large curtained doorway that led into the main foyer. They were nearly at the door when Rose-flower jumped out before them, brandishing a sub-machine gun.

"You'll get to Reverend Sun over my dead body!" the beefy Loonie announced boldly.

"I'll take that as an invitation," Remo said.

Leaping forward, he grabbed Roseflower by the throat, squeezing so tightly that neck and spine were crushed like an aluminum beer can. Both gun and Sunnie fell in a heap to the floor.

Remo and Chiun continued on to the staircase.

THE PLAIN WAS FADING at its most distant points. It was as if the area where the Pythia sat were an island surrounded by a sea of nothingness. Even the sky was gone. There was a great looming emptiness hovering just above his head.

The Pythia was still there. Weak. Racked with pain. It looked up at Sun with what had been its piercing yellow eyes. They were now dull, fading even as Sun watched.

"You failed," the Pythia said.

"The missiles were intercepted," Sun replied. He panted in this otherworldly place, just as his physical self was panting in the corporeal world.

"I did not foresee that," the Pythia admitted ruefully.

Sun was aghast. "You're a clairvoyant! The Oracle of Delphi! The most famous fortune-teller in the history of mankind! What do you mean you did not foresee that?"

The Pythia looked up. "I see much. Not all. What I gave you was *a* future. Not *the* future. I do much better with more immediate events. Like now." The floating smile above the cloud of yellow mist was deeply unsettling. "I see your future."

Eyes grew wide. "Yes?" Sun hissed. "What is it?"

The lopsided smile seemed indecisive. As if the Pythia was not sure whether to laugh or cry.

"Short," the spirit said.

There was an explosion of sound like snapping kindling from somewhere close by.

The vision receded in a flash of yellow. Sun was on his stool in his bedroom closet. He pulled the towel from his head, spying the remnants of his locked door lying in shards all around the floor. With horror, he saw Remo and Chiun standing in the open doorway.

"There's a familiar stink," Remo commented as he sniffed the fetid closet air. He nodded to the urn at Sun's feet from which the sickly sulfur smell was emanating.

Chiun's eyes condensed into slivers of pure rage. Hands clenched in thorns of vicious ivory at his sides, he began walking deliberately toward the seated cult leader.

As he looked at the two men who would deal him death, the yellow fire danced in the eyes of Man Hyung Sun.

"It was not me," Sun begged. "It was the minion of Apollo. He drove me to do these things."

Remo leaned against the door frame. "Possession is nine-tenths of the law," he said with a shrug.

Sun fell over backward off his stool. He struggled to his feet, falling against the far wall of the big closet. Hangers rattled against one another as he flattened his arms against the walls in terror.

"You deceived me," the Master of Sinanju said menacingly.

Grasping at mental straws, Sun suddenly struck on something that might save him. "Wealth!" he cried, his yellow eyes glowing brighter. "I can divine the future with the Pythia's aid. Together we can make you wealthier than you could ever imagine."

Chiun glanced over his shoulder at Remo. Remo pushed away from the door frame, standing upright, confused at the sudden attention. The Master of Sinanju looked back to Sun.

"I am already far wealthier than you can possibly imagine, dissembler."

Without warning, both of Chiun's hands slashed at angles before him, first the left, then the right. He looked like a demented orchestra conductor.

The raking paths left by his ten curved talons shredded the chest and abdomen of Man Hyung Sun. Blood and viscera poured out onto the floor as the cult leader collapsed.

Even as the body fell, a thick yellow mist began to pour from Sun's mouth and nose.

Remo knew from experience that the smoke signified possession. He and Chiun watched as the thick mist congealed into a tight, swirling ball. It rose dramatically to the ceiling, pausing for a moment.

All at once, the ball of smoke rocketed down toward Remo. He steeled himself against the attack.

As it brushed his skin, Remo felt the faintly familiar presence of the Pythia's consciousness. It was far weaker than he remembered it. Too weak for its purpose.

The spirit in the smoke was unable to take hold. It passed through Remo and back out into the room.

Still swirling—more slowly now—the smoke flew at Chiun. The Master of Sinanju rebuffed it easily.

Afterward, it rolled between the two of them for a long moment. Seemingly uncertain as to what to do. At long last, a decision appeared to be made.

With a final burst of energy, the smoke raced upward. It popped through the ceiling in a puff of yellow, disappearing from sight. A moment later, a terrible faraway cry rattled across the frozen lawns of the estate—as of one whose time had long since past finally expiring.

After glancing at one another, the two Masters of Sinanju crossed to the center of the room.

The smoke and smell were clearing. The strongest stink left in the room was the powerful odor of the noxious after-shave lotion Sun had used to block the stench of the yellow sulfur dust.

Wordlessly, Remo and Chiun looked down at the urn of the Pythia of Delphi. The dust no longer glowed.

33

"You were correct," Smith enthused. "The situation in the Koreas adjusted itself back to normal after you left."

"I think I might have had something to do with that, Smitty," Remo said, slightly annoyed.

He was on an outdoor pay phone on Cape Cod. Remo shifted the phone from one ear to another, searching for the Master of Sinanju on the nearby dock. He spotted the wizened Korean in heated conversation with a man in a thick Irish sweater.

"Kim Jong Il has virtually gone into hiding after the *Chosun* bombing incident," Smith persisted. "If the situation with Chiun was as you say, it is possible we will not hear much from the North for some time."

"What about the South?"

"There is a welcome calm after days of unrest," Smith said. "The student protestors and their pro-reunification sympathizers in the government were willing to argue their case as long as their fellow countrymen seemed to be sympathetic to their cause. Their outcry worked when it was the United States who had accidentally bombed Seoul National University. But with a bombing raid from the North stopped by the U.S., there are very few people willing to listen to them today.''

"So we're right back to square one.''

"I am content with the situation as resolved,'' Smith said. There was something almost bordering on chipper in his lemony tone. It was irritating in the extreme.

"By the way, I mailed you all the floppy disks I found at Sun's mansion,'' Remo said. "My guess is that the sailors on the U.S. and North Korean boats were Loonies. Probably the guys posing as New York cops at the rally, too.''

"I look forward to receiving them.''

Remo's face puckered. "Please, Smitty, do you have to be so damned happy? It's unnerving.''

"I believe I have a right to be happy. We have come out of a very dark cycle for CURE. I would think that you above all would appreciate a return to normalcy.''

Across the windswept wharf, Chiun had just finished berating the man in the sweater. The ruddy-faced man turned away in a huff, pulling a blue knit cap over his shock of white hair as he stepped onto a boat that was tethered to the dock. A nearby sign advertised M. Vineyard Whalewatch Charters, Inc.

"*Normal* is a relative term, Smitty," Remo said blandly as he hung up the phone.

Remo gathered up the heavy Delphic urn that had been resting at his feet near the pay phone. He hurried over to the Master of Sinanju.

"He demands we pay full price," Chiun complained, waving an angry hand to the boat. "I told him that if we were interested only in seeing whales we could sit on the dock and watch his lard-bellied passengers as they waddled on and off his garbage scow."

"I'm sure that was well received," Remo commented dryly. "Don't worry, I've got the money."

Remo paid the fee, and the two men climbed aboard the boat amid the throng of freezing passengers.

FORTY-FIVE MINUTES later, they were out in the churning black waters of the Atlantic Ocean.

Remo fended off the curious questions of people who had paid seventy-five dollars for the ride and had yet to see a single guppy by telling everyone who asked that the magnificent antique urn he was carrying contained the ashes of his dear departed Aunt Mildred. The people on board quietly thought that Aunt Mildred must have been as big as a house to warrant an urn that size.

When they were far enough from land, Remo began to ladle out heaping portions of yellow dust into the ocean. He used a spoon he had lifted from a restaurant the previous night, allowing each spoonful to dissolve fully in the frigid water before throwing in the next. It took more than half an hour for the big urn to nearly empty.

"Did you mean what you said to Sun yesterday?" Remo asked suddenly. The two of them had remained silent during the entire procedure.

"What did I say?" Chiun asked blandly.

"When he told you he could make you richer. You said you were already wealthier than he could possibly imagine. When you said it, I kind of thought you meant me."

Chiun pulled deeply at the cold salt air. The bleak horizon stretched out to an impossible distance before them.

"You are very important to me, Remo Williams," Chiun said eventually. His jaw was firmly set as he stared at the endless black sea.

"More important even than gold?"

Chiun tipped his head, considering deeply. Finally, he looked at Remo, a glimmer of warm mirth in his hazel eyes.

"You are in the running," he admitted. Repressing a smile, he looked back at the ocean.

Remo grinned, as well. In spite of the bitter cold, he felt a great swelling warmth within his chest. He turned his attention back to the urn.

There was only a small portion of yellow dust left.

"I hope we don't see the Pythia again," Remo said as he scooped out the last few portions.

Chiun shook his head. The tiny puffs of delicate white hair above his ears blew away from his parchment face in the stiff ocean wind.

"Did you not feel it, my son? His consciousness was all but lost." Chiun looked at the clumps of yellow powder as they dissolved and sank in sparkling crystalline patterns beneath the rolling dark waters of the Atlantic. "Even gods die," he said softly.

Remo did not respond. He waited until the last of the yellow dust was out of the stone container. Once it was empty, he brought the urn up to the railing of the boat and heaved it over.

It made hardly a splash as it disappeared below the waves. Forever.

In the Deathlands, power is the ultimate weapon....

JAMES AXLER

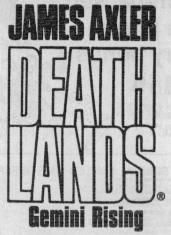

DEATHLANDS®

Gemini Rising

Ryan Cawdor comes home to West Virginia and his nephew Nathan, to whom Cawdor had entrusted the Cawdor barony. Waiting for Cawdor are two of his oldest enemies, ready to overtake the barony and the Cawdor name.

Unable to help an ailing Krysty Wroth, Cawdor must face this challenge to the future of the East Coast baronies on his own.

Book 1 in the Baronies Trilogy, three books that chronicle the strange attempts to unify the East Coast baronies—a bid for power in the midst of anarchy....

James Axler

OUTLANDERS™

NIGHT ETERNAL

Kane and his fellow warrior survivalists find themselves launched into an alternate reality where the nukecaust was averted—and the Archons have emerged as mankind's great benefactors.

The group sets out to help a small secret organization conduct a clandestine war against the forces of evil....

Book #2 in the new Lost Earth Saga, a trilogy that chronicles our heroes' paths through three very different alternate realities... where the struggle against the evil Archons goes on...

Follow Remo and Chiun on more of their extraordinary adventures....